Also by

An Ember of Darkness: Beyond the Veil Chronicles
(Audible audiobook available)
Primal Surrender: Knot Your Average Love Story
(Cypress City Seductions Series book one)
(Audiobook available)

Dedication

To those of us left behind.

Your found family is waiting.

Chapter One

MORNING TIDE

The shrill buzz of my alarm cut through the darkness of my silk sleep mask like a buzz saw through my skull. I groaned and rolled over, my hand blindly swatting at the nightstand until blessed silence returned. Just five more minutes. Please, universe, just five more—

BUZZ. BUZZ. BUZZ.

"Oh, gods. This is hell. I'm in *hell*," I muttered into my pillow, the words muffled by Egyptian cotton that suddenly felt like sandpaper against my face.

My mouth tasted like I'd been licking the bottom of a wine barrel. Which, considering how much Pinot Grigio I'd consumed last night while staring at that text message, wasn't far from the truth. The text still burned in my memory.

Trevone: Hey Twy, I know it's been a while, but I've been thinking about us. Can we talk?

Us. Like there had ever been an "us" worth salvaging after I'd caught him emptying my savings account to buy crypto that immediately tanked. It had been nearly two years since I'd thrown his shit on the lawn and changed the locks, and he wanted to "talk."

I reached for my phone to silence the alarm permanently when my bedroom door burst open with enough force to rattle the picture frames on my wall.

"Twyla, get up! We're going to be late! Kronos is already here to pick us up."

Alex stood in my doorway looking like he'd been dressed by a tornado with a hangover. His dark hair stuck up at impossible angles, defying both gravity and the industrial-strength gel he usually used to tame it. The morning light caught the blue of his eyes as he blinked at me sleepily. His white button-up was misbuttoned—the collar sat askew, one side higher than the other—and only half-tucked into his charcoal dress pants. A toothbrush hung out of his mouth like a cigarette, white foam dotting his chin and the corners of his lips.

"Go away," I mumbled, rolling toward the wall like that would make him disappear. The movement made my head throb with renewed vigor. "I'm dying. Possibly dead already. Hold my funeral without me."

The mattress dipped dramatically as Alex flopped down beside me, his weight bouncing me hard enough that my teeth clicked together. The springs in my ancient bed frame creaked in protest.

"Nope. No dice. You're going to miss E. Thalassos if you don't get your ass out of bed right now."

Even through my wine-induced misery, excitement flickered in my chest. E. Thalassos—the mysterious artist whose underwater paintings had been haunting my Instagram feed for months. The gallery had been keeping his identity under wraps, building anticipation for today's exclusive preview. I'd been looking forward to this for weeks.

But that was before the text. Before I'd decided wine was an acceptable dinner replacement.

"I'm serious, Twy," Alex said, tugging playfully at the edge of my bonnet. The silk tie loosened and the whole thing slipped sideways, threatening to expose my carefully protected braids to the humid coastal air. "We're leaving in ten minutes with or without you—"

"ALEX!" I bolted upright, my head spinning from the sudden movement. I clutched at the garment before it could fall completely off, shooting him a glare that could have melted steel. "You know better than to mess with the bonnet!"

His grin was completely unrepentant, the toothbrush bobbing as he spoke around it. "Then get up. I'm not kidding about leaving you behind."

I adjusted my sleep mask, so it sat properly on my forehead instead of hanging off one ear. "Since when do you care so much about art exhibitions? Last time I dragged you to one, you spent the entire time texting Kronos."

"This one matters to you." Alex pulled the toothbrush out of his mouth, gesturing with it like a conductor's baton. Little droplets of toothpaste flew through the air. "You've been obsessing over this artist for months. You literally have notifications turned on for his Instagram."

It was true—I'd become slightly obsessed with E. Thalassos's work. The way he captured water, the impossible colors, the sense of otherworldly beauty in every piece. It spoke to something in me.

"It's research," I said defensively. "I'm an artist too, you know. I'm allowed to admire technique."

"Uh-huh." Alex stood and shrugged off his suit jacket, tossing it onto the chair in the corner—the chair where clothes went to die in my room. It landed on top of a growing mountain of discarded outfits: the dress I'd tried on for last week's date that never happened, the cardigan I'd worn to the farmer's market and forgotten to hang up, Alex's own hoodie from the last time he'd crashed here after a fight with Kronos.

"Can I borrow that purple scarf of yours?" he asked, already opening my accessories drawer without waiting for permission. "This whole outfit feels too formal. Kronos picked it out."

Of course he did. Kronos had impeccable taste and the kind of old-money elegance that made expensive clothes look effortless. Sometimes I wondered if it came naturally to him or if it was something he'd learned over the years. Alex had never been forthcoming about his boyfriend's exact age or background, but there were hints—the way Kronos spoke sometimes, like he was translating from another era, the antique furnishings in his penthouse that looked original rather than reproduction. I didn't know if he was long-lived or if his family was just ridiculously into old-world customs. Honestly, it was probably the latter, Primals-aka werewolves who had interbred with humans and filtered down their powers-didn't really live longer than humans.

"Take your clothes with you when you leave," I said, padding toward my bathroom on bare feet. The hardwood floor was cold against my soles, sending a shiver up my spine. "There's more of your stuff in here than mine."

"Love you too, sunshine," Alex called after me, completely ignoring my request as he continued rummaging through my jewelry box.

I caught sight of myself in the bathroom mirror and immediately regretted it. My dark brown skin looked ashy despite my usual nighttime skincare routine, and my eyes were puffy from too much wine and not enough sleep. The micro braids had cost me two hundred dollars and six hours in the salon chair were still mostly contained in the silk bonnet, thank god, but I could see a few rebellious strands trying to escape around my hairline.

The coastal humidity was murder on natural hair. I'd learned that lesson the hard way during my first summer in Cypress City, when I'd stepped outside with freshly washed braids and returned looking like I'd stuck my finger in an electrical socket.

I pulled out my spray bottle—a mixture of leave-in conditioner, coconut oil, and a few drops of argan oil that smelled like heaven. Misting my braids lightly, I worked the product through with my fingers, being careful not to disturb the neat parts my stylist had created. The routine was meditative, a minor act of self-care that grounded me even when my head felt like it was stuffed with cotton.

While the leave-in set, I splashed cool water on my face, the shock of it helping to clear some of the fog from my brain. My skincare routine was streamlined but effective: vitamin C serum that stung slightly as it absorbed into my dehydrated skin, followed by a light-weight moisturizer with SPF that would protect me from the harsh sun.

Last came the body lotion—my favorite indulgence, a cashmere vanilla and sea salt blend that made me smell like expensive fall cookies and ocean breezes. As I worked it into my hands and arms, I traced small protection runes into the cream with my fingertips, the same symbols I painted on my nails in metallic polish.

The runes were probably overkill. Cypress City had been home to supernatural beings for decades now, ever since the Great Revelation when they'd stopped hiding among humans. Most of them were perfectly harmless—the selkie who ran the fish market, the wind elemental who worked at the weather station, the pack of werewolves who had the most successful landscaping business in the county.

But old habits died hard, and the runes made me feel safer, more prepared for whatever weirdness the day might bring.

"Twyla!" Alex's voice carried through the bathroom door, more urgent now. "Two minutes! Kronos is getting that look!"

I knew the look. The subtle tightening around Kronos's silver eyes that meant his patience was wearing thin. It wasn't anger, exactly—more like the disappointment of someone who valued punctuality and found himself constantly surrounded by people who didn't share that value. With as late as Alex always was, he had that look *a lot*.

"I'm coming!" I called back, grabbing my toothbrush and squeezing out a line of mint toothpaste. The fresh taste helped wash away the lingering wine flavor, though it did nothing for the low-grade nausea rolling in my stomach.

The excitement I'd been suppressing finally broke through my hangover haze. E. Thalassos. After months of admiring his work online, I was actually going to see it in person. Maybe even meet the artist himself, though the gallery had been maddeningly secretive about his identity.

There was something about his paintings that called to me on a visceral level. The way he captured water wasn't just technically impressive—it was emotional. Looking at his work felt like he'd painted the sensation of breathing underwater.

"Twyla!"

"Coming!" I called again, spitting out toothpaste foam and rinsing my mouth. I padded back into my bedroom to find Alex admiring himself in my full-length mirror, my purple silk scarf draped around his neck in a way that somehow made his entire outfit look perfectly put-together instead of like he'd been dressed by a drunk toddler.

"Better?" he asked, adjusting the scarf one more time.

"Much." I had to admit, Kronos had taught him well. The scarf added just enough color and texture to make the formal outfit look effortless. "Now get out so I can get dressed."

"What are you thinking of wearing?" Alex asked, not moving toward the door.

I surveyed my closet, trying to calculate how dressy this preview was supposed to be. Gallery openings in Cypress City ran the gamut from come-as-you-are casual to black-tie exclusive, and I'd made the mistake before of showing up underdressed to what turned out to be a society event.

"The purple dress with the wrap front," I decided. "Dressy enough for a fancy preview, comfortable enough to actually enjoy looking at art."

"Perfect choice." Alex finally headed for the door, pausing at the threshold. "And Twy? I'm really glad you're coming. It's been too long since we hung out outside of work."

He was right—between my shop, his relationship with Kronos, and the general business of adult life, we didn't get nearly as much time together as we used to. When Alex first came to work for me, fresh from escaping that awful club downtown, we'd spent hours talking while he learned the ins and outs of retail. Now he was confident and happy and deeply in love, which was everything I'd wanted for him. It just meant I had to share him now.

"Me too," I said. "Now seriously, get out. And tell Kronos I'll be down in five minutes."

"I'll tell him ten," Alex said with a grin.

The door closed behind him with a soft click, leaving me alone with my reflection and the growing excitement buzzing under my skin.

I pulled the purple dress from my closet and held it up against myself in the mirror. The color was perfect against my skin tone, and the wrap front was forgiving enough that I wouldn't have to worry about the extra bloating.

As I slipped the dress over my head, adjusting the tie at my waist, I caught myself smiling. Maybe it was the promise of exceptional art, or maybe it was the prospect of spending the day with my best friend and his boyfriend, who'd become something like family to me.

Either way, the text from my ex felt like a distant memory, easily pushed aside by the anticipation of discovery.

I grabbed my purse and keys, gave myself one last look in the mirror, and headed downstairs to meet whatever waited for me at the gallery.

Chapter Two

RIPPLES

I stared down at the embossed invitation, tracing my finger over the raised lettering. "Depths Unveiled: The Oceanic Visions of E. Thalassos." Fancy name for a fancy event. The thick cream-colored paper practically screamed expensive, making me wonder again if I belonged at something this upscale. I'd been dropped off at the door of the gallery, so I didn't have to walk too far in my heels. I appreciated the moment alone to gather my thoughts while they parked the car. While I loved them, it got to be a little much sometimes with the two of them together.

"Would you stop overthinking and come on?" Alex appeared beside me and gently grabbed my arm. "Are you contemplating throwing that into the nearest trash can?"

"I'm considering it," I admitted, tucking the invitation into my vintage beaded clutch. "Those people are *real* artists. What if someone asks me a question? I'll look like an idiot."

Alex rolled his eyes, but his smile was affectionate. "I promise Kronos will absolutely soak up all the attention. No one will even look at me and you." He hooked his arm through mine. "Besides, you've been following this artist on social media for months. Don't pretend you're not dying to see these paintings up close."

He had me there. I'd been obsessed with E. Thalassos's work ever since stumbling across it online in one of those promotional online galleries. While the underwater seascapes were excellently rendered, there was more to it. There was an air of melancholy that sucked in the viewer even through a screen. I could only imagine what it'd feel like in person. I *had* to meet the artist. Maybe some of his talent would rub off on me.

"Fine," I conceded, smoothing down my purple vintage dress. "But if anyone asks, I'm an eccentric art collector with mysterious connections."

"Twyla, your hair has beads that clack when you walk, and you've got protection runes on your nails. No one is going to mistake you for old money."

I glanced down at my newest nail art—protection runes outlined in metallic blue against a deep purple base. A witch at the nail salon had taught me which ones to include in my designs to protect me. Just in case. Cypress City was filled with Supes—supernatural people—and you never knew what kind of magic they'd be sporting. "Where's your boyfriend, anyway? Wasn't this whole gallery thing his idea?"

"Parking the car. He'll be in shortly," Alex replied, a soft smile playing at his lips. It still amazed me how much he'd changed since meeting Kronos. The guarded, skittish man who'd shown up at my shop desperate for work had transformed into someone who could actually smile without looking like it physically hurt. I loved how much happier he was, but I missed having him around all the time. It'd put a glaring spotlight on how small my world had become since I'd dumped my boyfriend more than a year ago. I'd thrown myself into focusing on my shop and Alex. Without him as my personal project…I was lonely.

We stepped through the gallery entrance, immediately enveloped in soft blue lighting designed to create the illusion of being underwater. Alex let out a low whistle.

"Damn, they went all out," he said, eyes sweeping over the transformed space. "Kronos wasn't kiddin' when he said this was the event of the season."

The crowd was exactly what you'd expect—women in designer dresses dripping with jewelry, men in bespoke suits discussing art like they were evaluating stock portfolios. A string quartet played something classical in the corner, nearly drowned out by the buzz of pretentious conversation.

Alex tensed beside me, his hand unconsciously moving to straighten his tie. *Looks like all that confidence was a front.* I squeezed his arm reassuringly.

"You look like you belong here more than half of these people," I told him. "Besides, you've got protection."

"Oh? You bringing those craft scissors out tonight?" he asked with a raised eyebrow.

I gestured to my nails. "Rune magic. If anyone tries to mess with us, they'll regret it."

"My heroes," a deep voice rumbled behind us. Kronos materialized as if he'd stepped out of a shadow, looking devastating in a charcoal suit that made his red hair look like fire and his silver eyes gleam like polished metal. He slid an arm around Alex's waist, drawing him close. "Though I doubt even supernatural troublemakers would risk the wrath of the gallery owner. Apparently she's a banshee."

"Good to know," I said dryly. "I'll try not to touch anything expensive."

Alex was already leaning into Kronos's touch, his eyes slightly unfocused in that way that told me they were about five minutes from ditching me to find a dark corner. Or not so dark. Those two weren't exactly subtle.

"Open bar's that way," Kronos said, nodding toward the back of the gallery. "The sylph by the bar makes an excellent dirty martini, if you're interested."

"I think I'll stick to champagne," I replied.

Kronos's laugh was warm. "Smart woman. Alex mentioned you're a fan of the artist?"

"She's obsessed," Alex supplied before I could answer. "Her MoonMarket explore page is nothing but underwater paintings and weird crafting videos."

"It's called research," I protested. "Some of us have non sex related hobbies…" I gestured vaguely at the two of them, "…instead of whatever supernatural hotness you two have going on."

Kronos's eyes gleamed with amusement, the corner of his mouth quirking up in a way that emphasized his sharp jawline. "Supernatural hotness?"

"You know what I mean." I waved dismissively. "Go look at art or whatever you two are actually planning to do here."

Alex had the decency to blush, but Kronos just smiled that seductive smile that made it very clear art appreciation was not his primary objective tonight.

"We'll catch up with you later," Alex promised as Kronos guided him toward a less crowded corner of the gallery. "Text if you need us."

"I won't," I called after them, already knowing I wouldn't see either of them again until tomorrow. The look that had passed between them was practically combustible.

Free of Alex's nervous energy and Kronos's intimidating presence, I could finally focus on what I'd actually come for—the art. Left to my own devices, I moved deeper into the exhibition space.

The first few pieces were impressive enough—stylized ocean scenes with unusual perspectives and colors too vibrant to be natural. But as I moved into the main gallery, the paintings transformed into something else entirely. Not just beautiful ocean scenes, but glimpses into another world.

I was drawn to a section toward the back of the gallery. One stopped me cold—a simple scene of a rocky tidal pool at twilight. Unlike the other paintings that showcased the fantastic and otherworldly, this one captured the liminal space where sea meets shore.

The technique was extraordinary. I could almost feel the cool evening air, hear the gentle lapping of waves against stone. But it was the emotional quality that held me transfixed—a profound sense of loneliness emanated from the canvas, as if the artist had somehow painted the feeling of being caught between two worlds and belonging to neither.

I lost track of time standing there, breathing in rhythm with the painted waves. My fingers itched with the familiar urge to create something in response—maybe a window display with sea glass and driftwood, or a jewelry collection inspired by tidal pools. Something to capture that exquisite sense of in-between.

"I take it you're a bit of a masochist." A voice said directly behind me, the sound so unexpectedly melodic it seemed to ripple through the air.

I jolted from the painting's spell. Before I could turn around, I felt a strange buzzing sensation wash over me, like standing too close to high-voltage wires, then fizzle out against my skin. The runes on my nails tingled in response.

"Only for art and jalapeno poppers." I said as I turned. Whatever else I was going to say died on my lips when I caught sight of who was talking to me.

He was, without exaggeration, the most beautiful person I'd ever seen. Loosely tied back, long, pale pink hair framed a face of impossible perfection, with a few strands escaping. His eyes were the same delicate seashell pink, set above high cheekbones and lips curved in a smile that belonged in a Renaissance painting. His flowing scarlet shirt was unbuttoned just enough to reveal a stretch of pale throat and collarbone, where I could see the faint shimmer of what looked like coral-colored scales.

His smile faltered slightly as our eyes met, then returned with doubled brilliance.

"You have an exceptional eye." His voice was musical, each word precisely chosen and delivered. "Few appreciate the power of the in-between."

Something about his tone suggested he expected me to hang on his every word with breathless admiration. I'd seen that expectation before, usually from men who thought their good looks excused a lack of substance.

With the spell of the painting broken, I took a deliberate step back. "It's beautifully rendered," I said neutrally. "The technique with the light on the water is particularly effective. I haven't been able to master that."

He tilted his head slightly, studying me with a piercing intensity. "You're an artist." It wasn't a question.

I shrugged. "I dabble. Nothing as grand as this."

"Art is art," he said, moving to stand beside me rather than behind me. His eyes flicked to my nails, then up to my purple micro-braids with subtle appreciation.

"I have to get going, sorry. My roommate is probably looking for me." My phone buzzed in my clutch before I could walk away. I pulled it out to see a text from Alex.

Alex: Heading home with K. You might want to stay out a while…this is going to get LOUD. Sorry!

I groaned, unable to help myself. So much for that escape route.

The beautiful stranger's eyes flicked to my phone screen, his smile turning mischievous. "It seems I get you all to myself, after all."

I was about to snap at him to back off when a woman in a sleek black pantsuit approached us

"Mr. Thalassos! The Hendersons just purchased 'Abyssal Court' and were hoping for a word. And—" she lowered her voice, "—the mayor's wife is asking about a *special* commission."

My jaw nearly hit the floor. *E. Thalassos.* I'd been about to blow off the creator of the very works I'd come to see.

He waved his hand dismissively. "Tell them I'll be over shortly, Clairen." His eyes never left my face. "I'm having a much more interesting conversation at the moment."

His publicist gave me a once-over that held equal parts curiosity and barely concealed annoyance before nodding and retreating.

"You're him," I said, feeling slightly off balance. My usual look wasn't star-struck, but I hadn't expected literally to bump into the creative mind behind these incredible visions.

"Enchante. Ezra Thalassos." He took my hand and brushed his lips against my knuckles, his touch lingering just a beat too long. "You are clearly the most fascinating person in this room, Ms...?"

"Twyla Knight," I supplied, withdrawing my hand despite the pleasant tingle his touch had left behind. "I own Twyla's Trinket & Trade downtown near the boardwalk."

"Ah, the eclectic little shop with the darling window displays?" His expression suggested he was filing away this information for future use. "Let me get you another drink, Twyla Knight. That champagne is atrocious—I've told them repeatedly to upgrade, but galleries never listen."

Before I could decline, he'd guided me toward the bar with a light touch at my elbow. He moved like water flowing over stones.

Despite my initial wariness, I found myself drawn into conversation with him. He was knowledgeable about art techniques, describing how he achieved certain effects in his underwater scenes. When I mentioned my college art classes, he listened with what seemed like genuine interest, asking thoughtful questions about my own creative process.

But every few minutes, we were interrupted. Women in revealing dresses and men would approach, clearly under the influence of whatever siren charm my runes had protected me from. They simpered and fawned, touching his arm or shoulder at every opportunity. Each time, Ezra would smile politely, but his attention would flick back to me as if checking I was still there.

After the fifth interruption—a woman who practically draped herself across him while asking for his 'personal insights' on a painting—I'd had enough. Beautiful or not, talented or not, I wasn't interested in being part of his adoring audience.

"I should get going," I said when the woman finally departed with his promised arrangement to discuss her art collection later.

"So soon?" His disappointment seemed genuine, which was almost annoying in itself.

"I have to be up for an early shipment tomorrow," I lied, gathering my clutch. "It was interesting meeting you, Mr. Thalassos."

"Ezra," he corrected, that perfect smile never faltering. "I'm sure we'll meet again, Twyla Knight."

As I left the gallery, the runes on my nails still tingled faintly, and I could feel him watching me as I left.

Was he beautiful, yes. Talented, certainly. But vain and self-absorbed? Absolutely. Not my type at all.

Chapter Three

SHALLOW WATERS

I tossed my keys onto the counter; the metal clinking against the ceramic bowl—a pathetically empty sound in my quiet apartment. My heels came off next, making me groan with relief as blood rushed back to my compressed toes. Whoever invented stilettos clearly hated women and feet equally.

I grabbed the remote and flipped on the TV for background noise while I changed. The news was on, showing footage of angry-looking protesters outside what appeared to be a fancy Greek-inspired temple near the harbor.

"...marks the third attack on the Temple of Oceanic Deities this month," the reporter was saying with practiced gravity. "Protesters calling themselves 'The Purifiers' claim that supernatural beings, particularly sirens and other sea-dwellers, should 'return to the depths where they belong.' Claiming that last year's hurricane was caused by their worship of the sea gods and their presence on land."

"Yeah, good luck with that," I muttered, rolling my eyes as they showed a pasty-faced man with a bullhorn shouting about "purity" and "natural order." As if 'supernatural' creatures are any less alive or natural than humans are. Some of them are reportedly even older than our species. How could it be said that we have sole rights in this world? I guess I can understand the fear, as humans are still adjusting to them, not just being stories. Most of us didn't know we shared a planet with 'Supes' until the grand reveal a few decades back. Some were furious and scared, while others were infatuated. That *is* how so many hybrids came to be, like the Primals.

The camera panned to show cops arresting some dude with a sign that read "HUMANS ONLY" in blood-red paint. *Creative.* I changed the channel, too tired to absorb more depressing evidence of humanity's stellar character.

But something about those protesters stuck with me as I peeled off my dress. The naked hatred in their eyes, the absolute conviction they were right. I'd seen that look before—in old photographs from my grandmother's civil rights albums, in documentaries about lunch counter sit-ins and bus boycotts. That same twisted certainty that some people were inherently less deserving of basic dignity.

As a black woman, my people had been the target of that kind of venom for centuries. Thankfully, most of society had moved past such blatant bigotry—or at least learned to keep it quieter. But humans, it seemed, needed someone to hate. Someone to blame for all the world's problems. Now that open racism was socially unacceptable in most circles, they'd found new targets.

Supes.

The world was changing—supernatural beings living openly among humans—but clearly some people would rather set themselves on fire than adapt.

Different faces, same ugly hearts.

My mood thoroughly killed, I flopped onto my bed just as the unmistakable sounds filtered through the wall—rhythmic thumping, breathless moans, and Alex's voice carrying with surprising clarity.

"OH *GOD*, RIGHT THERE!"

Heat rushed to my face. *Fuck,* Alex had warned me they'd be going at it by the time I got home. I pressed my palms against my ears, but it did nothing to block Kronos's answering growl. *Man, do I not want to hear Alex like this.* My stomach clenched with an uncomfortable mix of embarrassment and something else—a hollow ache I didn't want to name.

The drawer scraped as I yanked it open, fingers fumbling for earplugs. My shoulders tensed with each new sound filtering through the too-thin walls. Happy as I was for Alex, each enthusiastic cry hammered home how long it had been since anyone had touched me that way. Since I'd wanted anyone to. It'd just been easier to throw myself into work than to worry about dates since my breakup. I refused to even think the cheating bastard's name.

My stomach growled, the champagne from the gallery having long since worn off. No way was I staying here with this soundtrack. Worn jeans and a soft t-shirt felt like armor against the reminder of what I wasn't having tonight as I hurriedly dressed. I snatched up my keys again, the metal biting into my palm as I clutched them too tightly.

Outside, the night air hit my face like a gentle caress. I inhaled deeply, filling my lungs with the salt-sweet scent of the ocean carried on the breeze. My steps slowed as tension gradually melted from my shoulders, the sound of my sandals against the pavement replacing the echoes of the couple's pleasure.

The diner lights glowed warmly against the deepening blue of evening. Inside, the familiar smell of fried food and coffee wrapped around me like an old friend. I slid into my usual booth, the vinyl seat cool against the backs of my thighs.

"Clam chowder?" Marnie asked, already scribbling on her pad. She didn't wait for my nod. "Coming right up, hon."

"And a coffee," I said to her, nodding head as she walked away.

The rich, creamy soup warmed me from the inside out, but couldn't quite fill the strange emptiness that had settled in my chest. With each spoonful, the gallery exhibition replayed in my mind—the otherworldly paintings, the strange buzzing of magic against my skin, and those peculiar eyes watching me with unexpected intensity.

How could that tidal pool painting have come from someone so...superficial? The memory of it still pulled at something deep inside me—that sense of being caught between worlds, of belonging nowhere completely. I'd felt the artist's loneliness flowing from the canvas, raw and honest in a way Ezra himself hadn't seemed capable of being. He'd flip his hair and twirl it on his long pianist fingers and shamelessly flirt with every patron until they were so flustered they'd leave. He'd even done the finger on the chin thing! Where he'd lifted a man's chin with the tip of his finger, bringing their lips so close while he looked into the man's eyes and whispered to him, thanking him for buying the second most expensive painting in the gallery. I'd held my breath too, feeling like a fly on the wall in their private moment. I couldn't reconcile *that* Ezra with the serious, sorrowful, powerful feelings that emanated from that art.

I had a strong feeling that the paintings were enchanted, as my runes had sizzled every time I got close. Maybe that's how he evoked that feeling?

I paid my bill and stepped back into the night, but instead of turning toward home, my feet carried me toward the beach. The sand whispered beneath my steps as I kicked off my sandals, cool grains sliding between my toes. The ocean stretched before me, a vast darkness with moonlight dancing across its surface like scattered diamonds.

My shoulders ached from a day of hefting boxes, of rearranging displays, of carrying the subtle weight of worrying about Alex. Even with the Madam behind bars and her club permanently shuttered, I couldn't shake the habit of glancing over my shoulder, or checking in on him more often than he probably needed.

I sank onto the sand, a bone-deep weariness settling over me. The constant vigilance had become so familiar I barely noticed it anymore, but tonight it pressed down on me like a physical weight.

I leaned back on my hands, the sand still holding the day's warmth beneath the cooler surface. The vastness of the night sky opened above me, stars pricking through the darkness like tiny holes in a velvet curtain. Somewhere across town, Kronos embraced Alex in a way I'd never known.

Our movie nights had dwindled to almost nothing in recent months. I missed the weight of him curled against my side, his grudging laughter at the cheesy horror films I insisted on watching. The way he'd start the evening maintaining a careful distance, but inevitably end up pressed against me, tension gradually melting from his frame until he'd sometimes fall asleep with his head on my shoulder.

A year ago, I wouldn't have imagined him letting anyone get close like that. Now he was practically living at Kronos's place, coming home only to work shifts and change clothes. Soon enough, he wouldn't need the apartment next to mine at all.

The realization sent a pang through my chest so sharp it stole my breath. I wrapped my arms around myself, suddenly cold despite the mild night. I was genuinely happy for him—after everything he'd survived; he deserved someone who looked at him like he hung the moon—but that didn't stop the ache of impending loss.

A movement in the distance caught my eye—a figure walking where water met shore, silhouetted against the shimmer of moonlight on waves. Something about the way they moved held my gaze—too fluid to be human, each step flowing into the next like water. Long hair drifted around narrow hips, swaying with a rhythm that didn't quite match the gentle breeze.

Then the sound reached me—not carried by the wind, but somehow inside me, vibrating through bone and blood and breath. A voice unlike anything I'd ever heard, both ethereal and devastating in its beauty:

"Down in the dark, drifting from the shore,
A small silver scale lost forevermore,
Searching the depths, calling through the tide,
For a home that sleeps beneath the brine."

The melody wrapped around my heart and squeezed. I couldn't breathe, couldn't move, couldn't do anything but feel as the song pulled at something buried so deep I hadn't known it existed. My chest ached with emotions I couldn't name—longing and sorrow and a strange, sweet yearning for something I'd never had.

Wetness traced down my cheek, cool against my skin. I hadn't even realized I was crying.

The figure drew closer, and moonlight revealed what my body had already somehow recognized. Ezra walked barefoot through the shallow surf, water lapping around his ankles. He had rolled his pants to his knees, revealing glimpses of coral-pink scales appearing and vanishing with each wave's caress. His face tilted slightly skyward, eyes half-closed as the haunting melody poured from his lips.

Here, away from the gallery's carefully curated atmosphere, he looked wilder, more real. The polished charm had fallen away, revealing something ancient and otherworldly beneath. His hair moved in the breeze like living silk, catching moonlight in ripples of rose-gold.

His song ended abruptly as he noticed me, his expression narrowing before relaxing slightly as he gave a slight nod.

"Twyla." My name in his mouth sounded different now—no performance, just quiet recognition. He moved toward me with that liquid grace, stopping close enough that I could smell him—salt and something sweet like night-blooming flowers.

His gaze dropped to my cheek, where I could still feel the dampness of tears. Before I could pull away, his fingers brushed my skin, catching a tear about to roll down my chin. His skin was cool against mine, slightly rough like fine-grained sand.

My breath caught as he brought that finger to his lips, tasting my tears with an expression of such intense focus it made my skin prickle. The gesture was too intimate, too strange, and yet I couldn't look away.

A siren. The supernatural world had become more open in recent years, but sirens remained rare and misunderstood. Dangerous. Irresistible. Evil. I had never been one to listen to rumors. A person is a person, and should be able to prove themselves for who they are, not what they are. I shook my head. I had to shake these foolish thoughts loose.

"Couldn't sleep?" he asked, his voice low and intimate, like we were sharing secrets. The sound resonated inside my chest rather than just reaching my ears. This wasn't the practiced charm of the gallery; this was something deeper—the difference between a recorded song and live music that vibrates through your bones.

I forced myself to stand, brushing sand from my jeans. The movement broke whatever spell his voice had woven. "Just needed some air. Roommate has a *guest* over."

"Ah." A half-smile curved his lips as his gaze lingered on mine. "Your friends from the gallery. They were quite preoccupied with each other."

His tone held amusement, though his eyes remained fixed on me with an intensity that felt invasive.

"I should go," I said, gathering my sandals.

He tilted his head, studying me with those impossible eyes. "Stay," he said, nodding toward the water. "The beach is more interesting with company."

For a heartbeat, I imagined what it might be like to walk beside him in the moonlight, to hear more of that haunting music. *Yeah, that's enough of that.* I thought, forcing myself to let it go.

"Another time," I said, surprised to find I half-meant it.

I turned to leave, but something made me glance back after a few steps. The pleasant expression had vanished from his face. In its place was something blank yet terrifyingly focused. His eyes tracked my movement with the intensity of a hunter memorizing its prey. Nothing remained of the charming artist or the melancholy singer—only something ancient and hungry wearing a beautiful human disguise.

It lasted only a heartbeat. The mask slipped back into place with ease, his features rearranging into something warm and inviting once more. The transformation happened so quickly I might have doubted what I'd seen if not for the lingering chill.

"See you around, Twyla," he called after me, his voice carrying easily over the sound of waves.

The walk back to my apartment felt endless. The memory of that blank, hungry stare followed me all the way home, a stark contrast to the haunting melody that still echoed in my mind. I rubbed the protection runes on my nails, grateful for their earlier intervention at the gallery. Whatever he'd tried to do hadn't worked, and I intended to keep it that way.

I had enough complications in my life without adding a siren to the mix.

Relief washed over me when I entered my apartment building to blissful silence. Just the gentle hum of the ancient refrigerator and the soft ticking of the clock I'd rescued from a yard sale last summer.

I kicked off my sandals, gritty with beach sand, and padded to the freezer. The pint of wine ice cream—cabernet with dark chocolate chunks—had been my emergency stash for weeks. Tonight definitely qualified. I grabbed a spoon from the drawer, not bothering with a bowl.

Just as I was about to collapse onto my couch, a soft knock at the door made me freeze. My heart jumped into my throat. Had Ezra somehow followed me home? I hadn't noticed anyone behind me, but I'd been lost in thought, replaying that unsettling blank stare...

I approached the door cautiously, peering through the peephole. The tension drained from my shoulders when I saw Alex's familiar face.

"Hey," I said, swinging the door open. "I thought you'd be wrapped around wolf man for the rest of the night."

Alex leaned against the doorframe, looking thoroughly exhausted but radiating a quiet contentment that gave me a brief twinge of envy. His hair was still damp from a shower, and he'd changed into soft loungewear—Kronos's, judging by how the pants pooled around his ankles.

"We ordered way too much food," he said, holding up a plastic container that smelled suspiciously like my favorite Pad Thai. "Thought you might want some."

"You're a lifesaver," I said, accepting the offering. "I was about to have ice cream for dinner like a proper adult." I was pretty sure he hadn't ordered 'extra'. He'd ordered this to try to say sorry. *He is such a sweetie.*

Alex glanced at the pint in my other hand and snorted. "Wine ice cream doesn't count as dinner."

"Says who? It's got antioxidants."

A comfortable silence fell between us, the kind that only comes with genuine friendship. For a brief, disorienting moment, Ezra's face flashed in my mind—those pink eyes watching me with that strange intensity, the way his voice seemed to vibrate inside my chest. I shook the thought away immediately. No way was I going down that road. He might be fun for a night, but he couldn't possibly be actually interested in me. Men like that flirted as naturally as breathing.

"Earth to space cadet," Alex said, tapping my forehead with his finger. His blue eyes crinkled with amusement as he studied my face. "Ya still with me?"

I blinked, focusing on his face again. "Sorry. Did you need something else, or are you just here to make me smell the sex sweat on you?"

He smiled and ducked his head, a slight flush creeping up his neck. "We're about to watch that new rom-com—the one with the baker and the food critic. If you want to join…"

The invitation was genuine, his eyes holding a hint of concern that told me he'd noticed something in my expression. My heart squeezed with affection for him.

"I don't wanna be a third wheel twice in one day," I teased, lifting the ice cream. "Besides, I've got a hot date with cabernet and chocolate."

A flicker of guilt crossed his face. "Ya sure? We could make some time just for us soon—maybe that horror movie marathon you've been threatening me with?"

"I'd like that," I said, meaning it. "But for now, go back to your hunky boyfriend. Me and the wine ice cream have plans."

He hesitated, then nodded. "Okay. G'night."

"Night." I watched him head back down the hall to his apartment before closing my door.

As soon as the latch clicked into place, my smile slipped away. I ate a heaping spoonful of ice cream, savoring the rich wine flavor as it melted on my tongue. The takeout container was still warm as I settled onto the couch, tucking it between my thighs as I grabbed the remote.

I found an old movie I'd seen a dozen times, something I could half-watch while letting my mind wander. Before the opening credits had finished, my focus had already drifted. My phone was in my hand, thumb scrolling through TikTok as the familiar dialogue provided background noise.

Cute horse videos, dancing anime cosplayers, someone's elaborate pottery project—the endless scroll of content blurred together until something made me stop mid-swipe. My thumb froze over the screen, pulse quickening.

Ezra. Standing outside the gallery, illuminated by the soft glow of the entrance lights. The video had started as someone's attempt to show they were at the exclusive event, the camera panning to include both the videographer and the artist in the background.

What caught my attention wasn't Ezra himself, but his expression as he watched someone off-camera. That same dark, intent look I'd glimpsed on the beach—except this time, as the camera angle shifted, I could see who he was watching.

Me. Walking away from the gallery, completely unaware of him tracking my every move.

A chill ran down my spine despite the warmth of my apartment. Why was he so interested in me? I knew I was pretty enough, and my bright style usually stuck out in a crowd. However, supernatural men who looked like him rarely paid that kind of focused attention to women who looked like me.

Whatever. I set my phone aside with a sigh. The chances of seeing him again were slim to none. Cypress City was big enough that two people could easily avoid each other for years. Besides, I had inventory to sort through tomorrow morning, three custom orders to finish by Friday, and a window display that needed refreshing before the weekend tourists arrived.

I glanced at the clock—nearly midnight. My 6 AM alarm would ring whether or not I was ready. Running a business meant no time for whatever drama that man had in his life. The movie droned on in the background as I finished the last of my ice cream, my thoughts already turning to tomorrow's to-do list.

Chapter Four

CHANGING TIDE

The morning sun filtered through the shop windows, casting long rectangles of light across the polished wood floor. I'd been up since five, arranging my newest display of handcrafted jewelry and organizing the window installation that would replace the current nautical theme. Cypress City's summer season was in full swing, which meant steady business but precious little quiet time to work on creative projects.

I stepped back to examine the arrangement of sea glass and driftwood I'd assembled, mentally adjusting the color balance. The light blue pieces needed to be more prominent if I wanted to capture that perfect summer sky feeling. The bell over the door remained mercifully silent as I rearranged the display, the only sounds coming from the ancient ceiling fan whirring overhead and the distant call of seagulls from the boardwalk three blocks away.

The bell above the door jingled, and I glanced up to see Mira from Tempest Tea & Coffee weaving between displays with her usual grace. She carried a ceramic pot with a small, plump succulent and what was undoubtedly my usual order—double espresso with a splash of Amaretto.

"Delivery," she announced, setting both items on the counter with a flourish. "Coffee and a new friend to brighten up your day."

"You're an angel," I said, grabbing for the coffee like it contained the elixir of life. "But what's with the plant?"

"This," she declared proudly, "is Gertrude. She's practically immortal—perfect for someone who claims to have a black thumb." Mira adjusted the pot slightly, her fingers lingering on the counter near mine. "Consider it a thank you for those protection charms you made for the café. They've definitely kept the weirder customers in check."

I examined the squat little plant with its blue-green leaves. "She's cute. Low maintenance?"

"Practically indestructible," Mira promised with a smile that warmed her dark eyes. "And gorgeous, like you."

The compliment was delivered with enough warmth that I felt heat rise to my cheeks. Mira had been a regular presence since she had opened her café next door a few years ago. Our businesses supported each other in the sort of symbiotic relationship that small shop owners dream about. Lately, though, her visits had become more frequent, her smile lingering a little longer. I wondered if she wanted to become closer friends. That'd be nice, I didn't have any girl friends.

"Well, thanks. For both Gertrude and caffeine salvation." I took a sip of the perfectly prepared coffee. "How much do I owe you?"

"On the house," she insisted, backing toward the door. "Though you could stop by later if you want. I'm testing a new pumpkin bread recipe that needs an honest opinion."

After she left, I smiled at the little plant. It was nice to have friendly neighbors, especially ones who enabled my coffee addiction. I positioned Gertrude in a sunny spot on the counter, mentally betting myself how long it would take for me to accidentally kill it, despite its supposed indestructibility.

These early morning hours were my favorite part of owning Twyla's Trinket & Trade—peaceful moments when the shop was all mine, before visitors wandered in from the nearby casino hotels or locals stopped by to browse what was new. The scent of modeling clay and craft adhesive filled the air, mixing with the faint traces of sage and cedar from the protection sachets I'd tucked into the shop's corners.

I was halfway through arranging a series of felted ocean creatures for the children's section when my phone buzzed with a text from Alex.

Alex: Good morning! Don't kill me, but there's a surprise coming your way today. It was Kronos's idea.

I frowned at the screen. Alex's 'surprises' ranged from delightful (unexpected pastries from that bakery near the marina) to disastrous (the time he'd tried to install a new display case and somehow knocked out the power to the entire building).

Twyla: Should I be worried? I texted back.

The typing bubbles appeared and disappeared several times before his response came through.

Alex: Maybe? Just remember Kronos meant well.

That was not reassuring.

Before I could demand more details, the shop bell jingled. I looked up, ready with my practiced welcome smile, only to feel it freeze on my face.

Ezra Thalassos stood in my doorway, the morning light haloing his pale pink hair. He wore a loose white linen shirt that seemed to float around him, paired with fitted pants in a shade of blue so dark they were nearly black. A leather portfolio was tucked under one arm, and his eyes scanned the shop with quiet interest.

My stomach dropped. Three times in two days was no coincidence. Were all the hot men in this city stalkers?

"Good morning," he said, his voice carrying the same musical quality that had haunted my thoughts since the beach. "What a quaint little shop."

I straightened, setting down my phone with deliberate calm. "We don't open for another hour."

"I know." His smile was apologetic as he stepped further into the shop. "I was told to arrive early."

"Told by whom?" I kept the counter between us, my fingers instinctively touching the rune-marked bracelet at my wrist. With a quick touch to the runes, I would project a protective barrier to block him out. Or that's what it was supposed to do. I'd never actually tried it.

He tilted his head slightly. "Has Alex not told you?"

The text message suddenly made more sense. "What *exactly* does Alex have to do with *you* being in *my* shop?"

Before he could answer, the back door banged open. Alex appeared, carrying a cardboard tray with three coffee cups. He stopped short when he saw Ezra, his expression shifting from surprise to something more guarded.

"You're early," he said, his tone decidedly cooler than usual. He set the coffee tray down and moved to stand beside me, his shoulder brushing mine in what I recognized as a protective gesture. "We said nine thirty."

"My apologies." Ezra's smile didn't waver, though his eyes flickered between us with a keen assessment. "I prefer to get a feel for the space before beginning work."

"Beginning what work?" I asked, looking between them.

Alex sighed, running a hand through his hair. "That's the surprise I texted you about. Can we talk in the back for a minute?" He glanced pointedly at Ezra. "Don't touch anything."

I followed Alex through the curtained doorway that led to our small office and storage room, my confusion rapidly turning to irritation.

"What is goin' on?" I demanded once we were alone. "Why is E. Thalassos here at seven in the morning?"

Alex leaned against the desk, arms crossed. "Kronos commissioned him to do two portraits as a thank-you gift. One of me for Kronos, and one of you for the shop." He grimaced. "I tried to talk him out of it, but Kronos insisted he's the best in Cypress City. Not to mention his waiting list is months long, but Kronos pulled some strings. They're friends or something."

"And no one thought to ask me first?" I kept my voice low, though I wanted to shout.

"I know, I'm sorry." Alex held up his hands. "I told Kronos, but he was so excited about surprising you." He hesitated. "And honestly, I thought you'd be thrilled. You've been obsessed with his paintings for months."

"I liked his art, not him," I hissed. "There's a difference."

The memory of that blank, predatory stare on the beach flashed through my mind. Spending hours with him watching me? The idea made my skin crawl. Yet I could see the genuine guilt in Alex's eyes. He was trying to navigate between his best friend and his boyfriend, and I wasn't making it easy.

"Look," Alex said, lowering his voice further, "I don't trust him either." He shook his head. "But Kronos vouched for him professionally. He's done work for some pretty important Supes around here."

"That's not exactly comforting."

"I can stick around while he's here." Alex squeezed my arm. "Or we can cancel the whole thing. I'll deal with Kronos."

I considered it. Refusing would cause tension between Alex and Kronos, embarrassment for everyone involved, and probably waste whatever hefty deposit Kronos had already paid. All because I was unsettled by one strange encounter.

"It's fine," I sighed, not entirely meaning it. "But you owe me. Big time."

Relief washed over Alex's face. "Thank you. Really. I'll stay as long as I can, but I promised Kronos I'd help him with something this afternoon."

"Of course you did." I rolled my eyes, but couldn't maintain my annoyance at his sheepish expression. "Go. He's just a man. It'll be *fine*." I couldn't help the heavy southern twang exaggerating the last word.

When we returned to the main shop, Ezra was examining a handcrafted mobile I'd finished the previous week. His long fingers traced the delicate pieces of sea glass and driftwood that I'd balanced to spin gently in the shop's air currents.

"Your work is exceptional," he said without looking up. "The balance of these elements—" He paused, finally raising his eyes to meet mine. "You understand the power of liminal spaces too."

Something in the way he said it made me think he wasn't just talking about the design.

Alex cleared his throat loudly. "Ezra needs to observe before he starts the actual portrait."

"I prefer to understand my subjects in their natural environment," Ezra explained, delicately setting down the journal. "The best portraits capture essence rather than mere appearance."

Alex jolted as his phone started buzzing in his back pocket. He held up a finger as he checked it. "Kronos needs me earlier than expected." He looked between Ezra and I. "You sure you're okay with this?"

"I'll be fine," I repeated, more firmly this time. "Go help your man."

"Call me if—" he glanced at Ezra, not bothering to hide his wariness, "—if you need anything."

"I will."

Alex hesitated, then leaned close to whisper in my ear. "I can be back in a snap if anything funny happens." He pulled back, gave Ezra one last warning look, and headed for the door. "I'll check in later."

The bell jingled as he left, the sound unnaturally loud in the sudden silence. Ezra stood perfectly still, watching me with a mysteriously blank expression.

"He doesn't trust me," Ezra said, stating the obvious.

"Can you blame him?" I moved behind the counter, putting more space between us. "Your kind doesn't exactly have the best reputation."

"My kind." His smile held no humor. "And what do you know of *my kind*, Twyla Knight?"

The way he said my name sent an involuntary shiver down my spine—not entirely unpleasant. There was something about his voice, a musical quality that seemed to bypass my ears entirely and vibrate directly through my body. It made my pulse quicken and my skin flush, like he'd reached out and traced a finger along my neck instead of simply speaking. The sound rolled through me in waves, each syllable creating a warmth that pooled low in my belly and made my breath catch.

It was the kind of voice that could make grocery lists sound like poetry, that would make you lean closer without realizing you were moving. Something primal responded to it, something that whispered *yes* before my rational mind could catch up.

I pushed the feeling aside, chalking it up to good genetics and maybe an accent I couldn't quite place, though my body seemed reluctant to let go of the sensation.

"Enough to keep my distance," I said, returning to my display arrangement. "You can set up over there." I nodded toward a corner with decent light. "The shop opens at ten, so you'll have to work around customers."

"Of course." He sauntered to the indicated spot and plopped himself in the high-backed green velvet chair. As he began unpacking his supplies, I couldn't help watching from the corner of my eye. His movements were deliberate, almost ritualistic—arranging pencils, opening his sketchbook, adjusting his chair with precise care.

When he caught me looking, he didn't comment, just smiled a slightly knowing smile that made me think twice about letting him set up shop here.

It was going to be a very long day.

The morning passed in a strange dance of awareness and avoidance. I helped customers, restocked shelves, and tried to pretend I didn't feel his attention tracking my every movement. Whenever I glanced his way, his pencil was scratching across the page, his focus seemingly on his work rather than me.

By midafternoon, the steady stream of tourists had dwindled to the occasional browser. I used the lull to adjust the fairy lights I was planning to hang around the new window display. The strands had tangled overnight, and I muttered under my breath as I worked the knots free.

"You have an interesting approach to customer service," Ezra said, his voice breaking the silence we'd maintained most of the day.

I looked up to find his sketchbook closed on his lap, his full attention finally undisguised. "What's that supposed to mean?"

"You're kinder to the tourists looking for cheap souvenirs than to the locals who actually buy your hand-crafted pieces." His head tilted slightly. "I've watched you adjust your manners for each person who walks through that door."

"That's called readin' the room." I returned to my untangling. "Basic retail survival skill."

"Mmm." He rose from his seat, stretching in a way that made his loose shirt stretch taunt over his lithe form. "I think it's something more innate."

He wandered to the window, studying the street outside with an expression I couldn't read. The late afternoon sun caught his profile, turning his hair to flame and casting his features in sharp relief. For a moment, he looked carved from rose quartz rather than flesh.

"Do you always dress like that?" he asked suddenly.

The question caught me off guard, and a strand of lights dropped onto the table with a loud thud. "Excuse me?"

"That expression was adorable. Your nose scrunches—just there." His fingers tapped the bridge of his nose. "Especially when you're irritated."

"Are you irritatin' me on purpose, then?"

His smile was reflected in the window. "Perhaps."

I climbed the stepladder with the now-untangled fairy lights, determined to finish the display before closing. The top shelf was just out of comfortable reach, forcing me to stretch farther than was strictly safe.

"You should move the ladder," Ezra observed, still by the window.

"It'll be fine," I insisted, my southern accent thickening with concentration. I tugged my shirt down with one hand while stretching with the other, painfully aware that from his angle, he might get more of a view than I intended. Not that it would stop me—I'd be damned if I called for help over something as simple as hanging lights. "Just need to hook this over the—"

"That doesn't look stable." He said, moving to stand beside the ladder. "You're going to fall." He extended his hands as if to catch me.

"I know what I'm doing." I stretched further, fingers straining for the hook I'd installed last month.

The ladder wobbled. I felt the sickening sensation of balance lost, my body tipping sideways with nothing to grab onto. My stomach lurched as gravity took over.

Instead of the floor, arms wrapped around me, stopping my fall with surprising strength. My heart hammered against my ribs as I found myself cradled against Ezra's chest.

"Clearly an expert," he said dryly.

Our faces were inches apart, close enough that his breath warmed my skin with each exhale. My gaze dropped to his lips—their usual sardonic curve softened by surprise. A faint blush colored his cheeks, though his expression remained composed. The subtle movement in his throat as he swallowed drew my attention, the bob of his Adam's apple betraying the tension his calm demeanor tried to hide.

"You can put me down now," I managed, my voice embarrassingly breathless.

He set me carefully on my feet but didn't immediately step back. "You could have been seriously hurt."

"Are you okay?" I asked, noticing how he flexed his fingers. "That probably wasn't easy with your build."

A startled laugh escaped him. "My build? What does that mean?"

"Well, yeah." I gestured vaguely at his slender frame. "You look like you'd blow away in a strong breeze."

Something flickered across his face—amusement mixed with something darker, more challenging. "Appearances can be deceiving, Twyla Knight." He stepped closer, and despite our similar height, I suddenly felt small.

With deliberate slowness, he reached past me for his portfolio, his chest nearly touching mine as he gathered his supplies from the counter behind me. I held my breath, afraid to move as he took his time collecting each pencil, each piece of paper with meticulous care, tucking them into the leather case. The strange tension between us became almost unbearable, making the air feel thick and charged.

"You missed a spot," he said softly, portfolio now secured under one arm as he nodded toward the tangled fairy lights I'd abandoned on the table. "Allow me."

Before I could protest, he'd shifted the portfolio to tuck more securely under his arm and moved to the lights, his free hand working through the knots with surprising dexterity.

Damn him. And damn my body for reacting like this. As he stretched to reach a particularly stubborn tangle, his shirt rode up slightly, revealing a strip of surprisingly defined abs that made my mouth go dry. Those long, elegant fingers that had just been handling delicate art supplies were now working the lights free with careful, one-handed precision.

I bit my lip, pissed at myself for getting hot and bothered over something so simple. Since when did I turn into a cliché who got weak-kneed over a man handling basic tasks? It was just hanging lights, for Christ's sake. Not like he'd rescued me from a burning building. The fact that I couldn't tear my eyes from the way his pants hugged his ass as he turned away was downright embarrassing.

I forced my expression into something less thirsty when he turned back, though the knowing look he gave me made me wonder if my face had already given me away. *Great. Just what his ego needed.*

"Same time tomorrow?" He asked, turning back to me and cocking an amused brow.

"I suppose." I crossed my arms, uncomfortable with how flustered I felt. "If you must."

"I must." His smile didn't quite reach his eyes as he approached the counter where my phone lay. With startling quickness, he picked it up, fingers moving across the screen.

"What are you doing?"

"Insurance," he said, handing it back to me. "I texted myself, so now I have your number as well." He slid a business card across the counter—thick black cardstock with his name embossed in elegant red script. Beneath, simply 'Artist' and a phone number.

"In case you need to cancel," he explained, though his tone suggested he expected no such thing.

"I might," I warned, even as I slipped the card into my pocket.

His eyes lingered on mine for a moment longer than was comfortable. "We'll see."

He moved toward the door, pausing at the threshold to look back.

"Until tomorrow, Twyla Knight." His voice curled around my name like smoke. "Try not to fall off any more ladders in the meantime. I'd hate to add a cast to your portrait."

The bell jingled as he left, and I stared at the closed door. *Man, the ego on this guy is something else.*

I glanced at my phone, knowing his number was in there now, like he'd left a piece of himself behind. The fairy lights he'd hung cast a glow across the shop as the sun set.

What the hell had Kronos gotten me into?

Chapter Five

ROUGH CURRENTS

Days with Ezra fell into a maddening pattern. Each morning he'd arrive impeccably dressed in those flowing shirts that somehow made him look both delicate and imposing. He'd set up in the same corner, silent and focused as I opened the shop.

"Three inches to the left," he'd murmur, barely looking up from his sketchbook. Or, "Turn your face toward the window." An imperious command, never requests.

By the third day, he'd started asking for tea—not coffee like a normal person, but specific blends with precise steeping times. I'd had to purchase a few blends from Mira's shop next door. I was surprised to find that she even had tea in a coffee shop, but she was more than happy to help me.

"This is over-steeped," he informed me, wrinkling his nose at the cup I'd grudgingly prepared. "Earl Grey needs exactly four minutes, not a second more."

I snatched the cup back. "Then make it yourself next time."

He didn't respond, just returned to his sketching with a faint smile that made me want to dump the tea over his perfect hair.

The most infuriating part was that he'd suddenly transform without warning. One moment he'd be the haughty, hypercritical artist. The next moment , his entire demeanor would shift—voice dropping to a velvety register, movements becoming almost hypnotic as he prowled around my shop.

I could never get a decent read on him. The constant switching left me perpetually off-balance.

"Is there a reason you keep saying my name in every sentence?" I finally asked after he'd addressed me by my full name three times in one conversation.

His expression remained neutral, but amusement danced behind his eyes. "Does it bother you, Twyla Knight?"

"It sounds like you're addressing formal correspondence," I muttered, turning back to the display I was arranging. "Nobody uses both names in casual conversation."

"My dearest Twyla Knight," he replied, a hint of a smile playing at his lips. "I'm writing to inform you that your tea skills are subpar. However, I will let you make it up to me by permitting me to take you out this evening.

Looking forward to hearing from you. Ezra." He said it with such venom in his voice that I could tell he meant it as a jab and not a genuine offer.

"Dear Ezra, please choke on your tea bags. With regards, an annoyed shop owner." I rolled my eyes as I heard him chuckle, focusing on the arrangement of handcrafted jewelry instead of his scrutiny. Every time I glanced his way, his pencil was moving across the page with unwavering focus, though I could swear I felt his attention even when he appeared absorbed in his work.

The morning dragged on; the sun climbing higher as tourists wandered in and out, most just browsing to escape the growing heat outside. I'd just finished helping an older couple find souvenir gifts for their grandchildren when I noticed the shop had emptied. The sudden quiet was jarring after the constant jingle of the doorbell.

I used the lull to tidy the counter, reorganizing business cards and straightening the small display of impulse-buy items. The scratch of his pencil paused. I felt the shift in the room's energy before I even looked up—that peculiar tension that always preceded one of his mood changes.

"I need you to wear something pink tomorrow." His voice cut through the silence with calm authority, as if requesting a minor schedule change rather than dictating my wardrobe.

I glanced over my shoulder, pausing mid-motion with a stack of business cards in hand. "Excuse me?"

"Pink," he repeated, as if I hadn't heard rather than questioned the audacity. "It will complement the composition I'm planning."

"I don't take fashion advice from someone who dresses like a romance novel cover model," I said, gesturing to his billowing white shirt and fitted pants.

His lips quirked. "You think I look like a romance model?"

"That's what you took from that sentence?"

"It was the most interesting part." He stood, stretching like a cat waking from a nap. The movement was so sensual it should have been illegal before noon. "Wear pink. Please."

The unexpected 'please' caught me off guard more than the request itself.

"I might not own anything pink," I hedged.

"You have a salmon blouse hanging in your office," he countered. "I saw it when you left the door open yesterday."

The fact that he'd noticed made my stomach do a weird little flip. "Are you always this observant, or am I just special?"

"Maybe it's both." He started gathering his supplies, the movement oddly entrancing. Every gesture was deliberate, almost ritualistic. "I'll be leaving early today."

"Hot date?" The question slipped out before I could stop it.

"Would that bother you?" He glanced up, expression unreadable.

"Nope," I said too quickly. I hoped he didn't catch that. "Your social life is none of my business."

"Oh?" He tucked his sketchbook away. "I find myself increasingly interested in yours."

I snorted. "What social life? I work, I sleep, I occasionally watch bad reality TV with Alex."

"No romantic entanglements?" His tone was casual, but his gaze was anything but.

"Why? Are you planning to entangle me?" I meant it as a joke, but it came out more flirtatious than intended.

His eyes darkened as he moved closer, invading my space with a confidence that was both irritating and unnervingly attractive. "I've been considering it," he admitted, voice low enough that I had to lean in to hear him.

My stomach did an unexpected flip, and I tucked a strand of hair behind my ear nervously. I stepped back, bumping into the display table. "I don't appreciate being toyed with."

"You think I'm toying with you?"

"Of course I do," I shot back. "One minute you're cold and bossy, the next you're…" I gestured vaguely at his current stance. "This. It's confusing."

"Perhaps I find you confusing as well." He tilted his head, studying me with intense focus. He stepped closer still, boxing me in. "I think you're curious about what I see when I look at you. What's captured in my sketches."

He was right, damn him. I'd been dying to peek at his sketchbook for days. "I'm curious about lots of things," I deflected. "Doesn't mean I act on every impulse."

"Maybe you should." His finger traced the edge of the display table, inches from my hand. "Impulses can lead to unexpected pleasures."

My mouth went dry when I realized what he was referring to. "If you've still got energy for teasing, you can help me unpack these new arrivals." I nudged a box with my foot. "Unless those fancy hands of yours can't handle a little manual labor."

His gaze dropped to my lips for a heart-stopping moment before he smiled. "My hands are multi-talented."

"Prove it." I shoved the box toward him.

He accepted the challenge with a slight bow that was both mocking and elegant. "As the lady commands."

For the next hour, he unpacked fragile glass figurines with surprising dexterity, arranging them according to my instructions without complaint. The easy competence was almost more unsettling than his flirtation.

"You've worked retail before," I observed, watching him expertly wrap a purchase for an elderly customer who'd wandered in.

"I've had many occupations over the years." He handed the bag to the woman with a smile that had her practically giggling as she left.

"Like what?" I pressed, genuinely curious.

"That would spoil the mystery, wouldn't it?" He wiped his hands on a cloth, removing nonexistent dust. "Besides, you haven't earned those stories yet."

I laughed. "What do I need to do—pass a test?"

His smile turned mischievous. "Something like that."

I rolled my eyes, though part of me was intrigued by the challenge. "Fine, keep your secrets. I've got actual work to do."

"Of course." He returned to his corner, but didn't resume sketching. Instead, he watched me help customers with the same unnerving focus.

When he finally packed up to leave, I found myself oddly disappointed. Which was ridiculous—I'd been counting the hours until he'd go since he arrived this morning. I busied myself with inventory as he gathered his things, determined not to watch him leave like some lovesick teenager. Only when I heard him approach the counter did I look up.

"Tomorrow, then," he said, tucking his portfolio under his arm. "Don't forget. Pink."

"I'll wear whatever I feel like," I replied, just to be contrary.

His smile told me he saw right through me. "Of course you will." He turned to leave, then paused. "Oh, and Twyla?"

"What now?"

"You might want to return my pencil case before I leave."

I froze, hand instinctively moving toward my apron pocket where I'd slipped his expensive-looking pencil case while he was distracted. I'd planned to text him about it after he left, to see if I could lure him back for...I wasn't even sure what.

"I don't know what you're talking about," I lied, feeling my face warm.

He held out his hand, palm up, expression knowing. "Don't you?"

Busted. I pulled out the leather case, slapping it into his palm with as much dignity as I could muster. "It fell. I was keeping it safe."

"How considerate." His fingers brushed mine as he took it, the touch lingering. "If you wanted me to return, you could simply ask."

"I don't—"

"Lies don't become you," he interrupted gently. "Though your blush is quite charming."

Before I could plan a sufficiently cutting response, he was gone; the bell jingling in his wake. I pressed my hands to my heated cheeks, mentally kicking myself. He'd known exactly what I was doing. Worse, he seemed amused by it, like I was some transparent puzzle he'd already solved.

My phone buzzed minutes later with a text from his number.

Ezra: Next time, try stealing something less obvious. My watch, perhaps. I'd certainly come back for that.

I stared at the screen, caught between embarrassment and reluctant amusement. At least he wasn't angry. But his persistence was...unsettling. Flattering, maybe, in a weird way. But also confusing—was he actually interested, or just enjoying the game?

Either way, giving someone false hope was just cruel. If this was all some elaborate form of entertainment for him, I wasn't interested in being his plaything.

I shoved my phone back in my pocket without responding. Tomorrow I'd wear black, just to spite him.

Chapter Six

ARTISTIC UNDERTOW

I rummaged through my closet, pushing past a rainbow of oversized cardigans and patterned dresses until I found them—the most aggressively anti-pink items I owned. A custom crop top and high-waisted flared skirt set I'd made myself, both with a white background absolutely covered in bold black, electric green, and deep purple swirls that I'd hand-painted onto the fabric last summer. The combination clashed gloriously with pretty much everything, especially anything pink.

"Perfect," I muttered, pulling them on and pairing the outfit with my chunkiest turquoise jewelry and lime green glasses instead of my usual purple frames. The mirror reflected a color explosion that made me grin. My midriff peeked out between the hem of the crop top and the high waistband of the skirt, the swirling patterns creating an almost hypnotic effect when I moved. If Ezra wanted pink, I'd give him the polar opposite of pink—a walking kaleidoscope.

The outfit was actually one of my favorite creations—the crop top showed just enough skin to be sexy without being impractical, and the flared skirt swished delightfully when I moved, both pieces showcasing my hand-painted design work. I'd worn it to the craft fair last month and gotten compliments all day. Not that I was dressing for compliments from Ezra. This was purely about making a point.

At least, that's what I kept telling myself.

The morning was blissfully Ezra-free, as he'd said he'd arrive in the afternoon. I used the time to catch up on paperwork and online orders, savoring the quiet and trying not to glance at the clock every fifteen minutes. The lack of his presence was almost as distracting as when he was actually here, filling my shop with his contradictory energy.

At exactly 2:5PM5, I heard the creak of the stairs that led to my apartment above the shop. Alex appeared in the doorway, carrying a box of new leather journals he'd been working on. He stopped short when he saw me, eyes widening slightly.

"Holy color explosion, Batman," he said, setting the box on the counter. "You trying to induce seizures?"

"What do you think? Too subtle?" I replied, adjusting my lime glasses.

He laughed, shaking his head. "Yeah, real understated."

"He asked me to wear pink. I'm making a statement." I gestured to my outfit.

Alex's smile grew. "Oh, you're making a statement alright. Just not the one you think."

"You're reading too much into this," I protested. "This is just—"

"The nicest thing you own that isn't something you'd wear to a funeral," he finished for me. "I know your wardrobe, Twy. You're trying to impress him."

"I'm trying to *annoy* him," I corrected.

"If you say so." He started unpacking his box, carefully arranging the journals on the display rack. "Kronos thinks you two would make a cute couple."

I nearly dropped the receipt I was writing. "Excuse me? You've been discussing my love life with your boyfriend?"

Alex shrugged, unrepentant. "He brought it up. He said Ezra's been more inspired lately than he's seen in years. Apparently, that's a big deal."

"It's a *job*," I said flatly. "He's being paid to paint my portrait."

"And spending way more time here than he needs to." Alex gave me a meaningful look. "Kronos says he usually works from photographs for commissions like this."

That bit of information lodged itself in my brain like a splinter. If Ezra could have just taken photos rather than camping out in my shop for days, why hadn't he? The obvious answer made my stomach flutter in a way I refused to acknowledge.

"What else does Kronos say about him?" I asked, aiming for casual and missing by a mile.

Alex's grin turned knowing. "Oh, you're interested now, huh?"

"Just doing my due diligence on the man who's been haunting my shop."

"Not much," Alex admitted. "He's private about his past. Been in Cypress City about five years. Keeps to himself mostly, though his reputation in the art world is pretty significant." He paused, expression growing more serious. "Though Kronos said to be careful."

"Careful how?" I tried to ignore the chill that ran down my spine. "Did he say something specific?"

"Just that sirens are complicated." Alex arranged the last journal, his movements more deliberate. "Especially ones as old as Ezra."

"Old?" I frowned. "He doesn't look over thirty."

Alex's laugh held little humor. "Yeah, well, Kronos thinks he's older than the city."

The bell above the door jangled before I could process that bombshell. Alex and I both turned to see the subject of our conversation standing in the doorway, portfolio under his arm and eyes immediately fixing on me.

For a moment, no one spoke. He looked like he'd stepped out of a Renaissance painting—fitted vest in deep crimson velvet over a flowing shirt of palest pink silk, gold embroidery tracing intricate patterns across the fabric. Ezra's gaze traveled slowly from my lime green glasses down to my vibrant crop top and swirling-patterned skirt, the intensity of his appraisal making my skin prickle despite the shop's air conditioning. When his eyes finally returned to mine, his expression held a mixture of amusement and something darker.

"Not pink," he observed, voice neutral.

"Not even close," I agreed, adjusting my turquoise statement necklace with deliberate flair.

His lips twitched, fighting a smile. "Bold choice."

Alex looked between us, eyebrows raised. "Well, this is fun and not at *all* uncomfortable." He grabbed an empty box from behind the counter. "I'll just head back to my workroom before the sexual tension in here suffocates me."

"Alex!" I hissed, mortified.

He shot me an unrepentant grin before disappearing through the back curtain, leaving me alone with Ezra, whose expression had shifted to undisguised interest.

"Your friend is refreshingly direct," he commented, moving further into the shop. "A trait you share."

"Only when provoked." I perched on the edge of the counter, swinging one bare leg. "You're early."

"By five minutes." He set his portfolio down, the gold rings adorning several of his fingers glinting as he moved. "I appreciate punctuality."

"Is that why you've been lingering hours past when you should be done each day?"

He tossed his hair over his shoulder as he looked back at me. God, he was dramatic. "Perhaps I find the company worth lingering for."

I couldn't tell if he was flirting or simply amusing himself at my expense. "Where do you want me today?"

"The afternoon light through that window would be perfect." He nodded toward the reading nook I'd set up in the corner—a comfortable armchair surrounded by bookshelves filled with journals and craft books. "If you could sit there while I get set up."

It was a reasonable request, so I complied, settling into the chair with a stack of invoices I needed to review. The position gave me a clear line of sight to the front door for any customers, while still allowing me to catch up on paperwork.

Ezra set up an easel this time instead of his sketch-book. He placed an already prepped canvas with a base layer of paint in shades of deep blue-green and hints of gold. I watched from the corner of my eye as he arranged brushes and small containers of paint on a portable table.

"You're not sketching?" I asked, curiosity getting the better of me.

"The preliminaries are done." He didn't look up from his preparations. "Today, I bring you to life."

Something in the way he said it—like he was creating rather than capturing—sent a shiver through me.

"I'm already alive, thanks."

He glanced up then, studying me with that penetrating gaze. "Are you? Truly alive, I mean. Not just existing?"

The question caught me off guard. "What kind of philosophical bullshit is that supposed to be?"

"An observation." He selected a brush, testing its balance between his fingers. "You've built walls so high that very little gets in—or out. It's a kind of half-living."

Indignation flared hot and bright. "You don't know the first thing about my life."

"I know you're afraid of wanting things," he said, his focus returning to his canvas. "Afraid that if you acknowledge desire, the disappointment when it's not fulfilled will break you."

I stared at him, speechless. The casual accuracy of his assessment felt like a violation—as if he'd been reading my diary rather than just observing me for a few days.

"Stay still, please," he murmured, brush already moving across the canvas. "That expression is perfect."

I wanted to get up and walk away, just to prove I could. Instead, I remained frozen in place, pulse hammering as he worked in silence, occasionally glancing up to study some aspect of my face or posture before returning to his painting.

"You're doing it again," I said finally, unable to bear the quiet.

"Doing what?" he asked without pausing his brush.

"Acting like you know me."

"I don't know you fully." His tone was matter-of-fact. "But I see you more clearly than most."

"Because you're so special?" I couldn't keep the sarcasm from my voice.

His smile was fleeting. "Because I'm paying attention."

The shop bell jingled as two college-aged tourists wandered in, giggling over something on one of their phones. I rose to help them, grateful for the interruption.

For the next hour, I assisted a steady stream of customers while Ezra continued painting, seemingly unbothered by the surrounding activity. Occasionally I'd catch him watching me interact with someone, his expression thoughtful, before returning to his work.

By late afternoon, the flow of customers had dwindled again. I was drawn back to the armchair, curious despite myself about the progress of the portrait.

"May I see it?" I asked, nodding toward the canvas.

"Not yet." His answer was immediate, the brush never faltering. "It's not ready."

"It's *my* face," I pointed out. "I think I'm entitled to a peek."

"Patience is a virtue, Twyla Knight." He used both names again, deliberately this time, his eyes briefly meeting mine with amusement. "Good things come to those who wait."

"You're insufferable, you know that?" I huffed.

"So I've been told." He set down his brush, stretching slightly. "Would you mind making tea? Earl Grey, steeped for—"

"Four minutes exactly," I finished for him. "Yes, Your Highness. Anything else? Shall I fan you with palm fronds while you work?"

His laugh was rich and genuine—a sound I hadn't heard from him before. It transformed his face, softening the sharp angles and making him look almost human.

"That won't be necessary," he said, eyes still crinkled with mirth. "Though the image is charming."

"You have a strange definition of charming." I moved toward the small kitchenette in the back of the shop where I kept a kettle. I felt his gaze on my back as I prepared the tea, measuring loose leaves into the infuser with more care than I'd typically bother with. *Not because I care about his prissy tea preferences*, I told myself. Just because I took pride in doing things properly.

When I returned with the steaming cup, he was cleaning a brush with a cloth. He accepted the tea with a nod of thanks, testing the temperature with a cautious sip.

"Perfect," he pronounced, the simple approval causing an absurd flicker of satisfaction in my chest.

"Don't sound so surprised." I crossed my arms, leaning against the nearby bookshelf. "I'm capable of following basic instructions."

"When you choose to." His eyes traveled over my outfit again, one eyebrow raised in silent judgment.

I shrugged, unrepentant. "I don't take fashion orders from anyone, especially not men who dress like they're auditioning for a period drama."

His face lit up at that. "Touch a nerve, did I? How interesting."

"Don't flatter yourself," I scoffed.

But he was right, damn him. It bothered me, more than I wanted to admit. The comment about my appearance had hit exactly where I was most vulnerable, dragging me right back to middle school hallways and whispered insults behind cupped hands.

I'd always dressed differently—bold colors, unusual patterns, anything that felt like art instead of conformity. While other girls wore the same three brands in the same boring combinations, I'd shown up in vintage finds and handmade accessories that expressed something real about who I was inside.

The other kids had noticed. Of course they had.

Amanda Prescott had been the worst of them, the kind of pretty, popular girl who could smell insecurity from three lockers away. I could still hear her voice, high and sweet and absolutely vicious. "Oh my god, Twyla, you look like a fairy threw up glitter all over you." The laughter that followed had echoed in the bathroom where I'd been admiring my first attempt at body glitter, feeling magical and bold and beautiful for exactly thirty seconds before Amanda's words shredded my confidence.

I'd learned to armor myself after that, to own my choices so completely that criticism bounced off. But sometimes, when someone looked at me with that particular gleam in their eyes—the one that said they'd found a weakness to exploit—I was thirteen again, washing glitter down the sink drain and promising myself I'd never be that vulnerable again.

"Oooh, touchy." Ezra had that same predatory gleam that Amanda used to get when she'd found fresh material. The similarity made my skin crawl.

Lucky for me, his phone chimed with a text alert. When he checked it, his expression shifted from gleeful anticipation to clear annoyance. "I need to go," he said, already beginning to pack away his supplies with sharp, efficient movements. "We'll continue tomorrow."

"Oh we will, will we?" I couldn't resist asking, grateful for the reprieve but determined not to show it. "Should I wear green? Polka dots? Maybe something scandalous?"

"Wear whatever makes you feel powerful," he replied, not rising to my bait. "I find you captivating, regardless." The casual compliment threw me completely off balance. By the time I'd recovered, he had already covered the canvas with a cloth.

"Same time?" I asked, hating how eager I sounded.

He paused, studying me with that unnervingly direct gaze. "Does my presence no longer bother you, then? How interesting."

"It bothers me plenty," I lied. "I just want this finished so I can have my shop back."

"Of course." His expression told me he didn't believe me for a second. "Three o'clock, then."

He was nearly to the door when a thought occurred to me. "You could have just taken photographs," I called after him. "For the portrait. That's what you usually do, isn't it?"

He turned back, expression unreadable. "Who told you that?"

"Is it true?"

He considered for a moment, then nodded once. "For most commissions, yes." He rested his forehead on the door frame with a heavy sigh, as if my questions were draining the life from him.

"So why the daily visits? Why all this?" I gestured around the shop.

"I wanted to see more than a snapshot could capture." He just waved me off as if that should be enough of an explanation.

"Or you just like tormenting shop owners with ridiculous demands and cryptic statements," I countered, trying to lighten the suddenly serious atmosphere.

His smile returned, and he winked at me with a flourish. "Perhaps that too." He opened the door, pausing on the threshold. "Until tomorrow, Twyla Knight."

The bell jingled as the door closed behind him, leaving me standing there with the feeling that I'd somehow lost a game whose rules I didn't understand.

When I returned to the counter, I noticed something weird. Gertrude, the succulent, which had been thriving just that morning—a miracle given my black thumb—now looked distinctly...dead-ish. Several of her plump leaves had shriveled up like sad green raisins, turning an alarming shade of brown.

"What the hell?" I muttered, poking at the plant. It was as if someone had fast-forwarded its life cycle by about six months. I could have sworn I heard a faint musical hum right before Ezra left, but I'd been distracted organizing my supplies.

Surely he wouldn't have...No. That was ridiculous. Even Ezra I'm-So-Important Thalassos wouldn't be petty enough to murder a plant because the person who gave it to me flirts with me sometimes.

Would he?

"If you killed my plant out of jealousy," I informed the empty shop, "we are going to have words. Lots of them. None repeatable in polite company."

Alex emerged from the back room, eyebrows raised. "Well, that was intense. You okay?"

"Fine," I said automatically, still staring at poor dead Gertrude.

"Uh-huh." He didn't sound convinced. "Want to tell me why you're blushing?"

"I'm not—" I touched my cheeks, finding them warm beneath my fingers. "It's just hot in here." Was I blushing? Don't tell…that I actually felt flattered that he'd gotten so jealous? What in the hell is wrong with me?

He moved to adjust the air conditioning thermostat. "He was looking at you like you're his next meal."

The image his words conjured made me blush deeper. "He wasn't—"

"Oh, he absolutely was." Alex's expression turned serious. He glanced toward the covered canvas in the corner, the one Ezra had been working on all week. "What do you think he's got under there, anyway?"

"Something brilliant, I'm sure," I muttered, unable to keep the hint of envy from my voice.

Alex started moving toward it with casual curiosity. He rolled up his sleeves, revealing the intricate tattoo work that covered his forearms—designs he'd gotten after escaping that awful club, each one marking a piece of his freedom. From what he'd told me, he hadn't been allowed to get tattoos while working there as it lowered his 'value'. Just thinking about it and that Madam Michelle gave me the creeps.

"Alex, don't," I warned, staying firmly where I was. "Ezra specifically said it's not ready yet."

"Since when do you listen to men?" Alex asked, but he stopped anyway, respecting my request if not understanding it.

I shrugged, feeling awkward. "It's just...you know."

"I know you think the sun rises and sets on his artistic opinions," Alex said, leaning against the counter between trinket displays. "You know what would really throw him off his game? If you challenged him to some kind of art-off." He snorted at his own joke. "Can you imagine? Same subject, you two painting side by side, letting everyone see who's really got the goods."

I stared at him for a long moment, something clicking into place."

Alex's smile faltered. "Wait. You're not actually considering it, are you? I was kidding."

"Why not?" I asked, a strange new confidence blooming in my chest. "It would be...interesting."

"Interesting is one word for it," Alex muttered, looking slightly alarmed at the monster he'd created. "Terrifying is another."

He started backing toward the curtain that led to his workroom, shaking his head. "I'm going to pretend I never said anything and go finish those leather journals."

"Hey Alex," I called after him, a smile spreading across my face. "I'm closing up early tonight. Got some things to prepare for tomorrow."

His head poked back through the curtain, eyebrows raised. "Should I be worried?"

"Not you," I replied, the idea taking clearer shape with each passing second. "But Ezra should be."

Chapter Seven

BREAKING THE SURFACE

The bell chimed as I locked the shop door behind me, turning the OPEN sign to CLOSED a full two hours earlier than usual. Sacrificing afternoon sales wasn't something I did lightly, but desperate times called for desperate measures. And Ezra Thalassos was definitely a desperate time.

Cypress City's summer heat had turned my beat-up yellow Volkswagen Beetle into a miniature oven, and I cranked the AC to full blast while mentally running through my list. I needed supplies—and not the kind I kept stocked in my shop.

Spindle & Wool on Harbor Street was my destination. The massive store was a crafter's paradise, with everything from basic supplies to specialized materials you couldn't find anywhere else in the city. I needed high-quality watercolor paper, professional-grade pastels, and brushes thin enough for detail work.

I pulled into the parking lot and headed inside, the store's air conditioning a blessed relief after the sweltering heat. I grabbed a basket and made a beeline for the paper aisle, running my fingers over different textures and weights. I needed something substantial enough to hold layers of color, but not so heavy it would be unwieldy.

"Excuse me," I asked an employee stocking shelves nearby. "Do you have any cold-pressed watercolor paper, one hundred and forty pounds?"

The teenager pointed toward the back corner. "All the fancy stuff's over there. Just got a shipment of Arches yesterday."

"Thanks." I headed in that direction, mentally calculating how many sheets I'd need. As I rounded the corner into the premium paper aisle, I stopped short. Standing there, examining a pack of handmade paper with intense concentration, was the very person I was thinking about.

Ezra hadn't noticed me yet. He was still in the same outfit from earlier—that pale pink shirt and fitted pants—but he'd removed his jacket, revealing the elegant lines of his shoulders. A loose knot at the nape of his neck held back his hair, though a few strands framed his face.

I contemplated backing away before he spotted me, but it was too late. As if sensing my presence, he looked up in genuine surprise.

"Twyla." My name sounded different on his lips here, outside the confines of my shop. "This is unexpected."

"I could say the same," I replied, trying for casual while my heart did a somersault in my chest. "Are you stalking me now?"

His lips quirked. "If I were stalking you, I'd hardly look surprised to see you." He gestured to the paper in his hands. "I'm replenishing my supplies. Even I run out occasionally."

I moved past him to examine the watercolor paper, hyper-aware of his proximity in the narrow aisle. The scent of him drifted over me—night-blooming moonflowers and sea air, intoxicating enough to make my head spin.

"I didn't realize you shopped at places like this," I said, reaching for a stack of paper. "I figured you had some exclusive artist supply store where they only let you in if you can name-drop."

He laughed, the sound rich and genuine. "I appreciate quality wherever it's found. This place carries Japanese handmade paper I can't get anywhere else in the city." He tilted his head, studying my basket. "You're working on a project of your own?"

"Something like that," I hedged. "Just a creative itch."

I headed for the brush aisle next, and he followed naturally, as if we'd come to the store together. The store's fluorescent lights cast strange shadows, making everything feel slightly unreal. I kept peeking over my shoulder to see if he was still there. When he caught me, I'd pretend I was looking at something on a nearby shelf.

"Do you live around here? It's just weird we've never bumped into each other before today if we both shop here."

"No, I live on the other side of the city." He shrugged. I guess it wasn't that weird…he'd been at my shop all week. It made sense he'd do his shopping close to where he was already spending so much time. Though I don't know if I'd be as laid-back about changing my shopping habits. I could only imagine how overwhelmed I'd feel trying to figure out the layout of a new store.

The brush aisle was narrow, barely wide enough for two people to pass comfortably. Shelves towered on either side, bristling with every type of brush imaginable—from broad, flat ones for washes to the finest detail brushes with tips like eyelashes. I spotted what I needed on a higher shelf: detail brushes with sable tips perfect for the work I had planned.

I stretched up on tiptoes, fingers straining toward the package just beyond my reach. My crop top rode up slightly as I extended myself, revealing more of my midriff, and I felt rather than saw Ezra's gaze tracking the movement. The prickle of awareness slid down my spine like a physical touch.

"Need help?" His voice came low and close to my ear, his breath stirring the tiny hairs at my nape.

"I've got it," I insisted, stretching further. My fingertips just grazed the plastic packaging, nudging it slightly, but not enough to grab it.

Ezra reached up at the same moment I made another attempt, his body suddenly flush against my back as he extended his arm alongside mine. The full-body contact sent a jolt through me—his chest pressed against my shoulders, his hips aligned with mine. I froze, caught between the shelf and his body, my heart hammering so loudly I was sure he could hear it.

His fingers closed around the brush set just as I lost my balance. My heel slipped on the slick floor, and I pitched backward. Ezra tried to catch me, but the sudden shift in weight sent us both tumbling down in a tangle of limbs and art supplies. I landed hard on my back; the impact knocked the air from my lungs. Ezra came down on top of me, barely catching himself on his forearms to avoid crushing me completely.

For a moment, we both lay there, stunned. My basket had overturned, sending pastels and paper scattering across the floor. Ezra's weight pressed me into the cold linoleum, his face inches from mine. His leg had fallen between my thighs, pressing firmly against me through the thin fabric of my skirt.

"Are you okay?" he asked, his voice strained.

I couldn't answer immediately. The position had aligned his knee directly against my most sensitive area, and every tiny movement sent sparks of sensation racing through me. His hand had somehow ended up cupping my breast in the fall, his long fingers splayed across the side curve. I knew I should say something—push him away, make a joke, anything—but my body had other ideas, responding to his touch with embarrassing enthusiasm.

His eyes darkened as he registered our position, the innocent concern transforming into something hungry.

"Do you need a *hand*, miss?" His fingers moved slightly against my breast, a subtle pressure that could have been accidental—except for the deliberate way his knuckles grazed across my nipple, pinching it gently through the fabric. My mind went blank, every coherent thought scattered by that simple touch. I bit down on my lower lip to keep from making a sound, hyper-aware of every point where our bodies connected. I knew it wasn't the time or place, but it had just been *so* long, I couldn't help but be flustered.

"I–I think I might." Neither of us made a move to get up.

His knee moved gently between my legs, the slight rocking pressure making me realize just how long it had been since anyone had touched me like this. To anyone passing by, it would have looked like we were just struggling to disentangle ourselves from an awkward fall. But the lust in his eyes told a different story, and suddenly I understood that this was no accident.

"We should…" My voice failed me as his fingers shifted again, deliberately circling the hardened peak of my nipple with his thumb.

"What ever shall we do, Ms. Knight?" his voice dropping to that velvety register that made my toes curl. "With you trapped beneath me like this?"

I couldn't think. His thumb traced slow, maddening circles, while his knee maintained that perfect pressure between my thighs. Each tiny movement sent fresh waves of pleasure radiating outward. My hands had somehow found their way to his shoulders, neither pushing him away nor pulling him closer, just holding on as sensation threatened to overwhelm me.

The sound of a shopping cart at the end of the aisle broke through the fog of arousal. Ezra's head turned slightly, registering the approaching customer.

In one fluid movement, he slid his hand behind my neck and pulled me up with him. I thought—hoped, feared—he was going to kiss me, but he positioned us to look like he was simply helping me up from a fall. Which I suppose he was, technically.

His lips brushed my ear as he whispered, "Who knew Twyla Knight would let me touch her like that in public? I wonder what else you'd let me do to you."

A violent shiver raced through me at his words, my body clenching with unfulfilled want. He helped me to my feet just as an elderly woman rounded the corner with her cart, giving us a curious look.

"So sorry about that," Ezra said to her, his voice perfectly pleasant and normal. "Clumsy of me to knock into her like that."

The woman smiled vaguely and continued past us. I stood frozen, my body still humming with arousal, my mind struggling to process what had just happened. Ezra knelt to gather my scattered supplies, moving with that same deliberate grace that had captivated me from the beginning. From this angle, no one would guess that moments ago his hands and knees had been driving me to the edge of sanity.

"I believe these are yours," he said, handing me the basket with my now-collected items. His expression was composed, but his eyes still burned with unmistakable hunger. A hunger that matched the throbbing ache between my thighs.

"Thanks," I managed, taking the basket with hands that wouldn't stop trembling. *Holy crap.* My nipple still throbbed where he'd touched it, sending little electric tingles across my chest with each heartbeat. I could feel the ghost of his fingers through the thin fabric of my crop top, like he'd branded me somehow. The air conditioning suddenly felt nonexistent.

"My pleasure." Those two innocent words somehow sounded like the filthiest proposition I'd ever heard. His voice did that velvet-over-gravel thing that bypassed my brain and went straight between my legs. That slight accent got thicker when he was turned on, didn't it? Fantastic, another thing to obsess over at 3am.

I couldn't tear my eyes from the knowing smirk playing at the corners of his mouth. That stupidly perfect mouth. God, I wanted to either slap that smug look off his face or drag him behind the yarn display and climb him like a tree. Maybe both. Definitely both.

"I need to check out," I said, barely recognizing my voice—all breathy and high like some swooning heroine in a bad romance novel. *Get it together, Twyla.* I needed space, needed air that didn't smell like him.

"Of course." He reached past me—unnecessarily close—and selected a set of brushes from the shelf. "These will serve your purpose well. The tips are particularly... sensitive to pressure."

Jesus Christ! That wasn't even trying to be subtle. My cheeks burned so hot they probably matched the fire exit signs. I snatched the brushes from his hand, our fingers brushing in a way that sent another jolt straight to my core. No way in hell was I letting him see how badly he'd rattled me.

"I'll see you tomorrow, Ezra." *Keep it casual. Normal. Like my underwear isn't ruined and my heart isn't trying to jackhammer through my ribs.*

"I'm counting the hours," he replied, that damnable smirk still firmly in place, pink eyes tracking me like I was prey. "Until then."

I turned and walked away, willing my legs to carry me steadily despite the lingering tremors of arousal. My body felt like it belonged to someone else—hot, sensitized, and frustratingly unsatisfied.

At the checkout, I fumbled with my credit card, mind still replaying the feeling of Ezra's body pressed against mine, his knee applying that exquisite pressure, his fingers working magic through layers of fabric. The cashier had to ask me twice for my rewards card number, giving me an odd look when I finally snapped back to attention.

"Big project?" She asked, eyeing my supplies.

"You have no idea," I muttered, signing the receipt with a shaky hand.

By the time I reached my car, I'd almost regained my equilibrium. Almost. I cranked the AC to full blast, hoping the cold air would clear my head and cool my overheated skin.

I sat there for a moment, hands gripping the steering wheel as I forced myself to breathe deeply. I hadn't expected to see him there, and I certainly hadn't expected to respond so intensely to his touch. It was just attraction, I told myself. Nothing more.

My phone buzzed as I finally started the car. A text from Ezra.

Ezra: I'm already imagining your hands working with those pastels. See you at 4pm tomorrow. The golden-hour light suits you.

I stared at the message, heat staining across my skin all over again. The man was insufferable, arrogant, presumptuous—and God help me, I couldn't wait to see him again.

Tomorrow couldn't come soon enough.

Chapter Eight

UNCHARTED TERRITORY

I'd closed early, putting up the 'By Appointment Only' sign to ensure we wouldn't be interrupted. The easels stood facing each other like duelists at dawn—his professional-grade one that he'd brought with him yesterday, and my rickety craft store special I'd dragged down from my apartment.

"This is ridiculous," I muttered to myself, adjusting the angle of my easel for the third time. The pristine sheet of watercolor paper I'd attached to it seemed to mock me.

I rearranged my pastels by color, then scattered them again, trying for a casual disarray that didn't scream, "I spent an hour setting this up."

Last night, I'd stayed up until 2 AM watching watercolor tutorials on YouTube, as if cramming for an exam could somehow make me his equal. The memory of our encounter at the art supply store sent my heart to racing—his body against mine, his hands finding places that made me forget my name. I'd fled the store afterward, too confused and aroused to form a coherent sentence.

But today would be different. Today, I was in control. My territory, my rules.

The bell above the door jangled, sending a sharp bolt of anxiety through my chest. My shoulders tensed as I looked up, half-expecting to see pink hair and that infuriating smirk. Instead, I saw Mira from Tempest Tea & Coffee, carrying a little paper bag and my usual coffee order. A strange mix of relief and disappointment settled in my stomach—relief that I had more time to prepare, disappointment that it wasn't him.

"Pre-battle provisions," she announced with a bright smile that showed off her dimples. "You looked like you were setting up for something serious when I peeked through the window."

"You have no idea," I said, making grabby hands at the coffee. "I may have made a slightly questionable life choice."

"Those are the most interesting kind." She pushed the bag toward me. "Lemon scones. Extra glaze. Brain food."

"You're spoiling me," I said, taking a deep sip of the perfectly prepared coffee.

"That's the plan," She replied with a wink that was definitely flirtatious. "How's Gertrude doing?" She gestured to the potted succulent on my counter.

I'd hastily stuck the withered plant in a decorative pot this morning, hoping Mira wouldn't look too closely. "Oh, she's...um, thriving!"

Mira frowned, stepping closer to examine the plant. Her fingers hovered over the shriveled leaves. "Twyla, what happened? She's practically dead."

"Is she?" I feigned surprise poorly. "I just watered her yesterday…"

Mira's expression soured, and she gently touched one of the brown, withered leaves. "This wasn't neglect." She looked up at me sharply. "Someone deliberately killed this plant with magic."

My suspicions about Ezra were confirmed instantly, but I tried to keep my face neutral. "Really? How strange. Maybe it was some kind of…supernatural blight?"

Mira shook her head, clearly not buying it. "I can try to revive her. May I?" Her dryad heritage meant she had a deeper connection to plant life than most—something I'd learned when she'd first opened the café and couldn't help but nurture every struggling houseplant in the neighborhood.

"Please," I said, relief clear in my voice. Mira closed her eyes, placing both hands around the small pot. A subtle green glow emanated from her palms, seeping into the soil and up through the plant's stems. The withered leaves gradually plumped, color returning as they unfurled. It wasn't instantaneous—some leaves remained slightly brown at the edges—but Gertrude definitely looked alive again.

"There," Mira said, a light sheen of sweat on her forehead. "That was difficult. Whoever did this has some potent magic. Very specific, too—targeted life-draining. Not common."

I thanked her profusely, making a mental note to position the revived Gertrude front and center when Ezra arrived.

"You should come by the café later," she suggested, backing toward the door. "Tell me how whatever this is goes." She gestured to the dual easels I'd set up. "Looks like fun."

"I'll try," I promised, though I had no idea how long this showdown with Ezra would last.

After she left, I found myself smiling at the thoughtful gesture. Mira had been bringing me treats with increasing frequency, each delivery accompanied by that warm smile and lingering glance. If I didn't know better, I'd think she was hitting on me.

Ezra entered the shop with his usual graceful confidence, but froze mid-step when his eyes landed on my counter. Specifically, on the now-revived Gertrude sitting proudly in her pot.

"What a...*charming* addition to your workspace," he said, his voice tight with what I recognized as barely suppressed annoyance.

"Isn't she *lovely*?" I replied innocently, stroking one of Gertrude's plump leaves. "She had a bit of a magical mishap yesterday, but Mira was kind enough to help"

His jaw tightened almost imperceptibly. "Mira brought you a replacement?"

"Oh *no*," I said, enjoying his discomfort far too much. "This is the original Gertrude. Mira has quite the green thumb—or rather, green magic. She mentioned something fascinating about targeted life-draining magic. I wonder how that could have happened?"

Ezra tossed his head, pink hair sweeping dramatically over his shoulder as he turned away. "How fortunate for your plant." He moved to set up his easel, his movements slightly more stiff than usual. "Though I find succulents rather uninspiring as subjects."

I bit back a smile as I watched him fuss with his supplies, clearly trying to regain his composure. Score one for Gertrude—and for me.

He sighed and assessed the room. "You've been busy," he said, taking in my setup.

"I thought we could work side by side. You've been studying me for days. Seems only fair I get to study you, too." I replied, fighting to keep my voice steady.

His eyebrows rose slightly, but he set down his portfolio and moved to the easel I'd designated as his. "Mmm, fairness," he said, unpacking his supplies with that fluid grace that made even mundane movements look like choreography. "An interesting concept coming from you."

"Meaning?" I crossed my arms, immediately defensive.

"Just that you've been deliberately provocative since we met." He arranged his brushes methodically, not looking at me. "Wearing that scandalous outfit when I asked for pink. Stealing my pencil case. Purposefully incorrectly making my tea."

"I'm provocative?" I nearly choked on the word. "You dry-humped me in the middle of an art supply store!"

His smile widened, showing the edge of those too-sharp teeth. "You weren't exactly fighting me off."

"That was—I was—" I sputtered, furious at my inability to form a coherent defense. "That's not the point!"

"It was what it was," he said simply, popping the cap off a tube of paint. "No need to overthink it."

The casual dismissal stung more than it should have. I turned to my easel, unsealing a new set of pastels with more force than necessary. "Well, it won't be happening again, so you can put it out of your mind." I wasn't sure if I was trying to convince him or myself.

"As you wish." He squeezed paint onto his palette with precise movements. "Though I wonder who you're punishing with that declaration—me or yourself."

I ignored the jab, focusing on the blank paper before me. I'd planned to draw the view from my shop window—the old oak tree, the slice of ocean visible between buildings—but my hands refused to cooperate. Each line I attempted came out wrong, each stroke too hesitant.

Meanwhile, Ezra worked with quiet confidence, his brush moving across the canvas in sweeping strokes that captured the essence of water without being literal. I watched his hands more than my own work—the way his long fingers gripped the brush, how his wrist turned with each movement, the occasional flash of scales when his sleeve rode up.

After twenty minutes of frustrated attempts, I stepped back from my pathetic attempt at art, sighing loudly enough that he glanced over.

"Your brushstrokes are too hesitant," he said, his eyes tracking my movement across the canvas. "The sea doesn't apologize for its power. Neither should you."

I glanced over at him, taking in the fluid confidence of his hands as they danced across his own painting. "Not everyone sees the ocean the way you do."

"And how do I see it?" His voice softened, genuine curiosity replacing his usual imperious tone.

I set my brush down and studied his canvas—the vast expanse of water, beautiful but somehow hollow. Waves captured in mid-crash with no witnesses, no life, just endless blue stretching toward a vacant horizon.

"Like it's home and exile at the same time," I said, the words escaping before I could filter them. "Like you're homesick for somewhere that doesn't exist anymore."

His hand froze, brush suspended above the canvas. The sudden stillness was jarring—Ezra was always in motion, always flowing like the water he painted. His knuckles whitened around the brush handle, so much so that I worried it'd snap.

"I'm sorry," I said, reaching for my brush again, desperate to break the sudden tension. "I didn't mean to upset you."

"No." The word was rough, as if dragged across something sharp before reaching his lips. "You're more perceptive than most humans." He looked haunted and tired. The arrogance was washed away for the briefest moment to reveal the tears that had sprung down his cheeks. He quickly wiped them away, leaving no evidence of how moved he'd been.

"I don't think I am," I said, my voice barely above a whisper. I gestured at his canvas. "The ocean in your work is always empty. No boats, no people. Just water and sky."

His throat worked as he swallowed. He set his brush down with deliberate care, wiping paint from his fingers with a cloth. Blue smeared across his pale skin, making the scales at his wrist catch the light.

"There used to be more," he said finally. His voice had changed, the musical quality replaced by something that scraped like stone against stone. "Before."

"Before what?" I asked, taking a step closer to him.

The air between us felt charged, different from the tension that had been building for days. This was something deeper, more dangerous. His eyes met mine, and I saw him weighing if I deserved his truth.

Finally, he touched his throat lightly, long fingers resting against the scaled hollow at the base. "You've never heard me sing," he said.

"I heard you that night on the beach," I countered, remembering the haunting melody that had drawn tears I hadn't known I was crying. *Also, the hum when he'd tried to kill Gertrude*, but I didn't say that outloud.

"A shadow." His laugh held no humor. "A whisper. A memory of what a siren's song can be." His fingers pressed harder into his own throat, almost punishing. "What it was meant to be."

"I thought sirens sang to lure sailors to their deaths." The words tumbled out before I could catch them, and I immediately wished them back.

Something moved behind his eyes—an ancient darkness, like storm clouds gathering on a distant horizon. His face went terrifyingly blank, all expression wiped clean as if by an invisible hand.

"Is that what your history teaches?" His voice was soft, but carried an edge that made the hair on my arms stand up.

I swallowed hard. "I mean, that's the mythology, right?"

"Mythology." He repeated the word like it tasted bitter. "Yes, I suppose that's what humans would call it."

He turned back to his painting, adding a streak of midnight blue so dark it was nearly black. The brush moved with vicious precision, slashing across the peaceful sea he'd created.

"We didn't always call to drown sailors, Twyla Knight." My full name in his mouth sounded different now—not teasing or seductive, but formal, as if he needed the distance it created. "Once, we simply sang because it was beautiful. Because it was who we were." His shoulders hunched forward slightly, the only visible crack in his perfect posture. My chest ached at the sight.

"What happened?" I asked, my voice barely audible over the soft scrape of his brush.

The silence stretched so long I thought he wouldn't answer. His brush kept moving, but the strokes had changed—shorter, harder, each one etching pain onto the canvas.

"I was very young," he finally said. His voice had gone distant, as if he were speaking from the bottom of the ocean. "By your counting, perhaps six or seven summers." His hand trembled slightly, a tremor so small I wouldn't have noticed if I hadn't been studying him so intently. He steadied it with visible effort.

"It was before humans had names for the oceans, when their vessels were crude things of wood and hide." The brush slowed but didn't stop. Blue-black waves grew more turbulent beneath his hand. "A ship came to our waters. We'd seen humans before, but rarely so many together." The air in the shop felt thick, as if we were suddenly underwater ourselves.

"They heard us singing." His voice dropped lower, forcing me to lean closer. "My mother. My sisters. The others." His jaw clenched so hard I could see the muscle jumping beneath his skin. "We weren't calling to them. We were simply...being."

He inhaled sharply through his nose, a ragged sound that made my breath catch.

"But they came anyway."

The temperature in the shop seemed to plummet. Goosebumps erupted across my skin as cold understanding dawned.

"What did they do?" I asked again, though a part of me already knew.

Ezra's brush stilled completely. A drop of dark paint fell from the tip, blooming like a bruise across the canvas. "What men with power always do when they encounter beauty they cannot possess." His voice was utterly devoid of emotion now, the flatness more chilling than any rage could have been. "They took. By force."

My stomach lurched. The simple words carried centuries of pain, and images I didn't want filled my mind.

"My mother hid me beneath the waves when they came," he continued, each word measured and precise, as if reciting something memorized long ago. "But I saw...everything." His eyes had gone unfocused, seeing something beyond the canvas.

"My eldest sister fought back." His voice finally cracked, the veneer of control slipping for just a moment. "She was so strong—stronger than any of them individually. But there were many, and only one of her." His brush clattered to the floor. Neither of us moved to pick it up. A blue-black stain spread across the hardwood like spilled blood.

"They killed her for it." His hands curled into fists at his sides. "I watched from below as they drove a blade made from bone into her heart."

"Oh god," I whispered, horror washing through me. I reached toward him, then stopped, hand hovering in the space between us, suddenly unsure if touch would comfort or harm.

"After that day," he continued, his voice steadying again with visible effort, "we learned to use our voices as weapons. To protect ourselves. To ensure no ship would ever approach our waters again."

He finally looked at me, really looked at me, and the agony in his eyes struck me like a physical blow.

"I'm sorry," I said, knowing how wretchedly inadequate the words were.

"It was a very long time ago." He flexed his fingers, tiny scales at his knuckles catching the light as they rippled with the movement. "But that is why there are no ships in my oceans, Twyla. Some memories never fade, no matter how many lifetimes you live."

I looked back at his painting, understanding now what I was seeing—evidence of a wound so deep that millennia hadn't healed it.

"Thank you," I said softly, finally closing the distance between us. His skin was cool beneath my fingers, those impossible scales smooth against my palm. "For telling me." I moved to his canvas, drawn by an impulse I couldn't explain. I picked up his fallen brush, wiping away the excess paint on a cloth.

"May I?" I asked, brush hovering over his ocean.

He nodded, watching with an intensity that made my skin prickle as I touched brush to canvas. With careful strokes, I added a tiny glimmer of light to the darkest part of his ocean—not a ship or a person, but a small spark of something hopeful.

"Not everything that enters the water brings destruction," I said, offering the brush back to him.

Our fingers brushed as he took it, and the contact sent electricity racing up my arm. His eyes tracked from the light I'd added to my face, something new awakening in their depths.

"In three thousand years," he said, his voice rough with emotion, "no one has ever touched my paintings."

The weight of his words hit me like a physical blow. Three thousand years. My mind struggled to comprehend such vast stretches of time.

His hand lifted, hovering near my cheek, paint still staining his fingers. "You are quite extraordinary, Twyla Knight." The air between us had transformed again, charged with something that transcended mere attraction. When his fingers finally made contact with my skin, leaving a faint trace of blue-black paint on my cheek, it felt like permission—not just to touch, but to see him. Truly see him.

His pupils dilated, black nearly swallowing seashell pink as his gaze dropped to my lips. I felt my body sway toward him, drawn by something older than conscious thought.

"Ezra," I whispered, his name a question and an answer at once. His smile broke across his face like sunrise. His soft lips found mine, capturing whatever I might have said in a kiss that started gentle but quickly deepened into something more urgent.

I expected finesse from a creature as old as him, some calculated seduction perfected over centuries. What I got instead was raw hunger—his tongue pushing into my mouth, his teeth catching my lower lip hard enough to make me gasp.

"You're wearing too many clothes," he growled against my mouth, his hands finding the hem of my dress and yanking upward. The sound of fabric tearing filled the room as the seam gave way under his impatient grip.

"Asshole," I groaned, though I was already fumbling with the buttons of his shirt. "I liked that dress. That was vintage, you uncultured sea monster."

"I'll buy you ten more." His mouth moved to my neck, teeth scraping over my pulse point before biting down hard enough that I knew I'd have a mark tomorrow. When I struggled with a stubborn button, he simply ripped the shirt open, sending buttons flying across my shop like tiny missiles.

"Oh, for—at this rate we'll both be naked and broke," I muttered, but my annoyance evaporated as I got my first real look at his bare chest—lean muscle dusted with coral-pink scales that caught the light like something from a fever dream. I'd imagined what he looked like under those billowing shirts, but the reality put my imagination to shame.

My fingers traced the pattern of scales, fascinated by their texture—smoother than they looked, warm despite their alien appearance. "You're like a dream," I said before I could stop myself.

He laughed, the sound vibrating through both our bodies. "And you're overdressed."

His hands made quick work of my bra, tossing it somewhere over his shoulder where it knocked over a display of handcrafted earrings. Part of my brain made a note to reorganize them later, but that thought scattered when his mouth found my breast, his tongue—rougher than a human's, slightly textured—circling my nipple in a way that had me arching into him.

"Fuck," I breathed, my head falling back as sensation took over. I'd never been vocal during sex, too self-conscious about sounding ridiculous, but something about the way he touched me bypassed my usual filters. "Don't stop."

"I have no intention of stopping," he assured me, his voice rough as his hands slid down to grip my ass. "I've been dreaming of this since I first saw you glaring at me across that gallery."

"I wasn't glaring, I was—oh god!" My defense died as his teeth caught my nipple, the edge of pain sending a jolt straight to my core. My hands clutched at his shoulders, nails digging into skin that was inhumanly warm beneath my fingers.

He backed me against the counter, lifting me easily to sit on the edge. Art supplies scattered, brushes and pastels clattering to the floor. I'd normally be annoyed at the mess, but I couldn't bring myself to care as his hands pushed my thighs apart, positioning himself between them.

"I've imagined bending you over this counter," he said, voice dropping to a register that seemed to vibrate through my bones. "Listening to those smartass comments dissolve into begging."

"I would never beg. And that's bold—you haven't even gotten my underwear off yet," I shot back, though the breathiness of my voice undermined any attempt at sounding unaffected.

His smile turned predatory. "A problem easily remedied." His hands hooked into the waistband of my underwear, tearing the delicate fabric like tissue paper.

"That's getting expensive," I managed as his fingers were sliding through the wetness between my thighs, exploring with a precision that made my legs shake.

"Worth every penny," he chuckled. He brought the finger he'd slid inside me and licked it in one long drag. "You're soaked."

"Don't flatter yourself," I gasped, though we both knew I was lying. I'd been wet since his first kiss, maybe since he'd walked through my door with that imperious expression. "Just—fuck, do that again."

He obliged, fingers circling my clit with devastating accuracy. His other hand worked on his own pants, unfastening them to free his straining cock. My breath caught at the sight of him—thick and flushed, with ridges along the shaft that were decidedly not human.

"See something you like?" he asked, a hint of his usual arrogance returning. His eyes burned into mine as his hand traveled down the ridged planes of his abdomen, muscles tensing under his touch. He gripped his cock with deliberate slowness, the considerable length looking even more impressive in his large hand. A quiet groan escaped his throat as he stroked himself from base to tip, the ridges along his shaft pulsing subtly as blood rushed beneath the surface. Pre-cum beaded at the tip, glistening in the dim light as he circled his thumb over it, spreading the wetness down his length with another languid stroke.

"This is what you do to me," he purred, voice dropping to that register that seemed to vibrate directly between my legs. "I've been hard for you since I watched you bend over that display table." Another stroke, his wrist twisting slightly at the head in a way that made my inner walls clench.

My mouth watered as liquid heat flooded my core, watching him pleasure himself with sinful confidence. Each stroke of his hand made my thighs press together in desperation.

"I'm reserving judgment," I replied, my voice betraying me with its breathiness. "You still have to prove you know how to use that thing."

He didn't answer in words. Instead, he positioned himself at my entrance, the blunt head of his cock pressing against me without pushing in. His eyes locked with mine, seeking permission despite the raw hunger clear in every tense line of his body.

"Are you going to make me beg?" I challenged, wrapping my legs around his waist and pulling him closer. "Because that might take a while, fish-boy."

"You talk too much," he said, fingers digging into my hips hard enough to bruise.

"Make me stop," I dared him.

He surged forward in one powerful thrust, burying himself to the hilt inside me. The sudden fullness threw my head back, a sound I didn't recognize tearing from my throat. Those ridges I'd glimpsed created exquisite friction against places inside I hadn't known existed, sending sharp jolts of pleasure up my spine.

"Holy fuck," I breathed, adjusting to the sensation of being completely filled. Every smart remark I'd prepared vanished into nothing. My body registered only him—stretching me open, hands gripping me in place, breath scorching my neck.

"Still feeling chatty?" he asked, the strain in his voice revealing his struggle for control.

I might have had a comeback—something cutting about his ego—but he chose that moment to withdraw almost completely before slamming back in. Coherent thought fled entirely. The counter rattled beneath us as he set a punishing rhythm, each thrust hitting perfectly inside me.

"Ezra," I gasped, all pretense abandoned as pleasure built in waves. My nails carved into his shoulders, leaving marks that healed almost as they formed. "Harder."

He complied, sliding one hand beneath my ass to tilt my hips higher. The angle changed until he hit a spot that made stars explode behind my eyelids. I wouldn't last, not with him pounding into me this way, his cock filling me so completely I couldn't remember emptiness.

My arm knocked over a tray of pastels in my frenzy. The sticks shattered on impact, exploding into clouds of colored dust that swirled around us. Blues, golds, and purples settled on our sweat-slicked skin, transforming our fucking into living art.

"You're close," he observed without breaking rhythm. "I can feel you tightening around me."

"Don't stop," I warned, tension building to an unbearable peak. My thighs trembled against his waist, back arching as I chased the release just beyond reach. "Fuck, please don't stop."

Then, without warning, Ezra began to sing.

The sound wasn't human—a melody so raw and primal it vibrated directly through my bones into my core. My body responded instantly, walls clenching around him as every sensation magnified tenfold. The colors from the broken pastels pulsed with each note, pleasure spiraling higher than I thought possible.

I came with a cry that surely reached the café next door, my body convulsing around him as ecstasy crashed through me in relentless waves. Vision narrowed to pinpricks of light against darkness, every muscle drawing bowstring-tight before releasing in a rush that left me boneless.

He fucked me through it, his thrusts growing erratic as my inner walls pulsed around him. When he finally came, it was with a sound more animal than human, his body tensing as he drove deep one final time.

For several long minutes, neither of us moved. His forehead rested against mine, both of us breathing hard as reality slowly reasserted itself. When I finally found the strength to open my eyes, I faced the chaos we'd created—art supplies scattered across the floor, colored dust settling on every surface, our clothes in tatters.

"Well," I managed, looking down at our paint-streaked bodies. "That's one way to critique my art technique."

His laugh was genuine, shoulders shaking with mirth. "Your technique," he said, pressing a surprisingly gentle kiss to my temple, "is perfect exactly as it is."

As I took in the chaos we'd created—pastel dust hanging in the air like multicolored fog, water pooling on the floor, art supplies scattered everywhere, our clothes in tatters—I couldn't help but smile. Whatever was happening between us was messy and complicated and probably a terrible idea.

But sitting there on my counter, wrapped in the arms of a siren who looked at me like I was a masterpiece rather than a study, I couldn't bring myself to care.

Chapter Nine

DEEP DIVE

My apartment door banged shut behind us, the sound echoing in the sudden quiet. We stood facing each other in my cramped entryway, both of us covered in pastel dust and paint, breathing hard like we'd just run a marathon instead of simply climbing the stairs.

"Shower's through there," I said, gesturing toward the bathroom, desperate to break the strange tension. "I'll get you something to wear while your clothes wash."

Ezra nodded, those pink eyes tracking my every move as I edged past him toward my bedroom. The narrow hallway forced us close enough that I could feel the heat radiating from his skin. Flakes of dried blue paint fell from his hair, landing like strange confetti on my worn hardwood floor.

"You probably want to change. Alex leaves clothes here sometimes," I called over my shoulder, rummaging through my dresser for the emergency stash of men's clothes I kept for when my best friend crashed on my couch. "They might be a little small for you, but—"

I turned to find Ezra directly behind me, so close I nearly collided with his chest. I hadn't heard him move. His hand reached up to brush something from my hair—paint dust, probably—his fingers lingering against my cheek. The casual intimacy of the gesture made my heart stutter in my chest.

"You have paint on your face," he murmured, voice rough.

"You have it everywhere," I replied. Desperate to maintain some semblance of decorum, I shoved the borrowed clothes against his chest. "Shower's all yours. Towels are in the cabinet."

His fingers wrapped around mine before I could pull away, holding the clothes between us. "Join me."

It wasn't a question. The intensity of his gaze made my knees weak. "That's not a good idea," I said, even as I leaned into him.

"It's an excellent idea." His thumb traced circles on my wrist, finding my pulse point. Was he checking how fast my heart raced? "Conserving water would be the responsible thing to do."

A laugh escaped me before I could stop it. "Really? You're going with save the environment as your line?"

His smile was slow and predatory. "Is it working?"

"Maybe." I tried to sound casual, though we both knew I was going to. I tugged my hand free, taking a small step back. "But I get first dibs on the hot water."

"As you wish." He followed me toward the bathroom, his footsteps silent on my creaky floors.

The bathroom was barely big enough for one person, let alone two—especially when one was over six feet of lean, lithe muscle. Steam quickly filled the small space as I turned the shower to its hottest setting. When I turned back to face him, Ezra had already stripped off what remained of his shirt, revealing that expanse of scaled torso that had fascinated me earlier.

In the harsh fluorescent light of my bathroom, the scales looked different—more pronounced, catching the light in iridescent patterns that shifted with his breathing. They started as tiny flecks near his collarbone, gradually increasing in size as they trailed down his chest and disappeared beneath his waistband.

"If you stare any harder, I might burst into flames." he teased, the words at odds with the hunger in his expression.

"Just wondering how much drain cleaner I'll need after all this paint goes down my pipes." I turned away, focusing on peeling off my ruined dress rather than watching him undress further. The sound of his zipper was almost deafening in the small space.

His laugh was soft. "Is that so?"

I ignored the comment, stepping under the hot spray before I could lose my nerve. Water sluiced over me, all the colors mixing to a muddied brown before it sucked down in the whirling vortex of my shower drain. I closed my eyes, tilting my face into the stream. The heat felt good on my skin, melting away the fingerprints left embedded in paint.

The shower curtain rings scraped against the rod as Ezra stepped in behind me. My shower stall was barely big enough for my frame—with his added, his chest pressed against my back.

"Here," he said, reaching around me for the soap. His arm brushed my breast, sending a jolt of awareness through me despite the mess we must both look. "Let me help."

"I can wash myself," I protested weakly, even as I tilted my head to give him better access when his lips found my neck.

"You could," he agreed, lathering soap between his palms. "But where's the fun in that?" His hands slid over my shoulders, working in slow, deliberate circles. Paint and pastel dust swirled down the drain as he methodically cleaned every inch of my upper back. His touch was confident but surprisingly gentle, finding knots of tension and working them loose with the perfect pressure to make me melt.

"You're good at this," I murmured, embarrassed by how quickly I was melting under his ministrations.

"I've had a lot of time to practice," he replied, hands sliding lower to trace the curve of my spine. I shivered despite the steam surrounding us. The reminder of his vast age should have been unsettling, but it sent a thrill through me—the knowledge that this ancient, powerful being was focused entirely on me.

"Turn around," he instructed, hands settling on my hips to guide me.

Water droplets trickled down my spine as his fingers pressed into my skin. My heart skipped despite what we'd shared downstairs just moments ago. The tiny shower suddenly felt both too small and not small enough. The tile chilled my toes as I pivoted slowly.

I came face to face with him for the first time since we'd entered the shower. Water plastered his pink hair to his skull, creating rivulets that traced paths between scales and smooth skin. His eyes darkened before me, pupils expanding until only a thin ring of pink remained.

Steam swirled between us, fogging the small space. Each breath drew in his scent mixed with soap and hot water. He stood so close I could distinguish individual droplets clinging to his eyelashes. My breasts pressed flat against his chest, the contact shooting sparks through my nerves despite the cooling water. His hardness pressed insistently against my stomach, a physical reminder of how he'd felt inside me minutes before.

Our gazes locked as water streamed over both our faces. The shower walls confined us to mere inches of space - any movement brushed skin against skin. My fingers found their way to his waist, steadying myself as the spray pattered against my shoulder and ran in warm rivulets down my sensitized skin.

"Excellent." That single word vibrated from his chest into mine, sending a shiver through me despite the steam surrounding us.

His hands suddenly gripped my thighs, lifting me higher against the tile wall. My back hit the icy surface with a thud that emptied my lungs in a rush.

"Put your leg up," he commanded, his voice rough.

I hooked my right leg over his hip, bracing my foot against the opposite wall of the cramped shower. Water streamed between our bodies, my hair heavy against my shoulders. His eyes burned into mine as he positioned himself, one hand pinning my hip to the wall.

The first thrust had me seeing stars. My mouth fell open in a silent gasp, then transformed into a cry that bounced off the bathroom walls. My fingers dug into his shoulders, leaving crescent marks as he moved.

"God, yes," I hissed. My head knocked back against the tiles. Each point where the wall pressed painfully into my spine sent a counterpoint to the pleasure building inside me.

My hips bucked forward, meeting his movements. I circled and ground against him when he filled me completely. My micro braids slapped against my wet skin with each motion. One hand found his pink hair, fingers twisting in the soaked strands, yanking his mouth to mine. Our teeth clicked together before our tongues met, my moans disappearing into his mouth.

"Harder," I gasped against his lips. "I won't break."

A sound rumbled from deep in his chest—a growl that vibrated through me. His hand slammed against the wall near my head. His hips snapped forward with enough force that the breath rushed from my lungs with each thrust. My other leg wrapped around him, using the leverage to lift myself slightly. The new angle sent him deeper, hitting spots that made my vision swim. The tiles scraped against my back, water cascading over us as the steam billowed.

Heat coiled low in my belly, tightening with each movement. My inner muscles clenched around him, drawing a groan from his throat. His rhythm stuttered, his breathing harsh against my ear.

"Look at me," he commanded.

My heavy eyelids lifted. The intensity in his gaze—pupils blown wide, only a thin ring of pink remaining—pushed me over. My body arched against the tile, a hoarse cry tearing from my throat as waves of pleasure crashed over me. My vision blurred, limbs trembling.

His movements grew erratic. His body tensed against mine, face buried in my neck as he shuddered through his own release.

The only sounds filling the bathroom were our gasping breaths and the steady drum of water. My leg slid weakly from the wall, muscles quivering. He lowered me carefully to the floor, his hands steadying me when my knees wobbled.

"That wasn't exactly what I had planned," he said, his voice sandpaper-rough as his forehead pressed against mine.

A breathless laugh escaped me. I winced, realizing tender spots blooming across my back. Marks would match my hair by morning. "I'm not complaining."

His hands moved gentler now, fingers carefully working through my damp locks as we rinsed the last soap away. We stepped onto the bath mat minutes later, skin reddened from heat and exertion, water puddling at our feet.

Ezra grabbed a towel, but instead of drying himself, he wrapped it around me, using it to pull me against him once more. His mouth found my neck, teeth scraping gently over my pulse point as he backed me through the bathroom door toward my bedroom.

My legs hit the edge of the mattress, and I tumbled backward, pulling him down with me. Water from our still-damp bodies soaked into my quilt, but I couldn't bring myself to care as he settled his weight over me, one thigh pressing between mine.

"I haven't finished tasting you," he murmured against my throat, working his way down with open-mouthed kisses that left my skin tingling.

"Again? Already?" I didn't know if I could handle anymore, but I knew once he was done with me…he'd be done with me. I wasn't ready for this to end just yet.

When he reached my breast, he looked up, eyes locking with mine as his tongue flicked over the sensitive peak. The ridges I'd felt earlier were now visible—tiny, pearlescent bumps that ran the length of his tongue, catching against my skin in a way that made me arch off the bed.

"What—" I gasped, unable to complete the thought as he repeated the motion.

"Sirens are full of surprises," he explained, a wicked smile playing at his lips.

Before I could ask what other surprises might be in store, he continued his downward journey, hands spreading my thighs wider as he settled between them. The first stroke of that textured tongue against my core had me crying out, fingers clutching desperately at his still-damp hair.

"Too much?" He asked, looking up the length of my body with a concern that belied the predatory glint in his eyes.

"Don't you dare stop," I managed, hips tilting toward his mouth. I was embarrassed at how aroused I was.

His laugh was dark and pleased. "Oh, I have no intention of stopping. But I have a better idea." He rose to his knees, powerful thighs flexing as he repositioned himself. "I want you over me. On my face."

Heat flooded my cheeks at the blunt request. "I don't know…"

"Trust me," he said, rolling onto his back and pulling me with him until I was straddling his chest. His hands wrapped around my thighs, urging me forward. "I want to feel you lose control while I taste you."

"But what if I—" My insecurities bubbled up despite my arousal. "You won't be able to breathe like that—"

"Twyla." His voice cut through my nervous babbling. "If death comes for me while I'm buried between your thighs, it would be a worthy end." The words were teasing, but his eyes held a seriousness that made my breath catch. "I'm stronger than I look, and I want this. I want you."

"Okay," I whispered.

My thighs trembled as I moved forward, positioning myself above his face. The cool air brushed against my heated skin, heightening every sensation.

"Give me your hands," he commanded.

I extended my wrists toward him. His large hand encircled them both, drawing them firmly behind my back. My spine arched involuntarily, breasts thrust forward, exposed to the night air and his hungry gaze.

"Perfect. Now lower yourself onto my mouth."

For a heartbeat, I paused. Then, his free hand guided my hips downward until his tongue made contact. Lightning shot through me—those textured ridges creating friction that pulled a gasp from my lungs. His grip tightened around my wrists, holding me firmly as his tongue worked against me with devastating precision.

"Oh fuck," The words escaped as my thighs tensed. Pleasure spiraled through me faster than I could process.

A hum vibrated from his throat into my core, adding yet another layer to the already overwhelming sensations. His hand at my hip controlled my movements, setting a rhythm that left me struggling for breath. Each stroke of his tongue wound me tighter, the ridged texture finding spots I didn't know existed.

I strained against his grip, trying to move, to control the pace. His hold remained unyielding, forcing me to accept pleasure on his terms alone. Something about surrendering control sent another wave of lust rushing through me.

"Ezra," My voice sounded foreign to my ears as my thighs shook. "I'm going to–to–ah—"

The first notes of his song vibrated through me—the same haunting melody I'd heard before, but deeper, more resonant against my sensitive flesh. The sound penetrated my skin, weaving through my nerves until pleasure and music became indistinguishable. My eyes flew open at the familiar sensation, though this felt more intense, more direct.

His tongue moved faster as the melody built, each note amplifying sensations until they bordered on unbearable. The song worked its way through my body, turning my blood to liquid fire. I'd felt it before, but not like this—not with his mouth on me, creating a feedback loop of pleasure that defied comprehension.

My thighs clamped around his head as the first wave crashed through me. My body bucked against his restraining hands as the combined assault of his tongue and song transformed my release into something beyond physical. Colors burst behind my eyelids, pleasure radiating outward in pulses that seemed to match the rhythm of his melody.

Words spilled from my lips—his name, curses, pleas—I couldn't distinguish them through the symphony roaring in my ears. The orgasm stretched endlessly, his relentless tongue working through each aftershock while his song sustained the peak longer than should be physically possible.

When consciousness fully returned, I found myself slumped forward, one hand braced against the headboard. He released my wrists, his hands moving to steady my trembling hips.

"That," he said, voice rough with desire, lips glistening, "was just the beginning."

Before I could form words, he moved with an inhuman speed that still startled me. His hands lifted me as if I weighed nothing before placing me on my back in the center of the bed. His fingers wrapped around my ankles, raising them high and wide.

"What are you—" The question died as he folded me nearly in half, pressing my ankles back until they framed my face. The stretch burned slightly, surprising me with my own flexibility.

"Hold these," he guided my hands to my own ankles. "Don't let go."

My fingers curled around my ankles, holding myself open and exposed. Ezra knelt between my spread thighs, his eyes devouring every inch of me. His hands stroked the underside of my thighs. "You're exquisite like this."

His hardness pressed against me, hot against my sensitized flesh. I tried to roll my hips toward him, seeking connection, but the position restricted my movement. Completely at his mercy—exactly as he planned.

"Are you going to make me wait all night?" I challenged, frustration edging my voice.

"Tell me exactly what you want," he replied, the head of his cock teasing my entrance without pushing forward.

"I want you inside me," I managed, surprising myself with the command in my voice despite being folded in half. "Now."

His smile promised sin. "Like this?" He pushed forward, just enough to tease without satisfaction.

"More," I demanded, straining against my grip. "All of you."

"Since you asked so nicely..." In one powerful thrust, he buried himself to the hilt. The angle drove him so deep a shocked cry tore from my throat.

He froze, concern flickering across his features. "Too much?"

"Don't you dare stop," I gasped, tightening my grip on my ankles for stability.

Satisfaction gleamed in his eyes as he withdrew almost completely before driving forward again. Each thrust measured, hitting places inside me that made stars explode behind my eyelids.

"Faster," I urged, desperate for more.

"Patience," he chided, though strain lined his voice. "We have all night."

His pace increased gradually, each thrust harder and faster than the last, until the headboard slammed rhythmically against the wall. My world narrowed to the sensation of him inside me and the building pressure promising to eclipse my earlier release.

Then he slowed again, reducing his movements to a torturous grind that kept me balanced on the edge. A frustrated whimper escaped as I tried to chase the friction I needed.

"Not yet," he growled, one hand gripping my hip to hold me still. "I'm not finished with you." He leaned forward, using my ankles for leverage, his face hovering inches from mine. "Prepare yourself," his breath hot against my lips.

"For what?" Confusion cut momentarily through the fog of arousal.

Instead of answering, he captured my lips in a searing kiss. As his tongue distracted me, I felt something change. A subtle shift in pressure, a new fullness that pulled a gasp from my throat. I broke the kiss, looking down between our bodies.

What I saw widened my eyes. Where there had been one cock, there were now two—the second slightly smaller but equally rigid, positioned directly above the first. Both stretched me to the point of exquisite discomfort.

"What—how—" Words failed me.

"Another siren surprise," he murmured, watching my face intently. "Too much?"

I should have been frightened. Instead, my body adjusted to the new fullness in ways I hadn't thought possible.

"Where were you hiding that thing!" I managed between quick gasps as he shifted, causing both lengths to press against different spots inside me.

"I can control when it emerges," he explained, beginning to move again. "It takes a certain level of...exci tement."

The dual sensation overwhelmed me—too much and not enough simultaneously. Each careful thrust sent shockwaves through my body, building toward something more intense than before.

"Oh god," I moaned as his pace quickened. "That's—I can't—"

"You can," he assured me, voice rough with strain. He established a new rhythm, moving both lengths in counterpoint—one withdrawing as the other drove deep. Then, just as my body tightened around him, the first notes of his song filled the room again.

The melody wrapped around us, vibrating through every point of contact between our bodies. The notes seemed to penetrate my skin, amplifying every sensation until pleasure bordered on pain. Unlike before, this time I could feel how he controlled it, how he directed the waves of sound to intensify where our bodies joined.

The combination of physical and sonic stimulation pushed me beyond what I thought possible. The edges of my vision darkened as sensations built to impossible heights.

Then he stopped. Everything—movement, song—ceased completely.

"What the fuck?" I gasped, my body screaming for release. "Why did you stop?"

His smile turned wicked, sweat beading on his forehead from the effort of restraint. "Because I want you to ask for it."

"You've got to be kidding me," I groaned.

My hips strained against his grip, seeking the friction my body craved. His hands clasped me in place, denying even the smallest movement.

"Not at all." He withdrew slightly, then pushed forward in a single, torturous thrust that pulled a gasp from my lungs. Then stillness. "Tell me what you want."

"I want you to move." The words scraped through my clenched teeth as I glared up at him. "Now."

"So demanding," he murmured. Another deep thrust followed by that maddening stillness. "Perhaps I need more specific instructions."

"Fuck me or get off me so I can finish myself," my voice sharpened with frustration.

His eyes darkened at my words, pupils expanding until the pink nearly disappeared. "There she is," he whispered. Satisfaction colored his tone as he resumed movement—still at that infuriatingly slow pace that kept me teetering on the edge.

Time stretched and warped as he suspended me on the precipice—bringing me to the brink before changing angle or pace, denying the final push needed for release. Sweat slicked our bodies, my thighs burning with the strain of the position. Pleasure built beyond what seemed possible to withstand, hovering tantalizingly out of reach as he controlled my responses with calculated precision.

"Ezra," tears of frustration pricked at the corners of my eyes. "I can't take anymore."

He repeated the pattern in response—harder, deeper, then stopping just as the pressure peaked.

"Goddamnit!" My temper finally snapped. "Move, or I swear I'll flip you over and take what I need myself."

The threat ignited something within him. His expression transformed from controlled to feral in an instant. "I'd like to see you try." He challenged, pressing deeper.

"If you don't let me come right now," I hissed, nails digging into my own ankles where I still held them, "I'll never let you touch me again. I'll kick your ass out of my bed and find someone who knows how to finish what they started."

Something flashed across his features—triumph mixed with raw desire. "My fiery little sprite."

Before I could respond to the possessive words, he shifted position, angling his thrusts to hit exactly where I needed while his thumb found and circled the bundle of nerves above where we joined.

"Now," he commanded, pace increasing to something almost punishing.

The orgasm crashed through me like a tidal wave, and with such force my vision disappeared into white nothingness for several heartbeats. Words spilled from my lips—perhaps his name, perhaps curses, perhaps demands—lost in the overwhelming waves of pleasure that seemed endless, one peak flowing into the next without pause.

My release triggered his own. With a final, powerful thrust, he buried himself deep, his body tensing against mine. A sound escaped him—not quite human, something between a growl and a melody—that reverberated through my bones and somehow heightened the lingering pulses of my climax.

With careful movements, he lowered my legs, fingers massaging life back into muscles that quivered from exertion and satisfaction. He remained inside me as he gathered me against his chest, both of us breathing heavily in the aftermath.

For several minutes, neither of us spoke. His heartbeat thundered beneath my ear, gradually slowing to a steadier rhythm. His fingertips traced lazy patterns along my spine, leaving trails of pleasant shivers in their wake.

Reality crept back slowly—the dampness of sheets beneath me, traffic sounds filtering through the window, the mingled scents of paint and sex hanging in the air. Minor discomforts registered one by one—muscles complaining about unfamiliar positions, dried sweat making my skin feel tight and sticky.

I shifted, creating a space between us. "I need to clean up." My eyes focused on a point past his shoulder, avoiding direct contact as the weight of what we'd just done—again—settled over me.

His arms loosened reluctantly, allowing me to slide from the bed. My legs wobbled slightly as I crossed to the bathroom, his gaze a tangible heat against my bare skin.

The mirror reflected a stranger—my hair a wild tangle, lips red and swollen, skin decorated with marks from his mouth and hands. The woman staring back looked thoroughly claimed, completely satisfied, and oddly unfamiliar. Or perhaps this was the real me, usually kept carefully hidden.

When I returned to the bedroom, Ezra sat perched on the edge of the mattress. His expression remained unreadable as he watched me move. His unusual anatomy had disappeared, making him appear almost human despite the scales that caught the lamplight with each breath.

My fingers found the dresser drawer, pulling out fresh underwear and a simple t-shirt.

"Your clothes are probably still wet." My voice sounded steadier now as I collected the borrowed items from where they'd been abandoned earlier. I tossed them onto the bed beside him. "You can wear these."

He caught the clothes without shifting his gaze from me as I dressed. "Twyla." Something in his tone made me glance up. "That was—"

"Amazing," I forced a casual smile that didn't match the trembling in my chest. "Definitely a night to remember. Go team, am I right?"

His brow creased, confusion flickering across his face. "Yes, I thought perhaps we could—"

"You should probably head out before it gets too late," the words rushed out before I could stop them. My heart hammered against my ribs as I cut off whatever he might say next. I couldn't bear the careful letdown, the "this was fun but" speech I'd heard too many times before. "I've got early inventory tomorrow, and you've probably got...siren things to do."

His expression transformed, shock replacing confusion. "You're asking me to leave?"

I shrugged, keeping my movements loose despite the strange tightness spreading through my chest. "Unless you want to sleep in a wet bed. Besides, I figure you got what you came for." My hand gestured between us, then swept toward the rumpled sheets. "Mission accomplished, right?"

He rose slowly, something dangerous flickering behind his eyes. "You think this was about *conquest*?"

I arched a brow as I crossed my arms protectively over my chest. "You're not exactly subtle, Ezra. You like the chase, the challenge. Now you've had me." I injected a lightness into my voice that felt like glass in my throat. "No hard feelings. It was fun."

He stared, something unreadable moving across his features. When he finally spoke, his voice had chilled in a way I hadn't heard since our first meeting.

"You have no idea what this was to me." His fingers snatched the borrowed clothes with excessive force.

"Then enlighten me." I challenged.

He yanked on the borrowed pants—several inches too short for his frame—his movements sharp with anger. "Apparently," the t-shirt went over his head with a harsh pull, "not what I thought it was."

I couldn't decipher the emotion twisting his features—something between fury and another feeling I couldn't name. He tugged the shirt down, running fingers through his damp hair in a gesture that seemed jarringly human for the ancient being I now knew him to be.

"I should go." Stiffness replaced the earlier intimacy in his voice. "I've clearly overstayed my welcome."

My feet followed him to the entryway, uncertainty growing in the face of his obvious anger. This wasn't what I'd expected—I'd thought he'd welcome the easy out, the absence of clingy aftermath.

"Ezra—" The words died in my throat, intentions unclear even to myself.

"Goodnight, Ms. Knight." His hand gripped the doorknob.

Before I could respond, three sharp knocks startled us both. Ezra yanked the door open, revealing Alex and Kronos in the hallway, Alex's fist still raised mid-knock.

"Oh!" Alex's eyes darted between us, taking in Ezra's obvious anger and the borrowed clothes. "We, uh, heard—that is, the walls are kind of—"

"He was just leaving," I offered, attempting to dissolve the awkward tension.

Kronos's silver eyes narrowed as he assessed the situation, something passing between him and Ezra in silent exchange. "Everything alright?" The question addressed both of us while his gaze fixed on Ezra.

"Peachy." Ezra's voice clipped each syllable. He pushed past them into the hallway. "She's all yours."

We watched in stunned silence as he stormed down the stairs, his usual grace replaced by tightly controlled fury. The front door slammed hard enough to rattle the windows.

Alex turned to me, eyebrows nearly reaching his hairline. "What the hell was that about?"

I shrugged, ignoring the strange hollowness expanding in my chest. "Who knows?"

Kronos made a small noise that might have been disagreement but said nothing.

"Are you okay?" Concern deepened Alex's voice.

"I'm fine." The smile I forced felt brittle. "Everything's fine."

The apartment suddenly felt larger and emptier after I closed the door behind them minutes later, declining their offer to stay and talk. My feet carried me to the window, eyes tracking a familiar figure striding away down the darkened street below, pink hair unmistakable even in the dim glow of streetlights.

"Everything's fine," I repeated to the room, trying to convince myself that the tightness in my chest wasn't regret, but merely relief at avoiding what would have inevitably been a painful entanglement.

After all, men like Ezra—beautiful, talented, ancient—didn't fall for women like me. They conquered, they enjoyed, they moved on. I'd simply beaten him to the punch.

So why did my victory feel so hollow?

Chapter Ten

STORM SURGE

The silence that followed Ezra's dramatic exit pressed against my eardrums with crushing weight. I stood frozen in my entryway, the cool hardwood beneath my bare feet suddenly feeling like ice, when Alex cleared his throat behind me.

"Well," he said, his voice carefully neutral. "That was...intense."

"That's one word for it," I muttered, suddenly feeling exhausted.

"Come on," Alex said gently, his warm hand landing on my arm. "Let's sit down."

He guided me to the couch, and I sank into the familiar cushions with a plop. The worn fabric was soft against my skin, offering comfort I desperately needed. Kronos nestled beside Alex.

"So," Alex drew out the word, positioning himself between us on the couch. The old springs creaked softly under our combined weight. "What happened?"

I stared at my hands, wrapped around each other in my lap. "We had sex. Then I told him he could leave since he'd gotten what he wanted."

"Why?" Alex asked quietly.

"Because it's true," I said, though even I could hear how hollow the words sounded in my too-quiet apartment. "It was just sex."

Kronos went still beside Alex. When he spoke, his voice was carefully controlled. "Just sex."

"Yeah." I lifted my chin defiantly, though I couldn't quite meet his sharp gaze. "He got what he wanted; I got what I wanted. I don't see what the big deal is."

"Did you ask him if that's all he wanted?" There was a dangerous edge creeping into his voice.

"It's all men ever want." It felt like that to me, anyway. Not many men wanted much once the thrill of the chance wore off.

Kronos was quiet for a long moment, and I could practically see the gears turning behind his eyes.

When Kronos finally spoke, his voice had turned to winter steel.

"I've known Ezra for years," he said, each word cutting through the air. "In all that time, I have never—not once—seen him pursue anyone. He's had admirers, certainly. People throw themselves at him constantly. But he's never shown genuine interest in anyone." His eyes bored into mine. "Until you."

My throat felt raw. "That's not my fault."

"No," Kronos agreed, the single word sharp. "But what you just did to him is."

Alex gripped Kronos's arm, fingers pressing into the expensive fabric of his sleeve. I could see the tension radiating through Alex's shoulders. "Kro, maybe—"

"He trusted you," Kronos continued, steamrolling right over Alex's attempt at diplomacy. His voice was getting colder with each word. "Do you have any idea how rare that is? How vulnerable he made himself by coming here tonight?"

"Nobody asked him to!" The words exploded out of me before I could stop them, loud enough to make Alex flinch. The sound bounced off my walls, too harsh in the confined space. "I never promised him anything! We had sex; it was great, but that doesn't mean—"

"It doesn't mean what?" Kronos's voice dropped to barely above a whisper, which somehow made it more terrifying than if he'd shouted. The quiet rage made goosebumps rise along my arms. "That you owe him basic human decency? That you shouldn't treat someone like garbage the moment they become inconvenient?"

Heat burned my ears, and I couldn't make myself look at him. "You don't know what you're talking about."

Kronos leaned forward slightly, his movement predatory and controlled. "From where I'm sitting, it looks like you got scared the moment things became real and hurt him before he could hurt you."

My hands clenched into fists in my lap, nails digging into my palms hard enough to leave crescents. "You don't know me."

"I know you just broke his heart." Kronos straightened, his expression shifting from anger to something that looked almost like pity.

He stood abruptly, his movement fluid and graceful as he turned to Alex. Kronos's imposing build made the gentle way his hands cupped Alex's face even more striking.

"I have to go," Kronos said, pressing a soft kiss to Alex's lips. The sound of it—that tiny, intimate noise—made something twist painfully in my stomach. "Ezra shouldn't be alone right now."

"I know," Alex replied, leaning into the touch. "Go. Take care of him."

"I love you," Kronos murmured against Alex's mouth. "Call me if you need me," he told Alex, though his glare was clearly meant for me.

I watched him pull out his phone as he headed for the door, the device already at his ear before he'd even stepped into the hallway. "Ezra? Where are you?" I heard him say before the door closed behind him with a soft click that somehow sounded final.

The silence pressed against me from all sides, broken only by the distant hum of my refrigerator and the muffled sound of traffic two stories below.

Alex and I sat there in the sudden quiet, the weight of what had just happened settling between us.

"Okay," Alex said finally, his voice tired. "Want to tell me what really happened?"

I shifted deeper into the corner of the couch, pulling my knees up to my chest. "You heard him. According to Kronos, I'm a heartless bitch who destroys men."

"That's not what he said." Alex's voice carried that gentle but firm tone he used when he was trying to talk me down from a ledge.

"Close enough." I pushed myself up from the couch and moved to the kitchen, needing something to do with my hands before they started shaking. The bottle of wine I'd opened yesterday was still on the counter, the cork sitting beside it accusingly. I poured myself a generous glass without offering one to Alex, the dark red liquid sloshing against the sides. "Want some coffee? I could make coffee."

"Twyla." Alex's voice carried that note that meant he wasn't going to let me deflect. "Sit down. Talk to me."

"There's nothing to talk about." I took a long sip of wine, the familiar tart sweetness coating my tongue and warming my chest.

"Bullshit." The word came out sharper than Alex usually spoke, making me look at him in surprise. His expression was serious. "I've seen you after hookups, remember? That's not what this looks like. You look terrified."

I laughed, but it sounded hollow even to my own ears, echoing strangely in my too-quiet apartment. "Terrified of what? A guy with good cheekbones and an ego the size of Texas?"

Alex leaned forward, elbows on his knees, the leather of my couch creaking softly. "You care about him."

The wine turned bitter in my mouth. "I don't—"

"You do." Alex's voice was patient but relentless. "I can see it all over your face. Hell, I've been watching you get more and more wound up about him for weeks."

"So what if I do?" The admission slipped out before I could stop it, tasting sharp on my tongue. "So what if I think he's interesting and talented and..." I gestured vaguely with my wineglass, watching the liquid swirl, "...whatever. That doesn't change anything."

"You're being ridiculous." Alex crossed the small space between us. "This isn't even about him, is it? It's about Trevone."

The name hit me hard, making me flinch so violently I nearly dropped my wine glass. I set it down on the counter with a sharp clink, the sound too loud in the quiet kitchen. "Don't."

"He really did a number on you, didn't he?" Alex continued, ignoring my warning. His voice was gentle now, the way you'd talk to a wounded animal. "Not everyone is trying to hurt you, sweetie."

"They are!" The words exploded out of me, raw and ugly, tearing at my throat. My hands clenched into fists on the counter, knuckles going white. "That's what people do, Alex. They get close, they make you trust them, and then they fuck you over the first chance they get."

Alex was quiet for a moment, just watching me with those dark, understanding eyes. When he spoke again, his voice was soft. "Is that what you think I did?"

The question caught me completely off guard. "What?"

"When I started spending all my time with Kronos." Alex's expression was carefully neutral, but I could see the hurt lurking behind his eyes. "Do you think I abandoned you?"

My throat tightened. The kitchen suddenly felt too small, the walls pressing in on me from all sides. "I think people's priorities change when they fall in love. It's natural."

"That's not what I asked."

I stared at him, this person who'd become my closest friend, my chosen family. The person who'd shown up at my shop broken and scared and who I'd helped put back together piece by piece. The person who now split his time between me and someone who could offer him things I never could—money, status, a world I'd never be part of. I knew he didn't care about any of that stuff, but I was jealous that Kronos had stolen him away.

"Sometimes," I admitted quietly, the words scraping my throat raw. "Sometimes it feels like you don't need me anymore."

Alex's face crumpled slightly, as if I'd hit him. "Oh, honey."

"Which is stupid," I continued quickly, words tumbling over each other in my rush to get them out. "because that's how it should be. You're happy, you're in love, you have this whole new life. I want that for you. I do."

"But it makes you feel alone."

I nodded, not trusting my voice to work properly. The admission hung between us, bruised and tender.

Alex was quiet for a long moment, his fingers drumming against his thigh in that nervous habit he'd never quite shaken. When he spoke, his words were careful, handling something fragile. "Kronos didn't replace you. He filled a different space entirely. You're my best friend, my sister in all the ways that matter. That doesn't change just because I *fell in love*." He rolled his eyes at the last word.

"I know that," I said, though my bottom lip trembled.

"Do you?" Alex moved closer, close enough that I could smell his cologne—something warm and familiar that reminded me of coffee and safety. "Because from where I'm sitting, it looks like you've been so afraid of being left behind that you've been pushing people away before they can leave. I'd know a thing or two about that."

The observation stung, sharp and cleansing and painful all at once. "Maybe."

"Ezra isn't Trevone," Alex said gently, his hand reaching out to cover mine where it rested on the counter. His skin was warm, grounding me to something real. "And he's not me. He's not going to disappear just because he gets what he wants from you."

"How can you be sure?" The question came out smaller than I intended.

"As reluctant as I am to admit it," Alex replied, his thumb brushing across my knuckles. "I've seen the way his entire face changes when you walk into a room. That's not someone who's just interested in a quick fuck, Twy."

The words sent a jolt through me that started in my chest and spread outward, equal parts terror and something that might have been hope. "You don't know that."

"No one can really know someone else's heart," Alex conceded, giving my hand a gentle squeeze. "But I know what I saw tonight. And what I heard before the fighting." He wiggled his eyebrows at me, teasing me about how thin the walls between our apartments were.

Guilt twisted in my stomach, sharp and unwelcome. "I didn't mean to hurt him."

"I know." Alex tugged gently on my hand, leading me back toward the couch. "What are you going to do about it?"

I let him guide me back to the familiar cushions, curling up in the corner with my legs tucked under me. The fabric was soft against my skin, worn smooth from years of use, offering comfort only old, well-loved things could provide.

"I don't know how to do this," I admitted, my voice barely above a whisper. "The caring about someone thing. Letting them matter. What if I'm terrible at it?"

"What if you let yourself try and it turns out to be the best thing that ever happened to you?" Alex countered, settling beside me. The couch dipped under his weight, tilting me slightly toward him in a way that felt safe and familiar.

"What if it's not?" The fears tumbled out one after another, each one sharper than the last. "What if he gets bored, or finds someone better, or decides I'm too much work? What if I let myself fall for him and then he just...leaves?"

Alex was quiet for a moment, his fingers absently picking at a loose thread on the couch cushion. The small repetitive motion was soothing somehow. When he spoke, his voice was thoughtful.

"Then you'll survive it," he said finally. "The same way you survived Trevone, the same way you survived everything else that's tried to break you. But Twy, what if you don't let yourself try and you spend the rest of your life wondering what could have been?"

I stared down at my hands, wrapped around my now-empty wineglass. My reflection wavered in the curved surface, distorted and uncertain. "Kronos is furious with me."

"Kronos is protective of the people he cares about," Alex replied diplomatically, though I could hear the truth underneath—that Kronos had every right to be angry, that I'd hurt someone important to him. "Ezra is important to him. So are you, in your own way. He'll get over it once this gets sorted out."

"*If* it gets sorted out."

"It will if you want it to." Alex nudged my shoulder gently, the contact warm and reassuring against my skin. "The question is, do you want it to?"

I thought about Ezra's hands in my hair, gentle despite their strength. The way he looked at my art—like it mattered, like I mattered. The careful way he'd held me after we'd made love in my bed, treating me like something precious that might break if handled too roughly. His voice when he'd called me extraordinary, rough with an emotion I'd been too scared to name.

"Yeah," I whispered, the word barely audible even to myself. "I think I do."

"Then call him."

The suggestion sent panic racing through my veins, making my heart hammer against my ribs. My phone sat on the coffee table, silent and accusatory, its black screen reflecting the overhead light. "I can't. Not right now. He's probably with Kronos, and he's angry, and I don't even know what to say."

"Maybe start with 'I'm sorry,'" Alex suggested, his voice gentle but firm. "Go from there."

I shook my head; the movement making my still-damp hair stick to my neck uncomfortably. "What if he doesn't answer? What if he tells me to go to hell?"

"What if he doesn't?"

Outside my window, I could hear traffic, the distant crash of waves against the shore, and the normal sounds of a normal evening. As if the world hadn't just shifted on its axis, as if I hadn't just destroyed something beautiful because I was too afraid to let it exist.

The knowledge sat heavy in my chest, weighing down every breath. "I really fucked this up, didn't I?"

"Yeah," Alex said gently, his honesty somehow more comforting than false reassurance would have been. "You kind of did."

"Gee, thanks for the honesty."

"You asked." Alex bumped my shoulder again.

"I can't," I said, the words barely audible over the pounding of my heart. "Not yet. I'm not ready."

Alex sighed, a sound full of disappointment and understanding in equal measure. He didn't push, didn't try to force my hand or make me feel worse than I already did. "Okay. Don't wait too long, Twy. Some things can't be unfucked once too much time passes."

I nodded, knowing he was right but still unable to make myself move.

For now, the fear of hearing him tell me to go to hell was still stronger than my desire to make things right.

But maybe, if I was lucky, that would change before it was too late.

Chapter Eleven

TREACHEROUS WATERS

I moved through the shop in a fog, straightening displays, rearranging inventory. With the window installation looming half-finished, my spark was gone.

"You missed a spot." Alex pointed to a pastel smear under the counter. "Though why we're still cleaning is beyond me. We got most of the evidence yesterday."

I grabbed a rag and attacked the spot. "I like my shop clean."

"Since when?" His eyebrow shot up as he gestured to my creative chaos—supplies scattered everywhere, projects in various states of completion. "Besides, it's closing time. Nobody's inspecting under the counter."

My arm kept scrubbing at a stain older than my ownership of the shop. If I focused on this one spot, maybe I wouldn't have to think about anything else.

Alex leaned against the counter with a sigh. "Alright, what's going on with you?"

"Nothing." The rag flew into the sink with a wet slap. "I'm fine."

"Right. That's why you nearly bit Mrs. Henderson's head off when she asked about special orders."

"I did not."

"You told her, 'If you want custom work that badly, learn to do it yourself.'" His impression of me was annoyingly accurate. "To our best customer."

I winced. "I apologized."

"After I made you." Alex's expression softened. "Come *on*. Talk to me." He flipped the CLOSED sign and locked the door.

My hands were busy with the register, counting bills for the third time. "There's nothing to talk about."

"Is this about the siren? Because he hasn't been back?"

My fingers fumbled, quarters rolling across the counter and pinging onto the floor. Damn it. "I don't care that he hasn't been back."

"Maybe because you two practically redecorated the place." He gestured to a faded handprint on the wall.

My jaw clenched as I spotted the faded handprint on the wall. "I thought we cleaned those up."

"Mostly. I might've left one for evidence." Alex's grin faded when I didn't return it. "Seriously though, you look like hell. Did you sleep at all last night?"

I collapsed onto the stool behind the counter, exhaustion weighing down my limbs. "Not much."

Alex studied my face with concern. "You can't keep going like this."

"I know." I picked at a loose thread on my shirt.

"You already know my thoughts on the subject." He was about to say more when three sharp knots rattled the door. Alex peered through the glass, then shot me a loaded look. "Speak of the devil."

My heart slammed against my ribs as pink hair came into view. Alex swung the door open, and there he stood.

Ezra stepped in as if entering a royal court—chin high, shoulders squared. A deep crimson silk shirt with gold embroidery emphasized his impossible height, actual gold rings adorning several fingers. His hair was braided back, highlighting his prominent cheekbones that he'd dusted with gold flakes.

He was magnificent, untouchable, and pissed off.

"Ezra!" Alex's voice pitched unnaturally high. "What a surprise! I thought you'd finished the portrait commission."

"Not quite." His voice clipped each word, gaze sliding past me like I was furniture. "I'll need another session to complete the final details."

My spine snapped straight. "The shop's closed."

"I'm aware." He gestured to his portfolio. "This won't take long. I merely need to verify a few color elements."

The chill in his words could have frozen fire.

Alex glanced between us. "Well, I was just heading out. Kronos is waiting." He backed toward the door. "You two have fun with your...art."

The bell jangled during his hasty exit. *Coward.*

I'll revise to remove the immortal/age references and change to a pink dress.

Ezra set up his easel, fingers arranging brushes with the same intensity he did everything else.

"That's quite the outfit," I broke the silence. "Special occasion?"

"I had a meeting." He didn't look up. "Some of us take our professional appearances seriously."

The barb stung like salt on a paper cut. I glanced down at my paint-stained clothes, suddenly conscious of every smudge and worn spot. My shop, my rules—so why did I suddenly feel like I should apologize? The late afternoon light streamed through the window, highlighting every imperfection.

"Where would you like me?" I kept my voice steady despite my clenched jaw. A familiar tension headache threatened at my temples.

Now he looked up, pink eyes cold beneath those ridiculous lashes—so long they should have been comical but somehow weren't. "By the window."

I perched on the display table, pushing aside a half-finished dreamcatcher. The wood creaked beneath me, familiar and grounding. "Like this?"

"Turn your face slightly to the left."

I complied, watching dust motes dance in the sunbeams between us. The clock ticked relentlessly from the wall. Each second stretched like taffy, sweet and painful all at once. The silence pressed against my ears until I couldn't bear it.

"I didn't expect you to come back," I finally said. My voice sounded too loud in the quiet shop.

His hand stilled. I watched his knuckles whiten around the paintbrush. "Yet here I am."

"About the other night—"

"I'd rather not discuss it," he cut me off sharply. "A momentary lapse in judgment."

"Really?" My eyebrows shot up, irritation bubbling under my skin like water about to boil. "That's what you're going with?"

"Isn't that what you meant?" He finally met my eyes, a challenge written across his face. The afternoon light caught the scales at his temples, making them shimmer like opals.

Heat rushed to my cheeks. My skin felt too tight, too hot. "I didn't—"

"You did." The paintbrush clattered against the easel. The sound echoed in the shop, startling a small finch that had perched outside the window. "You made it perfectly clear I wasn't welcome once you'd gotten what you wanted."

"What *I* wanted?" I slid off the table, my feet hitting the floor with a thud. Indignation rose in me like a tide. "I could say the same of you!"

"What is that supposed to mean?" His voice rose to match mine, its usual melodic quality sharpening to something that made the glass jars on my shelves vibrate slightly.

"The you wanted the chase!" I threw my hands up, knocking against a hanging crystal that sent rainbow prisms scattering across the walls. "The novelty of it!"

"Is that what you think?" He stepped toward me, abandoning all pretense of painting. The floorboards creaked under his weight. "That after *everything*, I've nothing better to do than seduce you?"

"I don't know what to think! You never said what you wanted!" The words tasted bitter on my tongue. My hands clenched at my sides, nails digging into palms.

"I was here every day for *weeks*!" Two spots of color appeared high on his cheeks, making the pink of his eyes seem even more unnatural. "What more did you need?"

"Words, Ezra! Not everyone can read minds!" My pulse pounded in my ears, drowning out the ticking clock.

"Fine." He stepped closer, towering over me. The heat reached me before he did, supernatural warmth radiating from his skin. "I find you fascinating. Maddening."

Something fluttered in my chest, a bird trying to escape its cage.

"You pushed back. You challenged me. You saw past the glamour to the person beneath." His voice softened suddenly, the vibrato in it gentling to something that made my skin prickle with goosebumps. "Do you have any idea how rare that is?"

I swallowed hard, my throat suddenly dry. The shop felt too small, the air between us charged like before a lightning strike. "I thought..."

"You assumed I couldn't possibly be interested in someone like you." The bitterness in his voice caught me off-guard. "Your low self worth doesn't dictate what how I see you." One of his braids had come loose, a strand of pink hair falling across his face. "As if I haven't watched everything I've ever loved turn to dust." He said under his breath.

"Ezra—"

"Do you know how many people I've met?" He ran a hand through his hair, disheveling the perfect braids. One of his rings caught the light, blinding me momentarily. His eyes met mine, weary in a way that made him suddenly seem both older and younger. The pink seemed deeper now, layered like an ocean sunset. "Countless. Do you know how many saw me? Truly saw me, not just the magic, not just the beauty?" His voice dropped to nearly a whisper. *"One."*

What? Did he really just say that?

"I didn't ask you to leave because I was done with you," I admitted. My heart hammered against my ribs like it wanted to escape. "I thought I was protecting myself from getting in too deep with someone who'll disappear the moment things get messy. Because they always do." The way his expression shifted told me he understood exactly what I wasn't saying. "Stop looking at me like that," I muttered, heat crawling up my neck.

"Like what?"

"Like you can see right through me. It's unnerving."

"You don't think you're worth staying for," he said quietly.

"My last relationship ended with my bank account emptied and my trust shattered. And he was just a human disaster, not a—" I gestured vaguely at all of him, at the otherworldly beauty and the scales and the eyes that shouldn't exist.

A smile tugged at his lips. "I'll need to remember that one."

Despite everything, I felt my own lips twitch. The tension in the air shifted, lightened. "You know what I mean."

He stepped closer, close enough that I could count the individual scales along his jawline, see the subtle variations in their color. His body heat radiated toward me, chasing away the shop's persistent chill. "Trust is earned. I understand that better than most."

The afternoon light caught in his hair, turning it from pink to rose gold. His eyes studied me with an intensity that made me want to look away and never stop looking all at once.

"I should finish this," he said, gesturing to the canvas. "Though I find I've lost my focus for painting."

"Your concentration problem, not mine," I said, falling back on snark when feelings got too complicated.

His lips quirked again. "Indeed."

He turned back to the easel, and I studied the line of his shoulders, the way his shirt draped across his back. The silence that fell was different now—charged rather than cold, expectant rather than empty.

"You look like you're attending a royal coronation in that getup," I said, trying to lighten the mood further.

His lips curved into a fuller smile. "There's a reception at the Oceanographic Institute tonight. They're unveiling a marine conservation initiative I'm sponsoring."

"Marine conservation?" My interest sparked genuinely. I shifted my weight, the floorboard creaking beneath me. "I didn't know you were involved with that."

"The oceans are my home." His brush created gentle arcs of blue light on the canvas. The color was hypnotic, almost luminescent. "I've watched humans poison them for centuries. I won't any longer." He paused, brush hovering over the palette. Then, he set it down with deliberate care. "Come with me," he said, turning to face me fully. It wasn't a question, but it wasn't quite a command either.

"You want me to come to your fancy reception?" I raised an eyebrow, caught off-guard by the sudden shift. "In what—these paint-splattered jeans?"

His eyes traveled down my body slowly, lingering in ways that made me squirm. "I'm sure you have something more appropriate upstairs." His voice had dropped half an octave, making the words sound like a suggestion for something else entirely.

"I might," I replied, pulse quickening. "Though I'm not sure anything I own meets royal siren standards."

He stepped closer, abandoning the easel entirely. "I'd be happy to help you decide what to wear."

The innuendo hung in the air between us, heavy and unmistakable. My mouth went dry, memories of his hands on my skin flashing through my mind.

"That seems dangerous." I stepped toward him instead of away, the tension of minutes before transforming into something different but equally potent.

"I excel at dangerous." His smile was all predator now, sharp and hungry.

We stood inches apart, the air practically crackling. Part of me wanted to close the distance, to see if the electricity between us was as powerful as before. The more rational part knew exactly where that would lead, and we had unfinished business to address first.

"Nice try," I said, summoning my most teasing smile. "But if you come upstairs with me now, we both know we won't be leaving for that reception."

His eyes darkened further, confirming my suspicion. "Would that be so terrible?"

"No," I admitted, my voice huskier than intended. "But I think I'd like to see you in action at this conservation event."

Something shifted in his expression—surprise, maybe even approval. "Very well." He glanced at the antique clock on the wall. "The reception starts at eight. I can return in an hour to escort you."

"Great," I said, pleased with myself for maintaining some semblance of control. "That gives me just enough time to figure out what the hell I'm going to wear to a fancy institute event."

"Wear whatever you like," he said, gathering his supplies with swift efficiency. "Though I admit, I'm still hoping to see you in pink someday."

My eyes narrowed. "You're still on that? I told you during our first session—"

"That pink doesn't suit you. I disagree." That maddening smirk was back. "Wear what makes you comfortable. You'll outshine everyone, regardless."

The compliment caught me off guard, delivered so matter-of-factly. "Get out of my shop, Ezra. Come back in an hour."

He bowed slightly, the gesture oddly formal and completely at odds with the tension still simmering between us. "As you wish."

As soon as the door closed behind him, I flipped the sign to CLOSED and bolted for the stairs. My mind raced as I took the steps two at a time, panic replacing the earlier tension. A reception at the Oceanographic Institute? With Ezra? What the hell had I gotten myself into?

I burst into my apartment, heading straight for my closet. Nothing seemed right. Too casual, too weird, too me. I needed backup.

I grabbed my phone and called Alex, praying he'd answer.

"Hello?" His voice was wary. "Everything okay?"

"I need help," I said, skipping the pleasantries. "Ezra invited me to some fancy marine conservation reception tonight and I have exactly—" I checked the time "—fifty-three minutes to get ready."

Silence, then laughter. "Oh my god, you said yes? This I have to see."

"Alex, focus! Fashion emergency!"

"Okay, okay." I could hear the grin in his voice. "What about that black dress with the deep neck line?"

"No, I need something different." I hesitated, then admitted, "I was thinking about the pink dress."

More silence. "The pink dress? The one you bought for your cousin's wedding and never wore because 'pink makes you look like a bottle of Pepto-Bismol'?"

"That's the one." I pulled it from the back of my closet, where it had been hiding with the tags still on. A soft, dusky rose color with a subtle shimmer to the fabric. "He's been trying to get me to wear pink since day one. Said it would complement my skin tone."

Alex's voice took on a knowing tone that made me roll my eyes. "Look who's trying to please a man."

"Shut *up*. Will it work for a fancy institute reception or not?"

"With the right accessories, absolutely." His voice turned businesslike. "Those strappy gold sandals, minimal jewelry—just the hammered gold cuff. And for god's sake, use the good perfume, not the stuff you wear to the shop."

I breathed a sigh of relief. "You're a lifesaver."

"I know. I want details tomorrow. All of them."

I hung up and raced to the shower, my mind already several steps ahead. I was going on a date with Ezra.

Chapter Twelve

HARBOR LIGHTS

The Oceanographic Institute rose from the water like a fever dream—a massive fishbowl of curved glass and steel that shimmered in the twilight. Spotlights illuminated it from below, creating the illusion that the entire building was floating on light rather than concrete pylons. As our car approached along the narrow causeway, I pressed my face against the window like a kid at an aquarium.

"Holy shit," I muttered, fogging the glass. "You didn't say this place was straight out of a sci-fi movie."

"Where's the fun in spoiling the surprise?" Ezra purred, sounding entirely too pleased with himself.

I pulled back from the window to shoot him a look. "You just like teasing me."

"Guilty as charged," he said, his gaze sliding over my dress with obvious satisfaction. "And speaking of...p ink was an excellent choice."

My hand instinctively smoothed down the dress I'd spent forever agonizing over. The fabric suddenly felt too bright, too obvious against my dark skin. Ezra had been trying to get me to wear pink for his portrait for weeks. I'd resisted purely on principle, but when faced with a fancy event and limited wardrobe options... Well, I was going to deny until my dying day that I'd chosen it to please him.

"It was this or show up in paint-stained jeans," I lied.

His knowing smirk made it clear he didn't believe me for a second. "Naturally."

As we drew closer, I noticed fascinating details about the other guests. A woman whose hair seemed to ripple like seaweed despite the lack of wind. A tall man whose skin caught the light with a bluish iridescence that definitely wasn't makeup. Another, whose amber eyes reflected the spotlights like a cat's.

"You could have mentioned this was going to be a who's-who of supernatural society," I said, my artist's eye already cataloging colors and textures I rarely got to see up close. "I'd have brought my camera."

Ezra's eyebrow arched perfectly. "Would that have been appropriate?"

"Probably not," I admitted. "But think of all the reference material I'm missing. Alex is going to be so jealous—the most exotic thing at his dinner parties is Kronos glowering at people."

He glanced down at my gold sandals, then back to my face with unexpected sincerity. "You look beautiful, Twyla."

Something in his tone made my chest go tight. Before I could respond with my usual deflection, the car stopped, and I had to refocus. I was about to walk into a room full of beings from myth and legend, on the arm of a siren I was definitely not dating (despite what my brain whispered during late-night imaginings), wearing a pink dress bought on clearance that still cost more than I should have spent.

"Do these events usually have a human-to-supernatural ratio, or am I throwing off the curve?" I asked as the driver opened the door.

Ezra's laugh was genuine as his hand found the small of my back. "You'd be surprised how many humans are present."

We reached the entrance, where a woman with silver-white hair checked names against a tablet. When she looked up at Ezra, her eyes widened slightly.

"Mr. Thalassos," she said, her voice carrying that same musical quality I'd noticed in Ezra's. "How unexpected. We weren't certain you would attend."

"I wouldn't miss it, Nerissa." His hand remained steady at my back, warm through the thin fabric of my dress. "This is Twyla Knight, my guest."

Nerissa's eyes flicked to me, curiosity in their silver depths. "Ms. Knight. Welcome to the Institute." Her smile was polite but reserved, betraying nothing of what she might be thinking. But I could fill in the blanks: What's a human doing here with him?

We moved past her into a vast circular atrium that had me stopping in pure wonder. The domed ceiling soared overhead, made entirely of glass that revealed the night sky. But it was the floor that truly took my breath away—clear panels showed the ocean churning below, lit from beneath to reveal fish and other sea life darting through the darkness.

"This is incredible," I breathed, kneeling down to get a closer look at a spotted ray gliding beneath us. "I've seen aquarium tunnels before, but nothing like this."

"I thought you might appreciate it," Ezra replied, genuine pleasure in his voice at my reaction.

"I'm already mentally sketching designs based on this." I stood back up, my artist's brain cataloging the way light filtered through water, how the colors shifted and changed. "Do fish ever try to figure out what's above them? Like, are we their ceiling? Does it scare them?"

Ezra laughed, the sound surprisingly light. "It's so like you to worry about the fish."

The entire space made you feel underwater—with undulating glass walls, subtle blue lighting casting wave-like patterns across every surface. Servers glided through the crowd with trays of what looked like glowing drinks, and music that seemed to come from everywhere and nowhere filled the air—haunting melodies that reminded me of whale songs but arranged into something like classical music.

"The presentation will begin soon," Ezra said, accepting two glasses from a passing server and handing one to me. "Thaddeus likes to make an entrance, so we have time to explore first."

The glass felt strangely warm in my hand. "Is this safe for humans?"

"The blue is for gilled guests only," he nodded toward a different tray with golden-hued drinks. "Yours is the amber one—distilled from a rare algae, but quite safe. Actually considered a delicacy."

I took a cautious sip and was surprised by the taste—sweet at first, followed by something almost electric that tingled across my tongue. "That's...different."

"You don't have to drink it," Ezra said, scrutinizing my reaction.

"No, I like it," I admitted, taking another sip. "It's just not like anything I've had before."

His smile was pleased as he guided me through the crowd, his hand a constant presence at the small of my back. I noticed how other guests reacted to his presence—some with deference, others with barely concealed curiosity directed at me. Ezra acknowledged them with polite nods but didn't stop to chat, moving us purposefully toward the far side of the atrium where a stage had been arranged.

"Ezra!" A booming voice cut through the ambient sound. A barrel-chested man with a magnificent silver beard approached, arms outstretched.

"Thaddeus," Ezra greeted him, clasping the man's offered hand. "You look magnificent."

"Thank you, thank you," Thaddeus beamed, before turning his attention to me. "And who is this enchanting creature?"

"Twyla Knight," I supplied before Ezra could, extending my hand. "I own an art supply shop in town."

Thaddeus's eyebrows shot up as he took my hand. "How did you come to be acquainted with our reclusive benefactor here?"

"I'm painting her portrait," Ezra answered smoothly. "Twyla has been kind enough to indulge my artistic whims."

"Among other things, I'd wager," Thaddeus said with a wink that made my face burn.

"Actually, I mostly just tell him when his compositional choices are pretentious," I replied with a sweetness that made Ezra's lips twitch. "Someone has to keep him honest."

Thaddeus laughed, clearly delighted. "Marvelous! Well, you've arrived just in time. I should prepare my introduction. Ezra, you'll speak after me?"

"Of course," Ezra confirmed.

Thaddeus clapped him on the shoulder and disappeared back into the crowd.

"You'll be speaking?" I asked, surprised he hadn't mentioned this.

"Briefly," Ezra said, looking uncharacteristically self-conscious. "The Institute's new initiative was partly my idea. Plus, I'm funding a significant portion."

"Of course you are," I said, rolling my eyes, though I couldn't help being impressed. His smile was almost shy, a glimpse of vulnerability I rarely saw from him. Before he could respond, a soft chime sounded through the space.

"That's my cue," Ezra said, guiding me toward the gathering crowd. "Will you be alright here?"

"I think I can stand by myself for a few minutes." I assured him.

He squeezed my hand briefly before making his way to the stage, where Thaddeus waited with a few other important-looking individuals. I found a spot near the front, sipping my strange but increasingly appealing drink as Thaddeus welcomed everyone with practiced charm.

Ezra looked different under the spotlight—more formal, more commanding, yet still with that ethereal quality that set him apart. When it was his turn to speak, a hush fell over the crowd.

"The oceans have always connected us, even when we believed they divided us," he began, his voice carrying that musical quality that made it impossible not to listen. "They are not barriers but bridges—between continents, between species, between worlds that too often remain separate."

His speech was passionate but measured, laying out a vision for ocean conservation that clearly resonated with the crowd. I found myself captivated not just by his words but by how different he seemed in this setting—confident yet gracious, using his natural charisma not for seduction but for persuasion toward a greater cause.

As Ezra concluded his speech to enthusiastic applause, I noticed movement near one of the side entrances—security personnel speaking urgently into earpieces, their expressions tense. A moment later, Thaddeus appeared at Ezra's side, whispering something that made Ezra's posture stiffen.

He nodded once, sharply, then returned to the microphone. "Thank you all. Please enjoy the evening's refreshments while you explore the exhibits detailing our planned initiatives." His voice remained smooth, but I could see the tension in his jaw as he descended from the stage.

When he reached me, his expression was carefully neutral. "Twyla, I need to attend to something. Will you be alright on your own for a few minutes?"

"Of course," I said, though my curiosity was piqued. "Is everything okay?"

"Just a minor security concern," he replied, too smoothly. "Nothing to worry about."

Right. And I was secretly a mermaid. Before I could press further, he was gone, following Thaddeus through a door that seemed to materialize in the glass wall. I stood for a moment, contemplating whether to follow him anyway—I'd never been great at taking "stay here" instructions—but gave him a few minutes before I started causing trouble.

The finger food scattered across elegant serving stations caught my attention. Tiny works of art that seemed almost too beautiful to eat. My stomach growled, reminding me that nerves had prevented me from eating much before the event. I made my way to a display of what looked like sushi, but with colors and textures I'd never seen before.

"The blue ones are only for those with gills," a deep voice said from behind me, just as I was reaching for a particularly enticing piece dotted with electric blue pearls. "Unless you want your throat to close up."

I turned to look up at a man who could only be another siren. Broad shoulders strained against a tailored navy suit, and his hair—a pale blue-green that shifted like sea foam—was styled in tousled waves that framed a face that belonged on a Greek statue. Unlike Ezra, who kept his supernatural features carefully subdued in public, this siren did not hide the faint shimmer of scales along his jawline and the backs of his hands.

"Good thing you warned me," I said, withdrawing my hand from the dangerous sushi. "Though throat closing might have been a memorable way to liven up this party."

His laugh was unexpected—a rich, booming sound that drew glances from nearby guests. "Now that would have been entertaining. Rarely do humans provide such novel forms of amusement."

"Happy to keep the supernatural community entertained," I replied dryly. "It's my civic duty."

Interest flickered in those turquoise eyes as they swept over me with unconcealed appreciation. "You're Ezra's human," he said, not a question but a statement. He reached for a plate, loading it with selections from the non-lethal section of the display. "I've been watching you all evening. What makes you special enough to capture his attention?"

I bristled at being called Ezra's "human," like I was a pet or possession. "I have a name," I informed him. "It's Twyla, and I'm not Ezra's anything."

That earned me another laugh and a plate of food being pressed into my hands. "A spitfire, I see." He gestured toward a quieter corner of the room. "Come. Eat."

I should have politely declined and walked away. But curiosity—my perpetual downfall—and the genuine rumbling of my stomach had me following him to a small table near one of the massive aquarium walls.

"I'm Nereus," he offered as we sat. "Is this your first Supe event?"

"I work with supernatural clientele all the time," I said, sampling the shrimp sampler platter. "You stop being impressed after a while."

Nereus grinned, a flash of teeth slightly sharper than human. "A shopkeeper! Ezra didn't mention that part." He leaned forward, those ice-blue eyes suddenly more intense. "I'm curious—what does he tell you about sirens?"

"Enough," I replied vaguely, unwilling to share the personal stories Ezra had entrusted to me. "I know the myths humans tell aren't accurate."

"Myths rarely are." He selected something from my plate—a move so presumptuous it left me momentarily speechless—and popped it into his mouth. "I know a place where they serve seafood harvested from depths no human diver could reach. Flavors that don't exist in your world. I could take you sometime."

I was a little bit shocked that he so brazenly asked me out. I just sat there gaping at him like a fish. Luckily Ezra had returned, and his expression was thunderous. Even from this distance, I could see something different about him—a faint glow in his pink eyes, a tension in his frame that hadn't been there before. As he approached, patterns of scales rippled across his throat, appearing and disappearing as if he was struggling to keep his human form intact.

"Nereus," he said through gritted teeth. "I wasn't aware you'd be in attendance."

"Ezra." Nereus made no move to stand, swirling his drink lazily. "I rarely miss an opportunity to witness your conservation theater. Though I do admire how you've elevated your usual standards tonight." His eyes flicked to me with obvious appreciation.

Ezra's hand found my shoulder, fingers pressing possessively. "I see you've met my date."

"Oh, we've done more than meet, we're practically bosom buddies already." Nereus said, his smile turning predatory. "I was just telling Twyla about this marvelous little place I know. Perfect for someone with her refined palate." He looked directly at me. "I do hope you'll consider my invitation."

The temperature around us seemed to drop several degrees. Ezra's grip tightened. "We should find Thaddeus. He was asking for you specifically."

As I stood, Nereus caught my wrist with deceptive gentleness. "Until next time, Twyla," he murmured, his thumb tracing my pulse point with deliberate slowness. "I have a feeling it will be soon."

Ezra steered me away, and I could have sworn I heard him cursing beneath his breath. When I glanced back, Nereus was watching us with obvious amusement, raising his glass in a mocking toast.

"Friend of yours?" I asked once we were out of earshot, echoing the question I'd asked earlier about Thaddeus.

"No," Ezra replied, his voice tight. "What did he say to you?"

"Nothing important," I said, surprised by his obvious agitation. "Mostly prevented me from eating something that would have closed my throat. Then talked about food." I studied his face, noting the tension around his mouth. "What's wrong?"

For a moment, I thought he might actually explain. Then his expression smoothed over, the perfect mask sliding back into place. "Nothing to concern yourself with. The security matter is resolved, and we should enjoy the rest of the evening."

His hand rested on the small of my back, guiding me toward another exhibit. I couldn't help noticing it was unusually warm—almost hot—against my skin. When I caught his reflection in one of the glass walls, I could have sworn I saw patterns of scales shimmering across his face before disappearing again, like ripples on water.

Whatever was happening, it had something to do with Nereus. The look that had passed between them held centuries of history I knew nothing about, and judging by the way Ezra kept me close for the rest of the evening, occasionally scanning the crowd as if expecting trouble, that history wasn't friendly.

We didn't stay much longer. Ezra's mood had shifted completely—the warm openness from the start of the evening replaced by taut vigilance. He kept me at his side, his hand always maintaining contact with some part of me, as if afraid I might vanish if he let go. When Thaddeus approached to say goodbye, I noticed him giving Ezra a concerned look, his eyes flicking to the barely visible scale patterns that still occasionally rippled across Ezra's skin.

"Perhaps it's best if you call it an evening," Thaddeus suggested quietly, with a meaningful glance I couldn't interpret.

Ezra nodded sharply. "My thoughts exactly."

As we drove back along the causeway, the Institute's glowing dome receding behind us, my mind was still reeling from everything that had happened. The tension between Ezra and Nereus had been thick enough to cut with a knife, and now we were leaving early? Something was seriously wrong.

"Are you going to tell me what that was all about?" I finally asked, breaking the suffocating silence.

His profile was sharp against the darkness, jaw clenched as he focused on the road. "It's complicated."

"Try me," I challenged. I was getting tired of being kept in the dark.

He was quiet for so long I thought he might not answer. Finally, just as we turned onto the coastal road leading back to town, he spoke. "There was a threat to the Institute tonight. A bomb at one of the exits."

My blood turned to ice. "A bomb?" The word came out as barely a whisper. "Are you serious?"

"Security handled it—"

"A bomb, Ezra. An actual bomb." My heart was hammering now. "We could have died. Everyone there could have died." The elegant evening suddenly felt like a nightmare I'd narrowly escaped. "And you're just mentioning this now?"

"The situation was contained before anyone was in real danger—"

"That's not the point!" I twisted in my seat to face him fully. "Why didn't you tell me immediately? I had a right to know."

His jaw tightened further. "I didn't want to panic you. The evening was important for—"

"For what? Your image?" Anger was replacing the shock now, hot and sharp. "You let me walk around that place for hours not knowing there was a bomb somewhere in the building?"

"Twyla, this kind of thing happens a lot at our events—"

"No." I held up a hand, my voice shaking. "That's not okay. You don't get to hide things like this from me."

He was silent for a long moment, and I could see him processing my words. When he finally spoke, his voice was quieter. "I'm sorry."

The apology took some of the wind out of my sails, but I was still rattled. I pressed my palms against my knees to stop them from shaking. "Jesus, Ezra. A bomb."

"I know." His voice was gentler now. "Are you all right?"

I took a shaky breath. "I think so. It's just... processing it, you know?" The reality was finally sinking in, and with it came a delayed wave of fear that made my hands tremble.

"We're safe now," he said, and something in his tone made me believe him.

I nodded, trying to calm my racing heart. After a few more breaths, another thought occurred to me. "Wait. This whole thing tonight—is that why you and Nereus were at each other's throats? Does he have something to do with this?"

Ezra's hands tightened on the steering wheel again. "Not the bomb, no. Nereus sees me as competition. I've built something here—connections, influence, respect. He wants to tear that down and claim it for himself."

"Your investors?" I was starting to piece it together now.

"Among other things." His eyes flickered to me briefly before returning to the road. "He's been circling my contacts for months, trying to secure funding for his own ventures. Tonight was just another hunting expedition."

The possessive undertones weren't lost on me, and a chill that had nothing to do with the weather crept up my spine. "And now he's hunting me too."

"It would seem so."

We drove the rest of the way in silence, the only sounds being the rush of the ocean beside us and the rhythmic swish of the windshield wipers as a light rain began to fall.

When we reached my shop, Ezra cut the engine but made no move to exit the car. "I should go," he said, voice rough around the edges. "It's been an...eventful evening."

Something in his tone made me hesitate. I'd never seen him so tightly wound, so clearly struggling for control. "Are you okay to drive?"

"I'm fine," he snapped, though the white-knuckled grip on the steering wheel suggested otherwise.

I studied his profile in the dim light from the street lamp. The scales I'd glimpsed earlier were more pronounced now, a subtle shimmer across his cheekbones and down his throat that disappeared beneath his collar. His breathing seemed unusually measured, as if each inhale and exhale required conscious effort.

"Ezra," I whispered, reaching across to touch his arm. His skin was hot beneath my fingers, almost fever-warm. "What's happening to you?"

He turned to me then, and the raw emotion in his eyes took my breath away. "Nothing you need to concern yourself with," he said, though the strain in his voice belied the casual words. "I'll be fine by morning."

He walked me to my door, maintaining a careful distance that felt wrong after the possessive way he'd kept me close all evening. At the threshold, he hesitated, as if unsure of the appropriate goodbye.

I solved the dilemma by rising on tiptoes to press a quick kiss to his cheek. "Thanks for tonight," I said. "Even with the weird tension and mysterious security threats, I had fun."

Something like pain flashed across his features. "Goodnight, Twyla," he said, his voice containing that musical quality again, though it sounded almost broken now. Before I could respond, he was gone, striding back to his car with unusual haste.

I watched from my window as he drove away, wondering what secrets Ezra Thalassos was keeping, and why the appearance of another siren had caused such a dramatic change in him. I touched my lips, remembering the feel of his skin beneath them—hot and slightly textured with scales—and wondered, for the first time, if I might be in over my head.

As I turned away from the window, I couldn't shake the memory of Nereus's intense turquoise eyes, or the way he'd so brazenly flirted with me right in front of Ezra. The tension between the two sirens had been palpable, electric—like watching storm clouds gather over the ocean.

Whatever history lay between them, I had a feeling I'd just become caught in the middle of it.

Chapter Thirteen

Turning Tide

The shop bell chimed at 5:50 PM, just as I was counting down the register. I looked up to find Nereus in my doorway, looking like he'd stepped off a yacht—cream linen shirt open at the collar revealing the shimmer of scales along his collarbone, perfectly fitted dark jeans, that blue-green hair catching the late afternoon light streaming through my windows.

"We're about to close," I said, though I made no move to shoo him out.

"Perfect timing, then." He strode to the counter, pulling a small velvet box from his pocket. His rings caught the light as he moved—silver bands that complemented the subtle iridescence of the scales visible on the backs of his hands. "I have something for you."

I eyed the box warily, my hands still counting twenties. "What's that?"

He set it on the counter between us, not pushing it toward me. The velvet was deep ocean blue, expensive-looking. "Open it when you want to. No pressure."

Despite myself, curiosity won. I set down the stack of bills and lifted the lid. Inside, nestled in silk, were the most stunning earrings I'd ever seen—pearls that shifted from deep turquoise to pale pink to silver as they caught the light, like captured pieces of the ocean itself.

"Holy shit," I breathed, then caught myself. "I mean—they're beautiful. But I can't accept this."

"Why not?" He leaned against the counter, and I noticed he didn't hide the way the scales at his throat caught the overhead lights as he moved. Everything about him screamed confidence—in his appearance, his presence, his interest in me.

"Because..." I fumbled for the right words, my fingers hovering over the earrings without quite touching them. "It's complicated."

His head tilted slightly, turquoise eyes studying my face. "Has Ezra asked you to be exclusive? Are you two officially dating?"

The questions stung because they highlighted exactly what had been bothering me for days. I pulled out my phone; the screen lit up to show absolutely nothing new. No response to the texts I'd sent yesterday asking how his commissions were going, whether he wanted to grab coffee. Just radio silence stretching into its second day.

"I'll take that as a no," Nereus snorted. "Twyla, I'm not trying to complicate anything. I'm just being honest about what I want."

"Which is?" I set the phone facedown on the counter with more force than necessary.

"I'd like to take you to dinner. Tonight. Right now, if you'll have me." He straightened, and the movement made the scales along his jawline shimmer like sequins. "I know a place that makes the most incredible seafood you've ever tasted. Completely private, no crowds, no pressure. Just good food and conversation."

My phone buzzed against the counter. For a split second, hope flared—maybe Ezra—but when I flipped it over, I saw another text from Trevone. The third one this week.

Trevone: Hey beautiful, been thinking about you. Coffee sometime?

I shoved the phone back in my pocket, my jaw clenching. Like hell was I going to sit around pining while everyone else moved on with their lives.

"Okay," I said, the word coming out sharper than I'd intended.

Nereus's face lit up in pleasant surprise. "Really?"

"Yeah. I need a bit to close up and change." I gestured to my work clothes—paint-stained apron over a simple green dress that had seen better days.

"Take all the time you need." He was already heading for the door, moving with that fluid grace that reminded me he wasn't entirely human. "I'll bring the car around."

After he left, I quickly finished counting the register, my hands shaking slightly as I stacked the bills. What was I doing? This felt like standing at the edge of a cliff, but maybe it was time to jump instead of waiting for someone else to push me.

I was just grabbing my keys when the door chimed again.

"Sorry, we're—oh, Mira!" Relief flooded through me at the sight of my friend's familiar face, though something in her expression looked off. "What's up?"

"Just thought I'd see if you wanted to grab dinner," she said, glancing toward the back of the shop like she was looking for something. Her usual bright smile seemed forced. "That guy who just left...he seems kind of intense."

I laughed, though it sounded brittle even to my own ears. "Yeah, sirens are just like that, I think. Very...focu sed."

"Sirens?" Mira's eyebrows shot up, and she stepped closer to the counter. "As in multiple?"

Heat crept up my neck. I busied myself with putting the cash drawer back in the register. "It's not like that. I mean, not really. It's complicated."

"I see." Mira moved closer, her hands resting on the counter. The small potted plants scattered around the shop seemed to lean toward her, responding to her presence. "So dinner's off the table?"

"Actually, I've got plans with him tonight." The words felt strange in my mouth, like trying on clothes that didn't quite fit. "Rain check?"

Something flickered across Mira's face—disappointment, definitely disappointment. Her fingers drummed against the counter. "Sure. What about the pink, glittery guy? Did that not work out?"

I grabbed a cloth and started wiping down surfaces that didn't need cleaning. "I'm keeping my options open."

"Well, you know," Mira's voice was carefully neutral, but when I glanced up, her dark eyes were searching my face intently. "There are other options you might not have considered. Closer to home, maybe."

I paused in my cleaning, confused by the odd tone in her voice. "What do you mean?"

For a moment, Mira looked like she might say something important. Her mouth opened, then closed. She shook her head, reaching over to pat my hand gently. Her skin was always warm, like she'd been sitting in sunlight. "Nothing. Just...be careful tonight, okay? Trust your instincts."

She was almost to the door when Nereus reappeared, keys jingling in his hand. The overhead lights caught the scales scattered across his temples and cheekbones, making him look like he'd been dusted with crushed gemstones.

"Ready, gorgeous?" he asked, a confident smile spreading across his face.

As Mira passed him in the doorway, he muttered something under his breath—too low for me to catch, but Mira definitely heard it. One of the trailing vines from the potted plant by my door suddenly whipped out, smacking him smartly on the back of the head before recoiling innocently back into its pot.

"What the—" Nereus spun around, one hand going to his head, but Mira was already halfway down the sidewalk, not looking back.

"Huh," I said, staring after her retreating figure. "That was weird."

Nereus rubbed the back of his head, looking more amused than annoyed. The scales along his neck shifted color slightly—deeper blue, like irritation. He turned that brilliant smile on me, the scales lightening back to their usual turquoise. "Shall we go? Our table won't hold forever."

I grabbed my purse and pulled out my phone, fingers flying over the keyboard.

Twyla: Going to dinner with that other siren. Will text you when I'm home.

I hit send to Alex before I could second-guess myself, then followed Nereus out, locking the door behind me. The evening air was warm against my skin, carrying the salty scent of the ocean.

"You look good enough to eat," he said as we walked toward the sleek black sports car parked behind the building.

I glanced down at my simple green dress—nothing special, just what I'd worn to work. But the way he said it, the way his eyes traveled over me with obvious appreciation, made me feel like I was wearing designer silk.

"Thank you," I said, and meant it.

My phone buzzed as he opened the passenger door for me.

Alex: BE CAREFUL. Call if you need anything. Kronos says hi and also be careful.

I smiled despite my nerves and slipped the phone back into my purse. As I settled into the leather seat, I caught my reflection in the side window. My cheeks were flushed, my eyes bright with something that might have been excitement or might have been rebellion.

Either way, it felt good to be wanted.

Chapter Fourteen

DROWNING

"A food truck?" I asked, staring at the bright yellow vehicle parked at the end of the boardwalk. The hand-painted sign read "Coastal Catch" in cheerful blue letters, and the smell of butter and seafood made my mouth water despite my confusion.

"They have the best crab rolls on the entire coast," Nereus said, his hand settling naturally at the small of my back as we approached.

A weathered man with kind eyes and paint-stained fingers worked behind the window. When he saw Nereus, his face broke into a grin.

"Well, I'll be damned! Haven't seen you in months, son. The usual?"

"Two crab rolls, extra butter, and whatever she wants." Nereus gestured to me. "Joe, this is Twyla. Twyla, meet Joe—he makes the best seafood in three counties."

"Nice to meet you," I said, scanning the simple menu board. Everything looked amazing and reasonably priced. "I'll have the same."

"Coming right up. Find yourselves a spot and I'll bring them over."

We claimed a picnic table overlooking the water, the evening breeze carrying the salt scent of the ocean. Nereus stretched his long legs out, completely relaxed, the scales at his temples catching the setting sun like scattered jewels. There was something almost hypnotic about the way they shimmered, and I had to force myself to look away.

"So this is your idea of *fine* dining?" I teased, watching families stroll past with ice cream cones and cotton candy.

"Don't knock it until you try it," he said, leaning forward with his elbows on the table. "I have excellent taste."

The way he said it, with that knowing smile, made me suspect he wasn't just talking about food.

When Joe brought our orders, I understood why Nereus had been so confident. The crab roll was incredible—sweet, succulent meat piled high on a perfectly toasted bun, dressed with just enough mayo and butter to enhance rather than mask the flavor. I may have made an embarrassing sound of pleasure after the first bite.

"Good?" Nereus asked, and I could hear the smugness in his voice.

"Ridiculously good," I admitted, wiping butter from my chin. "How did you find this place?"

"I have my ways." He took another bite, somehow managing to look elegant even while dribbling butter down his chin. "You've been thinking about me, haven't you?"

The question was so direct it caught me completely off guard. Heat crept up my neck, and I was suddenly very interested in my food. "Maybe a little."

"Just a little?" His tone was playful, teasing. "I tried googling your name after we met, but without more details..." He shrugged with mock disappointment. "Not much came up either."

I looked up sharply. "You googled me?"

"Don't look so surprised. You're fascinating, Twyla." The way he said my name, like he was tasting it, made my stomach do something acrobatic. "I wanted to know more."

"Well, what did you find?"

"Your shop, some reviews. Nothing that told me what I really wanted to know." He leaned forward, his voice dropping to something more intimate. "Like what makes you laugh. What you're afraid of. What you want."

The intensity of his gaze made my mouth go dry. "That's pretty forward for a first date."

"Is that what this is?" His smile was pure mischief. "I wasn't sure you'd admit it."

I took a sip of my drink, trying to buy myself time to think of a clever response, but his words caught me so off guard that I nearly choked. Soda went down the wrong way, and I started coughing, my eyes watering as I frantically reached for a napkin.

"Smooth," I wheezed, my face burning with embarrassment. "Really making a great impression here."

Nereus was grinning now, not even trying to hide his amusement as he handed me another napkin. "Oh, you're making an impression alright."

"Shut up," I muttered, dabbing at my eyes, still feeling the sting. Could this get any more mortifying?

"If this is how you react to a simple question, I'm curious what happens when I really try to fluster you."

The teasing note in his voice made my stomach flip, and I was pretty sure my face couldn't get any redder. "You're enjoying this way too much."

"Guilty as charged," he said, standing and extending his hand with that infuriating smirk still plastered on his face. "Come on. Let's walk before you find another way to injure yourself."

I took his hand, hoping the evening air might cool the fire in my cheeks and that whatever he wanted to show me would help me forget how thoroughly I'd just embarrassed myself.

The boardwalk was busy with evening strollers, couples sharing funnel cake, and kids begging for one more ride on the carousel. Nereus kept up a steady stream of conversation as we walked, pointing out landmarks, telling stories about the various businesses we passed. His energy was infectious, making everything feel lighter, more fun.

"Want to head down to the beach?" he asked when we reached the far end of the boardwalk.

I glanced toward the water, remembering another evening, another beach. Ezra's voice floated across the waves, haunting and lonely, the way it had moved me to tears. I pushed the memory aside. "Sure."

We kicked off our shoes at the edge of the sand, Nereus rolling up his jeans to reveal more of those iridescent scales. The sand was still warm from the day's sun, soft between my toes. He caught my hand as we walked toward the water, his skin surprisingly warm.

"We should go for a swim," he suggested as we reached the water's edge. "The ocean's perfect tonight—not too cold, gentle waves."

I let the water lap at my feet, the foam cool against my skin. For a moment, I imagined it—diving beneath the surface, letting the water close over my head. But something held me back.

"I'm not dumb enough to get in the water with a siren on a first date," I said, trying to keep my tone light.

His laugh was bright and unguarded. "Smart woman. Though I promise my intentions are entirely honorable." The way he said it, with that wicked glint in his eyes, suggested his intentions were anything but.

We walked farther down the beach as the sun sank lower, painting the sky in shades of orange and pink. The crowds thinned out, leaving us mostly alone with the sound of waves and distant seagulls. Nereus began humming softly, something low and melodic that vibrated through the air between us.

"You have a beautiful voice," I said, and felt the faintest buzz from my protection runes—so subtle I almost missed it.

"I'd be a pretty terrible siren if I didn't," he said with a laugh, his thumb tracing circles on the back of my hand. "I appreciate the compliment though. Music is important to my kind. It's how we express what's building deep within our souls."

The humming continued, weaving around us like an invisible thread. My shoulders started to relax, tension I hadn't realized I was carrying slowly melting away. The sensation from my runes remained gentle, more like a soft warning than an alarm. I knew it should probably worry me more than it did, this clear sign that his siren abilities were affecting me, even mildly.

"This is nice," I said, surprised by how much I meant it. "I haven't done anything like this in... well, a long time."

"What, walked on a beach?"

"Had an actual date," I admitted before I could stop myself.

Something shifted in his expression, curiosity sharpening his features. "What do you mean?"

Heat crawled up my neck as I realized what I'd just revealed. "Nothing, it's not important—"

"Twyla." He stopped walking and turned to face me. "Are you telling me Ezra hasn't taken you on a proper date?"

My stomach dropped. "No."

"Where has he taken you? Dinner? Movies? Dancing?"

The questions hit like rapid-fire punches, each one highlighting exactly how pathetic my situation was. "The Institute reception was probably the closest thing."

"That wasn't a date. That was a work function where you were his guest." His voice was gentle, almost pitying, which somehow made it worse.

"I know that," I said, my voice coming out smaller than I intended.

His hand came up to cup my face, and warmth spread from where his palm touched my cheek. "So in all this time, he's never actually courted you? Never taken you somewhere just because he wanted to spend time with you?"

I could feel his humming shift to something deeper, more compelling. The buzz from my runes intensified slightly, a gentle thrum against my skin, though it felt distant compared to the heat pooling in my stomach from his touch.

"Not outside of my shop. He's busy—"

"We're all busy, Twyla," he said softly, his eyes searching mine. "The question is what we make time for."

His other arm slipped around my waist, pulling me closer until I could feel the hard lines of his body. The humming in his chest was stronger now, and I could feel it vibrating against my skin where we touched.

"Would Ezra do this?" he asked softly, his voice dropping to a register that resonated in my bones. "Would he bring you somewhere just to see you smile?"

I opened my mouth to answer, but no words came. The truth was too painful to voice—that Ezra had never done any of those things.

"You deserve someone who knows your worth." Nereus murmured, his lips so close to mine I could feel his breath.

When he kissed me again, my world tilted. His mouth moved against mine with clear intent, confident and claiming. His song vibrated directly from his lips into mine, and my knees went weak.

I kissed him back without thinking, my hands fisting in his shirt as he backed me away from the water. My heart was hammering so hard I was sure he could feel it against his chest. The rocky outcroppings rose around us, cutting us off from the rest of the beach.

"My private property starts here," he murmured against my lips, his breath warm on my skin. "No one can see us." He was shrugging out of his jacket, the expensive fabric settling onto the sand with a soft whisper. He pulled me down beside him, the sand was cool through the thin barrier of his jacket, grains shifting beneath my weight. His body covered mine, solid and warm and so much bigger than he'd seemed standing up. The breadth of his shoulders blocked out the moon as he leaned over me.

"You're so beautiful," he said, his voice rough in a way that made my stomach flip.

His mouth crashed against mine again, hungrier this time. His hands tangled in my hair, tugging just hard enough to make me gasp.

The sound seemed to encourage him. His mouth moved to my jaw, then down to my throat, his breath hot against my skin. When his teeth scraped the sensitive spot where my neck met my shoulder, electricity shot straight down my spine.

"Oh," I breathed, the word torn from my throat as my back arched involuntarily.

He bit down gently, and I felt the sharp points of teeth that were just a little too pointed to be human. The pain was brief, immediately soothed by his tongue—and that tongue, God, it was textured like Ezra's, ridged in a way that made the simple act of him licking my skin feel like lightning.

His hands were everywhere, sliding the straps of my dress down my shoulders, pushing the fabric aside to expose more skin to the cool night air and his burning touch. My nipples peaked instantly, partly from the cold, mostly from the way he was looking at me like I was something he wanted to devour.

"Nereus—" I started, but he silenced me with another kiss, this one desperate and consuming.

When he shifted his weight, settling more fully between my legs, I felt it—the unmistakable pressure of two hard lengths against my thigh through his jeans. *Just like Ezra.*

His knee nudged my legs apart, and I let him, my dress riding up around my hips. The buzz from my protection runes was getting stronger, a persistent vibration against my fingernails, but it felt distant compared to the song vibrating from his chest into mine.

His hand skimmed down my side, over my hip, then lower. When his fingers reached the edge of my underwear, I went completely still.

This was it. The point of no return.

His eyes found mine in the darkness, and for a heartbeat we just looked at each other. I could see the question there, the moment of choice. I could stop this. I should stop this.

Instead, I lifted my hips slightly, and his smile was downright sinful.

His fingers slipped beneath the fabric, pushing it aside rather than removing it entirely. The first touch of skin against skin sent a shock of heat straight through my core.

Holy shit.

His fingers traced along my inner thigh, ghosting over sensitive skin before moving higher. My breath hitched when he brushed along the curve of my hip bone, then traced a path back down. When his thumb swept across my clit, electricity shot up my spine and I had to dig my nails into his shoulders to ground myself. The sound that ripped from my throat was raw and desperate—definitely too loud for any beach, even a private one.

When he found my clit with his thumb, my entire body jolted like I'd been electrocuted. A sound escaped me I didn't recognize—high and desperate and definitely too loud for a public beach, even a private one.

"That's it," he said, his voice thick with satisfaction. His mouth worked at my throat while his hand worked between my legs, his thumb circling with devastating precision while his fingers teased at my entrance. The dual sensation was overwhelming, made more intense by his song vibrating through every point where our bodies touched.

I was losing myself completely. My hands clutched at his shoulders, nails digging into the expensive fabric of his shirt. My hips moved against his hand, chasing the pleasure he was building with surgical skill.

When he slipped one finger inside me, I cried out, my back arching so hard I thought I might snap in half. The intrusion was gentle but sure, and when he added a second finger, curling them just right, I saw stars behind my closed eyelids.

"God," I gasped, unable to form any other words.

He was going to make me come. Right here on the beach, on a first date. The rational part of my brain screamed that this was insane, that I barely knew him, that this wasn't like me at all. But my body didn't care about rational thoughts. My body only cared about the pressure building between my legs and the skilled fingers that knew exactly how to stoke it higher.

His thumb pressed down on my clit at the same moment his fingers found that spot inside me that made me see fireworks. The orgasm hit like a tidal wave, crashing over me with an intensity that left me shaking and gasping his name into the night air.

He guided me through it, his fingers gentle but persistent until the final tremor subsided, leaving me limp and breathless beneath him.

He pressed soft kisses to my throat as I struggled to remember how to breathe.

Through the haze of satisfaction, I watched him bring his fingers to his mouth. The ridged texture of his tongue was visible in the moonlight as he licked them clean, and the sight sent another pulse of heat through my already oversensitive body.

What the hell had just happened to me?

I lay there, my dress bunched around my waist, my hair full of sand, staring up at the star-filled sky and trying to process what I'd just let happen. The buzz from my protection runes had stopped completely, I realized with a start. When had that happened?

"We should go," Nereus said gently, helping me sit up and smooth my dress back down.

I nodded mutely, not trusting my voice. My legs felt like jelly as he helped me to my feet, his jacket draped carefully around my shoulders. I could smell his cologne on the fabric, mixed with salt air and the lingering scent of my arousal.

The walk back to his car was a blur of sensation and confusion. What had I done? What was I doing? And why did some traitorous part of me already want him to touch me again?

The drive back to my place passed in a haze of lingering touches and heated glances. Every red light brought his hand to my thigh, his thumb tracing circles on my skin that sent aftershocks through my still-sensitive body. His humming continued, softer now but still present, keeping me floating in that pleasant headspace where everything felt good and nothing felt complicated.

"I had an incredible time tonight," he said as we pulled up behind my building.

"Yeah," I managed, my voice still breathless. "Me too."

He walked me to my door, and I was acutely aware of how rumpled I must look, how thoroughly he'd claimed me on that beach. At my threshold, he caught a strand of hair that had escaped my careful style, tucking it behind my ear with infinite gentleness.

"Sweet dreams, Twyla," he said, leaning down to capture my lips in one final, searing kiss that left me breathless and aching for more.

I watched him drive away before climbing the stairs to my apartment, my legs still unsteady. It wasn't until I was safely inside, leaning against my closed door, that the fog cleared from my mind.

I'd put my phone on silent during dinner, and when I pulled it out, I saw a missed call from Ezra. One missed call, and a text that made my stomach drop.

Ezra: I guess you're sleeping. Sorry I have been so wrapped up in a painting for a client. Can't wait to see you. –E

I stared at the message, my heart clenching with something that might have been guilt or regret or longing. He'd finally reached out, finally made contact after three days of silence, and I'd been on a beach letting another man's hands map my body like territory to be claimed.

I caught sight of myself in the hallway mirror and winced. My hair was mussed, my lips were swollen from kissing, and a dark mark where Nereus had bitten me was visible on my neck even in the dim light.

A hickey.

Like I was seventeen again and sneaking around behind the gym. I touched the spot gingerly, and it was then that I noticed something else. The gentle buzz from my protection runes had stopped completely. I looked down at my nails, and my heart sank.

Tiny cracks ran through the polish on every finger; the carefully drawn runes fractured and broken. They must have given way during...during whatever had happened on that beach.

I'd been completely unprotected for who knows how long, completely vulnerable to whatever influence Nereus had been weaving around me. And I hadn't even noticed when they failed.

Standing there in my quiet apartment, staring at my broken defenses and feeling the throb of the mark on my neck, I felt the full weight of what I'd done hit me.

I allowed myself to be seduced, and the worst part?

Some traitorous part of me wanted to do it again.

Chapter Fifteen

BLOOD IN THE WATER

I woke up with sand in my hair.

Not just a few grains that had somehow survived my shower the night before, but actual, honest-to-god beach sand embedded in my braids despite my silk bonnet. I sat up in bed, my head pounding with what felt like the worst hangover of my life, though I'd barely had more than a beer with dinner.

The memory hit me like a freight train. Nereus. The beach. His hands on my body, his mouth on my throat, the way I'd come apart under his touch like some desperate teenager. My face burned with embarrassment as the full weight of what I'd done crashed over me.

"Jesus Christ, Twyla," I muttered, dragging myself out of bed. My reflection in the bathroom mirror confirmed my worst fears. My hair was a disaster, micro braids sticking out at odd angles despite the bonnet. My lips were still slightly swollen from kissing, and there—oh

187

god, there on my neck—was a dark purple mark that definitely hadn't been there yesterday morning.

I touched the spot gingerly, remembering the feel of his teeth scraping against my skin, the way he'd bitten down just hard enough to mark me. My hands were shaking as I reached for my makeup bag, digging through it for concealer. At least I could hide the evidence of my poor life choices. It took three layers of foundation and concealer to make the mark barely visible, and even then it was still noticeable if you knew what to look for.

I spent the next twenty minutes picking off the broken polish, my nails looking naked and vulnerable without their protective coating. I tried calling my nail tech, but her voicemail cheerfully informed me she was booked solid for the next three weeks. Three weeks without protection, in a city full of supernatural beings who could influence my mind with a look or a song.

I was trying not to have a panic attack when the knock came at my door. Probably another shipment of colorful yarn for the craft section. I'd told Alex to order some before Mrs. Jackson rioted about not having her tinsel yarn. I trudged downstairs, my body still aching in places that reminded me exactly what I'd been doing the night before.

The delivery woman was practically hidden behind a massive floral arrangement. These were elegant—deep red roses mixed with white lilies and greenery, arranged in a sleek black vase that probably cost more than my monthly grocery budget.

"Twyla Knight?" she asked, peering around the bouquet.

"That's me," I sighed, accepting the arrangement with resignation. At least these didn't hurt to look at.

The card was tucked discreetly among the flowers. I waited until the delivery woman left before opening it, my stomach clenching with a mixture of anticipation and dread.

I can't stop thinking about you. -N

I stared at the message, my face burning all over again. The words were direct, but they carried the weight of everything that had happened between us. He wasn't just thinking about me—he was thinking about the way I'd responded to his touch, the sounds I'd made, the way I'd arched beneath him on the sand.

I set the flowers on my counter, trying to ignore how beautiful they were. Everything about Nereus seemed designed to remind me of what we'd shared, to keep me thinking about him just as much as he was apparently thinking about me.

My phone rang, startling me out of my brooding. Ezra's name flashed on the screen, and guilt crashed over me like a wave.

"Hey," I answered, trying to sound normal despite the anxiety clawing at my throat.

"Good morning." His voice was warm, genuinely pleased to hear from me. "I hope I didn't wake you."

"No, I've been up for a while." I touched the concealer covering my neck, paranoid that he could somehow see it through the phone. "How are you?"

"Better now that I'm talking to you." There was something different in his voice today, softer somehow. "I wanted to apologize for the other night. Though things were tense, I shouldn't have snapped at you. I do hope you can forgive me."

"You don't need to apologize," I said, though the words felt like ash in my mouth. He was apologizing to me while I was standing in my kitchen, staring at flowers from another man.

The silence that followed was comfortable, and it made the guilt in my chest burn even brighter. How could I have let another man touch me when Ezra could make me feel like this just by talking to me?

"I should let you get on with your day," he said finally. "I have several commissions to finish, including the one for Alex and Kronos. I'll be quite busy for the next few days."

"Of course." The words came out more bitter than I'd intended. Of course he'd be busy.

"Twyla?" His voice was concerned. "Is everything alright?"

"I'm fine," I lied. "Just tired."

"Get some rest," he said gently. "I'll call you soon."

The line went dead, leaving me staring at my phone and feeling like the worst person in the world. He was being sweet, considerate, everything I should want in a man.

My phone rang again almost immediately. Unknown number.

I almost didn't answer, but something made me swipe to accept the call.

"Hello?"

"Good morning, beautiful." Nereus's voice was like warm honey, instantly recognizable and sending an unwelcome shiver down my spine.

I almost dropped the phone. "Nereus."

"You sound surprised. Did you think last night was a dream?" There was amusement in his voice. "I suppose I am rather dreamy."

Heat burned my ears as memories of the beach crashed over me again. "What do you want?"

"Direct as always. I like that about you." I could practically hear his smile. "I wanted to make sure you received my flowers."

I glanced at the red roses. "They're beautiful."

"Not nearly as beautiful as you looked beneath me." His voice dropped to a register that vibrated directly through my bones, even over the phone. "The way you looked in the moonlight, the sounds you made..."

"Stop," I said weakly, my body responding despite my embarrassment.

"Why? You enjoyed it." His tone was matter-of-fact, completely unapologetic. "I certainly hope you're not having regrets."

Was I? I honestly wasn't sure.

"I don't know, maybe?" I said finally.

"I know what I want, Twyla. I want you. And unless I'm very much mistaken, you want me too."

I couldn't deny it. My body's response to just hearing his voice was proof enough that whatever had happened between us wasn't going away anytime soon.

"What do you want from me?" I asked.

"My club is having its grand opening tonight. I'd like you to be there."

"I don't know—"

"Think about it," he interrupted. "When was the last time you went dancing?"

I couldn't remember. Certainly, before my shop took off. Before Alex and his drama had consumed my free time. Before I'd started spending all my energy trying to decode Ezra's mixed signals.

"This isn't about Ezra, if that's what you're worried about." Nereus continued, as if reading my thoughts. "You deserve to have fun, Twyla. You deserve to feel good."

The intimate way he said it reminded me of exactly how good he could make me feel. My treacherous body was already responding to the memory, to the promise in his voice.

"I shouldn't," I said, but even I could hear the weakness in my protest.

"You're not committed to anyone, are you? You're free to make your own choices."

He was right, and that was the worst part. I wasn't committed to Ezra, despite whatever possessive words he'd used on the phone. We'd never defined what we were, never had that conversation. Technically, I was free to do whatever—and whomever—I wanted.

"Where?" I heard myself asking.

"Salt & Smoke, in the marina district. Ten o'clock." His satisfaction was audible. "Ask for me at the VIP entrance. And Twyla?"

"Yeah?"

"I can't wait to dance with you."

The line went dead before I could respond, leaving me standing in my kitchen with my heart racing and my body humming with anticipation.

I stared at the flowers, at the card with its simple message. *Can't stop thinking about you.*

The truth was, I couldn't stop thinking about him either. The way he'd touched me, the way he'd made me feel desired and beautiful and reckless.

I touched the concealer covering my neck, remembering the feel of his teeth against my skin. Tonight. I could go tonight, dance with him, let him touch me again. Let him make me forget about mixed signals and undefined relationships and the crushing weight of waiting for someone to decide I was worth fighting for.

My fingers traced the edge of the card, and I made my decision.

Tonight, I was going to be reckless.

Chapter Sixteen

FEEDING FRENZY

Saturday night found me idling in my beat-up Beetle outside Salt & Smoke, wondering if I'd completely lost my mind.

The guilt had been eating at me all day. Every time I caught sight of myself in a mirror, the concealer covering Nereus's mark on my neck seemed to mock me. Every time my phone buzzed, I expected it to be Ezra somehow knowing what I'd done, what I was about to do again.

Nereus had texted earlier, suggesting he send a car for me. I'd politely declined. I wanted my own wheels in case tonight went sideways—though honestly, after what had happened on the beach, I wasn't sure there was anywhere left to go but down.

Nereus: You sure? ;) After last night, I thought you might trust me a little more.

Twyla: I'm good. See you there.

I'd answered, trying to sound casual.

He bounced back quickly.

Nereus: Can't wait to see you again. Wear a dress that shows off your neck.

I'd stared at that message for a full minute, my hand flying to the concealed hickey. He wanted people to see his mark on me. The possessiveness should have been a red flag, but instead it sent a thrill through my body.

So here I was at 10:15 PM, dressed in the indigo dress he'd requested—the one with the deep neckline that would show his mark if I let my hair fall the right way. I sat in my car trying to talk myself into—or out of—going inside. The building glowed with an otherworldly blue light, its façade transformed from an old warehouse into something that looked like it belonged underwater.

I hadn't told anyone where I was going tonight. Not Alex, not Mira, definitely not Ezra. The secrecy made it feel even more like I was doing something wrong, which was ridiculous. Ezra and I weren't exclusive. We weren't even officially dating.

So why did my stomach feel like I'd swallowed a butterfly sanctuary?

Because you know this is wrong, but you can't stop yourself. my conscience whispered.

"Screw it," I muttered, grabbing my clutch and getting out of the car. I was already damned. Might as well enjoy it.

The VIP entrance was tucked around the side, a glowing turquoise door guarded by a mountain of a man with gills visible on his neck. When I approached, his expression immediately shifted to recognition.

"Ms. Knight," he said before I could even introduce myself. "Mr. Nereus has been expecting you. He asked me to escort you to him personally."

Of course he had.

The space was breathtaking. Shimmering fabrics draped across the rafters. The music vibrated through my body in a way that felt more like being submerged in an ocean of sound. The lighting shifted between deep blues and soft teals, casting rippling patterns across every surface. It wasn't gross or seedy like the places Alex used to work—this was elegant, sophisticated, beautiful.

And dangerous. Without my runes, I could feel the supernatural energy in the air like electricity before a storm.

The bouncer led me through the crowd, past the main bar toward a raised VIP section overlooking the dance floor. Nereus stood with his back to us, talking to someone I couldn't see, but I'd recognize those broad shoulders anywhere. When he turned and saw me, his face lit up with pure satisfaction.

"Hey, there's trouble," he said playfully, dismissing whoever he'd been talking to with a wave.

He moved toward me with that fluid confidence, and I felt my resolve wavering already. In the blue light of the club, his scales caught the illumination like scattered jewels, and his turquoise eyes seemed to glow from within. When he reached me, his hands went immediately to my waist, pulling me close.

"You look incredible," he murmured against my ear, his breath warm against my skin. "Though I notice you covered up my work."

His finger traced along my neckline, dangerously close to where his mark lay hidden beneath concealer.

"I work with the public," I said weakly. "I can't walk around looking like I've been mauled."

"Mauled?" He chuckled. "It's a love bite at best."

Heat flooded my face as memories of the beach crashed over me. "Nereus—"

"I prefer 'claimed,'" he continued, his voice dropping to a register that bypassed my brain and went straight between my legs. "Or 'thoroughly pleased.' But we can work on your vocabulary later."

Before I could respond, he was guiding me toward the bar, his hand never leaving my back. "Drink first. Then I want to show you off on my dance floor."

The bartender—a woman with iridescent scales dusting her cheekbones—immediately prepared something without being asked. When she set it before me, it was unlike anything I'd ever seen—what looked like a blooming lotus made entirely of delicate blue spun sugar, filled with shimmering liquid.

Nereus lifted the delicate creation, holding it out to me. "Try it," he said, his voice low and intimate. His eyes never left my face as I took a tentative sip.

The drink was sweet with a hint of salt, like what I imagined mermaid tears might taste like. Complex and layered, with flavors I couldn't quite identify. I closed my eyes, savoring it, and when I opened them, found him watching me with hungry intensity.

"Good?" he asked, stepping closer until his body nearly pressed against mine.

I nodded, not trusting my voice. He reached out, fingers delicately snapping off one of the sugar petals from the cup. The piece was translucent blue, catching the club's lighting like a tiny piece of sea glass.

"Open," he murmured, his free hand cupping my jaw.

I parted my lips, and he leaned in, so close I could feel his breath against my skin. His mouth touched mine as he placed the sugar petal on my tongue with his own, the sweet flavor dissolving instantly and mixing with the taste of him.

The kiss was brief but devastating, leaving me breathless and wanting more. I tried to take a half step back, suddenly feeling dizzy, but his arm tightened around my waist, keeping me pressed against him.

"It's good," I managed, my voice barely above a whisper.

"You seem tense," his thumb was tracing circles on my lower back. "Still thinking about him?"

I didn't need to ask who he meant. "I'm ok."

"Good," he interrupted, setting my drink aside and taking my hand. "I want to be the only siren on your mind tonight."

He pulled me toward the dance floor, weaving through the crowd with confidence. The bass thrummed through the floor, vibrating up through my bones as he drew me into his arms. Without my protection runes, his song hit me like a drug, making every nerve ending come alive under his touch.

His hands settled on my hips, fingers digging in just hard enough to guide my movements. I moved against him like I was made for it, my body responding to his rhythm before my brain could catch up.

"That's my girl," he murmured against my ear, his voice rough with approval. "Let me see you move."

I rolled my hips against his, and the low groan that escaped his throat made me dizzy with power. His hands were everywhere—sliding up my sides, tangling in my hair, pulling me closer until I could feel every hard line of his body pressed against mine.

He spun me around, my back flush against his chest, his arms caging me in as we moved together. I could feel him growing hard against my lower back, could feel the vibration of his song resonating through my ribs, making my skin hypersensitive to every shift and grind of his hips.

"God, you're perfect," he growled in my ear, one hand splaying across my stomach to hold me tight against him. "I think I'll keep you."

I was drowning in sensation—the possessive grip of his hands, the way his mouth found the sensitive spot behind my ear and made me shiver. My head fell back against his shoulder, a soft moan escaping as his teeth grazed my neck right over his hidden mark.

"You don't even need to say anything," he whispered against my skin. "Your body tells me everything I need to know."

I was completely lost in the haze of his song, letting him move my body however he wanted, when a voice cut through the music like a blade.

"Twyla Knight."

My name, spoken in that familiar musical tone, snapped me partially back to awareness. I blinked, trying to focus through the fog, and saw him across the club.

Ezra.

He sat partially hidden by the undulating fabric hangings, but I'd recognize that pink hair anywhere. He wasn't alone. A stunning woman with silver-white hair sat close to him, her hand resting intimately on his arm as she leaned in to whisper something in his ear.

But his attention wasn't on her. Even through the haze of Nereus's song, I could see Ezra's eyes locked on me with a frightening intensity. They were glowing—not their usual soft pink, but a fierce, burning magenta that seemed to cut through the club's dim lighting.

"I see we have an audience," Nereus murmured against my ear, his satisfaction clear. His hands grew more possessive, one sliding down to cup my ass while the other traced the neckline of my dress in full view of anyone watching. "Let's give him a show."

The fog in my head thickened as his song intensified, but some part of me tried to resist. "We should stop—"

"I don't think so." His thumb traced along my jawline, then deliberately pressed against my neck where his mark lay hidden. The pressure made me gasp, and I felt the concealer give way under his touch, revealing the dark bruise beneath.

He spun me so we were directly facing Ezra's table, his body pressed against my back as we moved. His hands roamed freely—one splayed possessively across my stomach, fingers dipping dangerously low, while the other slid up to graze the underside of my breast through my dress. Every touch was calculated, intimate, designed to show exactly how well he knew my body.

Across the club, I saw Ezra stand abruptly, his chair scraping back. The woman beside him looked confused as he started moving toward us, his expression murderous. But then something changed. His steps faltered, one hand going to his chest as his face contorted in pain.

I caught sight of Nereus's reflection in the mirrored wall behind the bar, and his smile was pure evil. Cold satisfaction gleamed in his eyes as he watched Ezra struggle.

"Perfect," he breathed against my neck. "Right on schedule."

That sinister expression cut through some of the fog clouding my mind. Something was very wrong here. This wasn't just jealousy—Nereus had planned this, whatever this was.

I watched in growing alarm as Ezra doubled over slightly, his skin flushed and sweaty even from this distance. He was in actual pain, and somehow Nereus was enjoying every second.

"Let me go," I said, trying to pull away, but my limbs felt heavy, uncooperative.

"Why would I do that when we're having so much fun?" Nereus's voice was smooth honey, but his grip was iron. "Look how much he wants you now. Pity it's too late."

I forced myself to move, stumbling away from him despite the way his song tried to pull me back. My head spun with each step, like I was fighting through thick syrup, but I had to get to Ezra.

"Twyla," Nereus called after me, his voice carrying that hypnotic quality that made my knees buckle. "Come back and dance with me. We're not finished."

His dark chuckle followed me as I fought through the crowd, but I didn't look back.

I burst through the main entrance, gasping as the cool night air hit me like a splash of cold water. Without the constant pressure of supernatural songs and the overwhelming sensory input of the club, my head cleared.

I had to find Ezra. Whatever was happening to him, whatever had caused that look of pain on his face, I couldn't just walk away. Not when he might need help.

Drawing in a deep breath, I ran into the night, my heart pounding as I tried to figure out which direction he might have gone.

Chapter Seventeen

CAPSIZE

The first drops of rain hit my face as I raced down the street, my eyes frantically scanning the shadows. I had no clue which way Ezra had gone. My heart hammered against my ribs, panic rising with each passing second.

Thunder rumbled overhead, and the light sprinkle quickly turned into a downpour. *Great. Just perfect.* Within seconds, the rain plastered my carefully styled hair to my face and soaked my dress, making it cling to me like a second skin. I turned down a side street, cursing under my breath.

A noise stopped me—something between a growl and a curse, coming from a narrow alley between two buildings. I peered into the darkness, blinking against the rain. A flash of lightning illuminated the space for a split second, and I caught a glimpse of pink.

"Ezra?" I called, moving cautiously forward.

Another flash revealed him more clearly. He slumped against the brick wall, clutching one hand to his chest, his face twisted with fury and pain. His hair, which was usually perfect, was plastered to his skull, and I could see his flushed, almost fevered skin even in the dim light.

I rushed toward him, but he held up his free hand to stop me.

"Don't," he snarled, his usually melodic voice rough and strained. "Just...don't."

"What's wrong? Are you hurt?" I ignored his warning and knelt beside him, reaching for his forehead.

He jerked away from my touch like I'd burned him. "Go back inside. I'm sure your shark is wondering where you've gotten to."

The venom in his voice made me recoil. "Are you seriously giving me attitude right now? You're clearly having some kind of medical emergency!"

He let out a bitter laugh that turned into a grimace of pain. "Sure, let's call it that."

I looked at him more closely. His ears had.. . changed. They were no longer human-shaped but elongated into delicate, translucent fins that pulsed with a faint pink glow. The scales I'd always seen at his throat had spread, now covering most of his neck in a shimmering pattern that seemed to shift and spread even as I watched.

"Holy shit, Ezra. What's happening to you?"

"Nothing that concerns you." He tried to push himself up the wall, his legs giving out almost immediately. "Shouldn't you be letting that overgrown shark paw at you?"

Heat flared in my chest. "Oh, you've got to be kidding me. You're going to be jealous NOW? After ignoring me for days?"

"I told you I was working—"

"You disappeared!" I shot back, rain dripping from my hair onto his legs. "No calls, no texts, nothing! What was I supposed to think?"

"That maybe I meant what I said instead of running off with another man!"

"At least he actually asked me out! At least he was clear about what he wanted instead of playing mysterious artist and leaving me to guess!"

Ezra went still, his breathing harsh. When he spoke again, his voice was deadly quiet. "You think I don't want you? Are you serious?"

"I don't know what to think! You've never actually said—" I gestured helplessly between us. "We've never talked about what this is, what you want from me. And then Nereus shows up, and he's direct and interested and—"

"And you let him mark you." His voice had turned cold, his eyes fixed on my neck where I knew the concealer had washed away in the rain.

My hand flew to the spot instinctively. "That's not—it's complicated—"

"Looks pretty simple from where I'm sitting." He made another attempt to stand, this time making it to his feet through sheer stubborn will. "You made your choice. Go back to him."

"You are the most infuriating—" I grabbed his arm as he swayed dangerously. "Stop being an idiot and let me help you!"

"I don't need your help." But even as he said it, his knees buckled again. I caught him before he could hit the ground, his weight nearly taking us both down.

"Clearly," I said dryly, slinging his arm around my shoulders. "You're doing great on your own. Now shut up and let me get you out of this rain before you drown in a puddle."

"Where exactly do you plan to take me?" he asked, but he was leaning heavily against me now, his earlier resistance crumbling.

"Your place. Where do you live?"

He hesitated, pride warring with practicality. Finally, he sighed in defeat. "Lighthouse Point. The blue house with the copper roof."

"Of course you do," I muttered, starting the awkward journey back toward my car. "Can't live somewhere normal like the rest of us."

"My apologies for not meeting your standards of normalcy," he said, his voice dripping sarcasm despite his obvious pain.

"Oh, believe me, normal went out the window the day I met you."

Getting him to my Beetle was like wrestling with a very attractive, very stubborn octopus. He kept trying to pull away, muttering things about not needing help and how I should go back to my "new friend," while simultaneously being unable to walk in a straight line.

"Get in the car, Ezra," I said, opening the passenger door.

"I'm fine—"

"Get in the goddamn car or I'm calling an ambulance and explaining to the paramedics why you're growing gills!"

That shut him up. He folded his long frame into my tiny car with as much dignity as he could muster, which wasn't much considering he was soaking wet and clearly running a fever.

I cranked the seat back as far as it would go and started the engine, the heater immediately fogging up the windows. The silence stretched between us, broken only by his labored breathing and the sound of rain against the windshield.

"So," I said finally, pulling out of the alley. "Are we going to talk about what's actually happening here, or are you going to keep pouting?"

"I don't pout," he said stiffly.

"Right. My mistake. You brood dramatically. Much more sophisticated."

His jaw clenched, but I caught the slight twitch at the corner of his mouth. His head turned toward the window. "I was trying to be careful."

"Careful of what?"

"Of this." He gestured vaguely at himself, at the scales visible on his neck, at whatever was happening to his body. "I thought if I kept busy, kept my distance, maybe I could get control of this before..." He trailed off, his breathing growing more labored. "Before something awful happened to you."

"Control of what?"

His hand pressed harder against his chest. "You saw how they looked at you at the Institute." His voice was strained. "Being close to me puts a target on your back. Other supernaturals see you as a way to get to me. And humans in general are horrible, bigoted creatures." His eyes met mine briefly before looking away. "I thought if I stayed back, if we seemed less...connected, maybe they'd lose interest."

"So you were protecting me by ignoring me?" I scoffed, tightening my grip on the wheel.

"I was trying to." His laugh was bitter. "Clearly, that worked out perfectly."

I could feel him watching me, waiting for my reaction. I couldn't let myself look at him though, or he'd see the guilt painting my features. I felt like an idiot.

We'd reached Lighthouse Point, the exclusive peninsula stretching out into the churning sea. His house was exactly what I'd expected—all glass and clean lines, perched dramatically at the edge of the point like something from an architectural magazine.

I pulled into the circular driveway and killed the engine. "We're here."

He made no move to get out, just sat there staring at his house like it was a prison.

"Ezra," I breathed. "Whatever's happening to you, whatever this is—I'm here. But you have to let me help."

He turned to look at me then, his eyes bright in the car's darkness. "You don't understand what you're offering."

"Then tell me."

For a moment, I thought he might. His mouth opened, then closed, and something shifted in his expression. The fever flush on his cheeks deepened, and his breathing grew more labored.

"We need to get inside," he said finally. "Now."

This time when I helped him out of the car, he didn't pull away. He leaned into me, his skin burning hot even through our wet clothes, his body trembling with something that might have been fever or might have been something else entirely.

Whatever was about to happen, I had the feeling there would be no going back from it.

Chapter Eighteen

UNDERTOW

Just as we stepped inside, a tremendous crack of thunder shook the house, and the lights flickered once before going out completely.

"Is there a generator?"

"No," he said, his voice slightly stronger now that we were inside. "There's a fireplace through there."

I helped him into what had to be the most gorgeous living room I'd ever seen. Floor-to-ceiling windows faced the churning ocean, though in the darkness I could only make out the vague shapes of furniture. A massive stone fireplace dominated one wall.

"Matches are on the mantle," Ezra said, sinking onto a nearby couch. "Wood's already set."

I found the matches by feel and lit the kindling. As the fire caught and grew, the room was slowly illuminated in a warm, flickering glow. Despite the circumstances, I couldn't help but notice how beautiful everything was—clean lines, expensive but not showy furniture, and artwork that looked original and valuable.

"I'm going to find some ice for your fever," I said, once I was sure he wasn't going to immediately collapse. "Where's your kitchen?"

He gestured vaguely down a hallway. "Don't bother. It won't help."

I ignored him and followed the hall until I found a state-of-the-art kitchen. After some rummaging, I located a freezer drawer full of ice and fashioned a makeshift cold pack using a dish towel. When I hurried back to the living room, I stopped dead in my tracks.

Ezra was on his knees in front of the fireplace, his shirt discarded on the floor beside him. The firelight played across his bare torso, highlighting the pattern of scales that now covered not just his neck but swept across his shoulders and down his chest. His head was thrown back, eyes closed, body trembling.

"Um," I said eloquently, clutching the ice pack like a shield. "I think getting out of wet clothes is actually a good idea if you've got a fever. But maybe we should get you to bed?"

His eyes snapped open at the sound of my voice, locking onto me with an intensity that made my breath catch. "No. I can't...contain this much longer."

I approached slowly, kneeling beside him to press the ice pack to his forehead. "Contain what? Ezra, please, tell me what's happening to you."

He leaned into my touch, a sound somewhere between a groan and a purr rumbling from his chest. His hand came up to catch my wrist, his grip surprisingly strong, given his condition. Slowly, deliberately, he guided my palm to his cheek, then down his neck to rest against his chest.

"Ezra," I said warningly, though I didn't pull away. His skin burned beneath my fingers, the scales smooth and strangely pleasant to touch.

"I can't stop," he murmured, leaning closer until his face was buried in my neck. His breath was hot against my skin, his lips brushing my collarbone. "I'm sorry, Twyla. I'm trying, but I can't..."

His hands moved to my waist, strong and insistent, pulling me closer. One slid up my back while the other dropped to my thigh, fingers splaying possessively over the damp fabric of my dress.

"Stop what?" I asked, my voice embarrassingly breathless. "What's happening to you?"

He pulled back just enough to meet my eyes, his own glowing brighter than I'd ever seen them. "I'm in heat," he ground out, the word clearly costing him tremendous effort. "You need to go. Now. Before I—"

"Heat? Like Alpha/Omega werewolf novels?" My mind raced, trying to process this information while very distracted by his hands, which hadn't stopped their exploration of my body despite his warning.

"Oh gods don't start in with that, I hear enough from Kronos about that tripe," he snapped, then immediately softened. "The threat of another male...triggered it." His fingers tangled in my hair, tugging gently to expose more of my neck. When his mouth found the spot where Nereus had marked me, he went completely still.

His nostrils flared, and a low growl rumbled from his chest that raised every hair on my arms. "I can taste him on your skin." he said, his voice dropping to something barely human.

Before I could respond, his mouth found the exact spot where Nereus's hickey lay hidden beneath my ruined makeup. His tongue was rough with growing ridges as he licked over the mark, then his teeth sank in, claiming the spot for himself.

The possessive claiming sent liquid heat racing through my veins. "Ezra—"

My phone, abandoned somewhere on the floor, buzzed with an incoming text. The sound seemed to cut through his haze for a moment, and I saw him glance toward it with confusion before his expression darkened.

I reached for it without thinking, my fingers closing around the device. The screen lit up with a message from Nereus: *You can't run from what we started, beautiful. I'll be waiting when you're ready to finish it.*

Ezra's reaction was instant and violent. A guttural snarl tore from his throat, and his hand shot out to knock the phone from my grasp. It skittered across the floor as he loomed over me, his expression transformed into something primal and dangerous.

"The audacity," Ezra said, his voice deadly quiet despite the fury burning in his eyes.

Understanding dawned. "This heat—it's related to him somehow."

But Ezra was beyond conversation now. With a swift movement, he flipped me onto my stomach, his body covering mine from behind. His hand snaked around to unfasten my bra while the other pushed my hips up, positioning me on my knees.

"Ezra," I gasped, not out of protest but surprise at his roughness.

"I need you," he said against my ear, his voice rough silk and barely controlled power. "I need to be inside you, to feel you come apart around me until you forget he ever touched you. Tell me to stop," he added, his voice strained as if the words were being torn from him. "Tell me now, Twyla, or I won't be able to—"

"Don't stop," I said immediately. That was all it took. With a sound like a dam breaking, he tore away the last of my underwear and freed himself from his pants. There was no gentle preparation, no teasing preamble—just the blunt pressure of him pushing inside me in one powerful thrust.

I cried out, fingers digging into the rug beneath us. He was bigger than before—ridges more pronounced, his body changed by whatever was happening to him. The stretch bordered on painful, but my body was more than ready for him, already slick and eager.

"You feel incredible," he groaned, his voice breaking on the words as he stilled inside me. "I could stay buried in you forever."

His rhythm started slow, deliberate, each thrust calculated to drive me to madness. The ridges along his length created exquisite friction against places inside me

I didn't know existed, sending jolts of electricity up my spine with every movement.

"Look at you," he murmured, his voice like dark honey as one hand tangled in my hair, pulling my head back so he could see my face. "Look how beautiful you are when you let go. This is how you should always be—beneath me, around me, taking everything I give you."

His words sent shockwaves through me, filthy and eloquent all at once. Each thrust pushed me forward on the rug, the friction against my knees a distant sensation compared to the overwhelming pleasure building inside me.

The combination of his voice, his touch, his body moving inside me with increasing urgency—it was too much. When his fingers worked that bundle of nerves while his cock continued its relentless assault, I felt myself climbing toward something that would shatter me completely.

"Come for me," he commanded, his voice dropping to that register that seemed to vibrate directly through my core.

The climax hit me like a tidal wave, my body clenching around him as pleasure ripped through every nerve ending. I screamed his name, my voice echoing off the walls as wave after wave of sensation crashed over me.

He worked me through it, his rhythm never faltering, extending my release until I was sobbing with the intensity of it. Only when the last aftershock faded did his own control finally snap.

His movements became erratic, desperate, and I felt his body beginning to change against mine—scales erupting across his skin, fins forming along his arms as the transformation the heat had been building toward finally began.

"The water," he gasped, his voice already changing. "I need to get to the water. *Now*."

"In there?" I asked, gesturing to the small closest at the edge of the room.

He nodded, and I threw his arm over my shoulder, supporting him as we stumbled toward the door. Inside looked like a closet, but the floor opened up to reveal a circular hole filled with dark water—a hatch to the sea.

"Help me," he pleaded, his voice distorting as the gills at his neck fully opened.

I lowered him to the edge of the hatch, his now scaly legs already dangling into the water. Relief visibly washed over him as he made contact with the sea, but when I tried to step back, his grip on my wrist tightened.

"What are you doing?" I asked, trying to pull away from him.

But he wasn't listening. With one powerful movement, he pulled me forward and plunged into the dark water, dragging me with him into the depths below.

Chapter Nineteen

DEPTHS OF DESIRE

The shock of cold water stole my breath. Darkness closed around me as we plunged deeper, Ezra's grip unyielding despite my frantic struggles. My lungs were already burning, panic clawing through me as the surface light receded above. I'd never been good at holding my breath.

I thrashed against him, my nails scraping uselessly against his scales. My rational mind had shut down completely, replaced by pure terror. Had I been wrong about him all along? Was this how sirens truly were—luring humans to watery deaths?

His arms wrapped around me from behind, pinning mine to my sides as we descended. When I tried to kick, my legs tangled with his—or rather, what had been his legs, now fused into a powerful, muscular tail. My chest felt like it would explode, black spots dancing across my vision.

Just as unconsciousness threatened to claim me, Ezra spun me around to face him. His transformed face was almost alien—gills fluttering at his neck, fin-like appendages where his ears had been, his eyes entirely magenta and seeming to glow in the darkness. He crushed his mouth to mine, forcing my lips open.

Instead of water rushing in, I felt something else—a tingling, effervescent sensation that spread from my mouth through my entire body. My lungs suddenly expanded, the burning sensation replaced by blessed relief.

I could breathe.

Ezra released me cautiously, hovering just beyond arm's reach. His voice reached me strangely—not muffled as I would have expected underwater, but resonating directly in my mind.

"I'm sorry," he said, the words carrying genuine remorse.

I touched my throat, then my lips, utterly bewildered. My terror receded, replaced by astonishment. My hair floated around my head like a cloud, my torn dress billowing in the gentle current.

"You're safe," Ezra continued, his mental voice soothing. *"The kiss—it's temporary, but it lets you breathe underwater. It won't last forever, but long enough."*

I tried to respond, but no sound emerged. My voice couldn't work here, even if my lungs somehow could.

Ezra drifted farther back, giving me space. *"I'll stay away until you're calm. I won't hurt you, Twyla. I would never hurt you."*

I nodded slowly, my racing heart gradually steadying. As my panic subsided, I began to notice my surroundings. We weren't in total darkness as I'd initially thought. A faint, ethereal light emanated from patches of what looked like coral and plant life along the rocky walls of what must be an underwater cave system beneath Ezra's home. The bioluminescent glow cast everything in shades of blue and green, creating a dreamy atmosphere.

The water wasn't as cold as the first shocking plunge had suggested. Or perhaps my body was adjusting, the adrenaline keeping me warm. I explored this strange new ability to breathe underwater, taking experimental breaths that felt nothing like breathing air but somehow satisfied my lungs just the same.

Movement caught my eye—Ezra, swimming in a wide circle around the periphery of the cave. Seeing him like this, in his natural form, was nothing short of breathtaking.

His upper body remained recognizably humanoid, though now covered in shimmering scales that caught the bioluminescent light with every movement. Where his legs had been was now a powerful tail, at least six feet long, tapering to a delicate fin that propelled him through the water with effortless grace. Additional fins extended from his forearms and back, translucent and elegantly shaped. His pink hair had transformed too, becoming something between hair and tendrils that floated around his head like a living crown.

He was magnificent. Terrifying and beautiful at once. I could understand how sailors of old would have followed such a creature to their deaths willingly, enchanted by the mere sight of him.

Ezra circled closer, watching me cautiously. *"Better?* " He asked.

I nodded, then pointed to my throat and shook my head, trying to communicate that I couldn't speak.

"I know," he replied. *"Human vocal cords don't work underwater. But I can hear your thoughts if you direct them at me. Try."*

I concentrated, focusing my thoughts toward him. *"Like this?"*

His eyes widened, a smile revealing teeth that were now significantly sharper than before. *"Yes! Exactly like that."*

"What's happening? " I asked, still taking in his transformed appearance.

His expression tensed, a pulse of color moving through his scales like a wave of emotion. His eyes blazed brighter, and I could see he was struggling to maintain even this much control.

"I want you." Was all he communicated, swimming closer.

The raw desire in his mental voice sent a shiver through me that had nothing to do with the water temperature. Despite the strangeness of our situation, despite my recent fear, I felt an undeniable pull toward him.

"Can I help?" I asked, the question carrying all my uncertainty but also my willingness.

"Yes," he replied, the single word laden with hunger and barely restrained need. *"But only if you want to."*

I swam toward him, closing the distance between us. My movements were clumsy compared to his underwater grace, but I managed to reach him, my hands finding his shoulders.

"I want to try," I told him, surprising myself with how much I meant it.

His eyes flared brighter, his tail curling around my legs in a possessive gesture. *"You're sure?"*

I answered by pressing my lips to his, a rush of tingling energy passing between us with the contact. His response was immediate and overwhelming, his mouth claiming mine with a hunger that bordered on desperation.

The tattered remains of my dress and underwear drifted away, leaving me bare in his arms. The contrast between my soft skin and his sleek scales created a friction unlike anything I'd experienced before. His hands seemed to be everywhere at once, exploring my body with an urgency that took my breath away—or would have, if breathing were still necessary.

Then…he sang.

Unlike the subtle influence he'd exerted before, this was his true siren song—raw, primal, and devastatingly powerful. The melody didn't come through my ears but vibrated directly through my body, setting every nerve ending alight. Colors swirled in. Whether real or hallucinated, I couldn't tell.

The song stripped away all defenses, all reservations. Under its influence, I felt my desire amplify to almost unbearable levels. My body responded to his every touch as if he'd been playing me my entire life, knowing exactly where and how to elicit the most intense reactions.

We spun slowly in the water, his tail wrapping more securely around my legs as his mouth moved down my neck, across my collarbone, and lower still. The cool water against my heated skin created a delicious contrast, heightening every sensation.

I gasped silently when I felt him pressing against me—not one but two distinct pressures seeking entrance. I looked down between our bodies and saw what I'd only felt during his partial transformation on land. In his full siren form, he possessed two thick, pulsing cocks, both fully aroused and ridged in a way that promised exquisite friction.

My body felt weirdly malleable in the water, like gravity and physical limits had taken a vacation. I nodded my consent, wrapping my arms around his neck and my legs around his waist as best I could with his tail still snaked around my calves.

Ezra's eyes burned into mine as he positioned himself. I felt the first push and nearly lost my mind right then. Holy hell. The ridges along his first shaft caught against spots inside me I didn't know existed, sending jolts of electricity from my core to my fingertips. My back arched so hard I thought it might snap, my head falling back as pleasure slammed through me, right on the edge of too much.

Before I could even process that first invasion, I felt his second shaft pressing insistently against my other entrance. In any other situation, I'd have thought it impossible—but underwater, with his siren magic pulsing through me, my body opened eagerly, accepting him in ways that defied every law of physics I knew.

The surrounding water shifted, creating a kind of supernatural lubricant that eased his passage. I gasped silently as he pushed deeper, the pressure both terrifying and exhilarating. The unique ridges of his second member sent shockwaves of sensation through nerves I didn't even know I had. What would have been painful, maybe even tearing on land somehow transformed into mind-bending pleasure as my body adapted to his inhuman anatomy. His song seemed to relax my muscles while simultaneously heightening every sensation, making me yield to him completely.

The fullness was mind-blowing. I felt stretched, claimed, filled beyond capacity, my nerve endings firing so rapidly I couldn't distinguish between pleasure and pain anymore. They'd become the same overwhelming sensation, consuming me entirely.

For a single breathless moment, we hung suspended, the impossible connection between us so intense I thought I might black out.

Then he shifted his hips, and I lost whatever remaining sanity I had.

His rhythm was ruthless—one shaft pulling back as the other pushed deeper, never giving me a second's emptiness, never allowing me a moment to breathe or think or do anything but feel. The scales on his tail scraped deliciously against my thighs as he controlled every movement, using my body with a primal intensity that should have terrified me, but drove me higher.

His song intensified, no longer just sound but something physical that rushed through my bloodstream like liquid pleasure. Each note matched perfectly with each thrust, doubling the sensation until I couldn't tell where his song ended and my body began. The glowing plants pulsed in time with his melody, casting his face in eerie blue light, his eyes blazing like pink fire against the shadows.

I completely lost myself. Time? Gone. Self-awareness? Bye. There was only this—his body claiming mine, his song claiming my mind, the twin invasions reducing me to nothing but raw sensation and desperate need. My thoughts scattered like startled fish, impossible to catch or hold.

His movements got rougher, deeper, more urgent. One hand fisted in my floating hair, yanking my head back to expose my throat. His teeth scraped along my pulse point, not quite breaking skin but definitely reminding me how sharp they were.

When I finally came, it wasn't like anything I'd experienced before. It wasn't the sharp release I was used to, but an endless, building wave that seemed to start everywhere at once—a full-body explosion that kept going and going. My inner walls clenched around both his shafts, milking them rhythmically as colors I couldn't name burst behind my eyelids. My whole body convulsed so hard I probably hurt myself if not for the water supporting us.

Ezra completely lost it. His last shred of control vanished as his movements turned wild, almost violent. The song rose to a crescendo that seemed to make the cave itself vibrate. His tail tightened around my legs as he drove impossibly deeper, his whole body going rigid as he came. I felt the hot pulse of his release filling me from both sides; the sensation triggering another orgasm that crashed through me like a tsunami.

We drifted slowly in the aftermath, still joined, his tail now wrapped around me more protectively than possessively. The fierce glow in his eyes gradually dimmed to a softer pink, his expression shifting from feral hunger to something softer, almost reverent as he looked at me.

"Mine," his voice whispered in my mind, the word settling into me like it had always belonged there.

"Better?" I asked when I could form coherent thoughts again.

"Yes," he replied, touching my face with surprising tenderness, given the wildness of moments before. *"The heat is passing."*

"Good," I thought, suddenly aware of how tired I was, how the water no longer felt neutral but distinctly cold against my skin.

Ezra noticed my shiver immediately. *"The breathing spell is fading too. We need to get you back to the surface."*

I nodded, my limbs feeling heavy and uncooperative. The intensity of what we'd just experienced had drained me completely. Ezra disentangled himself carefully, then gathered me in his arms.

"Hold on to me," he instructed.

The journey up seemed much shorter than the descent, or perhaps I was simply drifting in and out of awareness. Before I knew it, we were breaking the surface in the water-filled chamber where this had all begun. Ezra lifted me out first, then pulled himself up with surprising agility despite his transformed state.

Once out of the water, a visible shudder ran through his body. Scales receded, his tail painfully separating back into legs. I wanted to help somehow, but my body refused to cooperate, my teeth chattering as the air hit my wet skin.

"S-so c-cold," I managed, my voice returning now that we were above water.

Ezra, still only partially transformed back, gathered me in his arms. "I know. Let me get you warm."

He carried me through the house to what must be his bedroom—a spacious room with the same floor-to-ceiling windows as the living area. The storm still raged outside, lightning occasionally illuminating the churning sea beyond the glass. Without electricity, the room was dark save for these brief flashes and the faint glow still emanating from Ezra's not-quite-human eyes.

He set me on the enormous bed, wrapping me in plush blankets before climbing in beside me. His body radiated heat again, though not at the feverish temperature from before.

"I'm sorry," he said, pulling me against his chest. "I never meant for any of this to happen."

I snuggled closer, seeking his warmth. "Does this mean the heat is over?"

"For now." His arms tightened around me. "But I need to keep you close. If we separate too soon, it could trigger again."

"So I'm stuck with you," I murmured, already feeling sleep tugging at me.

I felt rather than saw his smile as he pressed a kiss to my forehead. "For tonight, at least. Is that so terrible?"

"Not terrible," I admitted, my eyes drifting closed. "Actually, kind of perfect."

The last thing I remembered before sleep claimed me was Ezra's whispered response. "Yes. Perfect."

Chapter Twenty

SUNRISE

I woke to sunlight streaming across my face. For a moment, I couldn't remember where I was—the bed beneath me was too soft, the sheets too silky to be my own. Then memories flooded back: the club, finding Ezra in the alley, the storm, and everything that had happened underwater.

My eyes flew open. I was alone in Ezra's massive bed, wrapped in a cocoon of expensive blankets. My body ached pleasantly in places I hadn't known could ache, a physical reminder that last night hadn't been some bizarre dream.

"Ezra?" I called, my voice sounding strangely normal after the telepathic communication we'd shared underwater.

No answer came, but I heard movement elsewhere in the house. I sat up, noticing for the first time that I was wearing an oversized shirt that definitely wasn't mine. Ezra must have dressed me while I slept.

The bedroom looked even more impressive in daylight. One entire wall was glass, offering a panoramic view of the ocean stretching to the horizon. The storm had passed, leaving behind a pristine blue sky and calm seas that belied the chaos of last night.

Slipping out of bed, I padded barefoot across the hardwood floors to explore. An en-suite bathroom beckoned, all marble and glass, with a shower big enough for four people. I caught sight of myself in the mirror and winced—my hair was a disaster, tangled and dried with salt water. Dark circles shadowed my eyes, and several minor bruises dotted my neck and collarbones.

"Well, hello hot mess," I muttered to my reflection.

The sound of footsteps approaching sent me scurrying back to the bed, suddenly self-conscious about my appearance. Ezra appeared in the doorway moments later, carrying a tray laden with food and coffee. He looked entirely normal—no scales, no fins, no evidence of the creature he'd been hours before. Just a gorgeous man in sweatpants and a t-shirt, his pink hair tied back in a loose knot.

"You're awake," he said, sounding relieved. "How do you feel?"

"Like I got dragged to the bottom of the ocean, had mind-blowing sex, and then passed out for—" I glanced at the bedside clock. "—ten hours, apparently."

His lips quirked into a smile. "So...not great?"

"Actually, pretty good, all things considered." I eyed the tray he carried. "Please tell me that coffee is for sharing."

"All for you." He set the tray on the bed beside me. "I thought you might be hungry."

The spread was impressive—fresh fruit, pastries, and a large mug of coffee that smelled heavenly. My stomach growled on cue.

"You're a lifesaver," I said, reaching immediately for the coffee. The first sip was pure bliss, exactly how I liked it—strong, with just a hint of sweetness. "Okay, either this is a lucky guess, or you've been paying attention."

"I pay attention to everything about you," he replied simply, perching on the edge of the bed. "How could I not?"

The sincerity in his voice made my chest tighten strangely. I busied myself with a pastry to avoid meeting his eyes.

"So," I said between bites, "are we going to talk about what happened last night?"

He tensed slightly. "Which part?"

"All of it. The club, Nereus, you going into 'heat' like some kind of supernatural salmon, dragging me into your personal aquarium..." I ticked off each item on my fingers. "Plus the whole telepathic communication thing, and whatever that was that happened underwater."

"Mating," he supplied, his voice neutral, but his eyes intent on my face. "That was mating."

I nearly choked on my coffee. "Mating. Right. So tell me more about this 'heat' business. Is that normally a thing for sirens, or...?"

Ezra shifted his position, clearly organizing his thoughts. "It's natural for us, yes, but usually more controlled and predictable. What happened to me was... unusual."

"Because of Nereus," I guessed.

He nodded. "Sirens are territorial by nature. When another male showed interest in someone I have feelings for, it triggered my cycle prematurely and intensified it."

"So you recognized me as your potential mate before all this?"

His eyes met mine, something ancient and powerful flickering behind them. "My body did. Sirens have instincts that operate beyond conscious thought sometimes." He hesitated. "When we shift forms, those instincts become harder to control."

"And that's why you went all fish-man on me after we started..." I waved my hand.

A smile tugged at his lips. "Fish-man is hardly the preferred terminology, but essentially, yes. The heat speeds up the transformation."

"And underwater? Why could I breathe down there? And the telepathy?"

"The kiss," he explained. "It temporarily allows humans to breathe underwater—an adaptation that evolved for...well, for exactly the situation we found ourselves in." His expression grew more serious. "As for the telepathy, that's how sirens communicate beneath the waves. Your mind adapted to receive it."

I took a moment to process this. "And the mating itself? Does that...mean something specific in siren terms?"

Ezra was quiet for a long moment, weighing his words. "It can. Traditionally, it would establish a bond. A permanent one."

"Like marriage?" I asked, my voice higher than usual.

"It's more binding than marriage," he said. "Though it's not formed unless both parties intend it. Your consent was to the act, not to the bond. I wouldn't presume—"

"Hang on." I set my coffee down. "Let me get this straight. Last night, we potentially got supernatural-married, but maybe not because I didn't know that's what we were doing?"

He nodded. "Essentially, yes."

"And if the bond had formed?"

His eyes met mine, something ancient and powerful flickering behind them. "It would mean we're connected. That I could always sense you, to find you. That no other siren could ever claim you." He hesitated. "It would also mean I couldn't mate with anyone else. Ever."

"That's...a lot." I pulled the blanket tighter around myself, feeling exposed despite being covered. "Do you know whether it happened? The bond?"

"No." His voice was soft. "Only you would know. You would feel it—a pull toward me, a sense of my presence even when we're apart."

I thought about the strange awareness I'd always had of him. I could feel his mood shift even before seeing his expression. Had that been the beginning of such a bond, or just a normal attraction?

"What if I don't want it?" I asked, then backtracked at the flash of hurt in his eyes. "I mean, not that I don't want... I just meant if someone didn't want it."

"It would fade. Without mutual acknowledgment, it cannot fully form." His fingers traced patterns on the bedspread, not meeting my eyes. "I would never hold you to something you didn't choose, Twyla."

Using my name, so simple yet intimate, coming from him, made something inside me soften. "What do you want, Ezra?"

Now he looked up, his gaze direct and unwavering. "I think I've made that rather clear. I want you. I have since the moment you stood in my gallery, refusing to be charmed like everyone else."

"Is that why you kept asking me to wear pink? Some siren mating ritual involving color coordination?"

His laugh was unexpected and genuine. "No. Pink complements your complexion. I *am* still an artist, after all."

I smiled, relief easing some of the tension. This was still Ezra—frustrating, talented, enigmatic Ezra. Though I had a feeling he was lying about the pink thing.

"We should talk about Nereus," I said, my smile fading. "He triggered your heat cycle. Was that deliberate?"

Ezra's expression darkened. "Almost certainly. He might not have known how I would react, but he knew showing interest in you would provoke me."

"But why? What's his game here?"

"Power. Territory. Status." Ezra shrugged, though the casual gesture didn't match the intensity in his eyes. "Sirens are hierarchical by nature. If he could steal what another male had claimed..."

"I'm not property to be stolen," I hissed.

"Of course not." Ezra's hand found mine, his touch gentle. "I don't see you that way. But Nereus is younger. His impulses are harder to control, and he may not even have experienced a heat yet. However, he would know what it would do to me."

I processed this, trying to reconcile the puppy-like enthusiasm Nereus had initially shown with this calculating behavior. "Will he try again?"

"No." The certainty in Ezra's voice was chilling. "He'll sense what happened. No siren would challenge a completed mating heat."

"Good." I squeezed his hand, then withdrew to reach for more coffee. "Because I didn't appreciate being used as a pawn in some supernatural pissing contest."

Ezra's smile was rueful. "Understandable."

A comfortable silence fell between us as I finished my breakfast. The sun climbed higher, casting the room in warm golden light. It felt strangely domestic.

"I should get home," I said, though I made no move to leave. "Alex will wonder where I am."

"I texted him from your phone," Ezra admitted. "Just said you were safe and staying with a friend. I hope that wasn't overstepping."

"No, that was thoughtful." I glanced around. "Speaking of my phone, where is it?"

"Living room floor, I think. Along with what remains of your dress." He winced. "I'll replace it, of course."

"You'd better. You still owe me ten other vintage dresses." I stretched, enjoying the pleasant soreness in my muscles. "I should also shower. I smell like I took a swim in the ocean. Oh wait, I did."

Ezra stood, extending his hand to help me up. "Shower's through there. Use whatever you need. I put some clothes out that might fit you."

I took his hand but didn't let go once standing. "Thank you. For everything. Even the underwater part, which was terrifying at first, but then...not."

His expression softened. "I am sorry about how it happened. The heat—it doesn't leave much room for explanation or gentleness."

"Hey, I'm not complaining about the lack of gentleness," I said, trying to lighten the mood. "That was pretty spectacular."

The word hung between us, weighted with new meaning. Ezra's eyes darkened slightly, his grip on my hand tightening. "Yes. It was."

Warmth spread through me that had nothing to do with the morning sun. I stepped closer, drawn by a pull I couldn't quite name. "I should shower."

"You should," he agreed, not moving away.

"Alone," I clarified, though with little conviction.

"If you insist." His free hand came up to cup my face, thumb brushing across my cheekbone.

I leaned into his touch. "I'm still processing...everything."

"Take all the time you need," he said softly. "I've waited millennia for you, Twyla Knight. I can be patient a little longer."

Something about the way he said it—like a vow, like a promise spanning longer than I could comprehend—made my breath catch. The pull I'd felt toward him seemed to strengthen, a golden warmth spreading from my chest outward.

Oh, I thought. So that's what a bond feels like.

I didn't say it aloud, not yet. But from the widening of Ezra's eyes, the sudden intake of his breath, I suspected he felt it too—the subtle shift solidifying between us.

"Shower," I repeated, stepping back with reluctance. "Then we'll talk."

He nodded, releasing me with visible effort. "I'll be here."

The bathroom was a sanctuary of marble and glass, with the shower large enough for a small party. As hot water cascaded over me, washing away the salt and sand from our underwater encounter, my mind finally had space to process everything that had happened.

The way Ezra had claimed me so completely, erasing every trace of Nereus's touch. I touched my neck where new marks bloomed over the old ones, and for the first time since this all started, I didn't try to hide them. What was the point? The person I'd been worried about seeing them already knew, had already covered them with his own.

But that brought up other complications. What did this mean for my normal life? For my shop, my friends, my carefully constructed independence? And what about everything I hadn't told Ezra about that night with Nereus? He could see the evidence on my skin, could probably guess enough. Did I need to hurt him with details when he'd already staked his claim so thoroughly?

My phone buzzed from the bedroom, probably more texts I'd missed. The thought of returning to the real world, of explaining any of this, felt overwhelming. I needed perspective. I needed my best friend.

When I emerged from the bathroom, wrapped in one of Ezra's fluffy towels, he was sitting by the window looking out at the ocean. He'd changed into fresh clothes and looked perfectly human again, though I could still feel that golden thread connecting us.

"Everything alright?" he asked, turning to face me.

"Yeah, just..." I gestured vaguely. "A lot to process."

He stood, moving toward me with that fluid grace. "We don't have to figure everything out today."

"I know. I just..." I looked down at my hands, then back up at him. "I think I need to talk to Alex. About all of this. He's the only one who knows me well enough to help me sort through...everything."

Understanding flickered in Ezra's eyes. "Of course. You should talk to whomever you need to."

I found my phone on the nightstand and quickly typed out a text to Alex.

Twyla: Can we meet up later? Just us? I need to talk through some stuff that happened last night. Beach maybe?

His response came almost immediately.

Alex: Everything okay? Yes, of course. 2pm at our usual spot?

Perfect. Thanks.

I looked up to find Ezra watching me with an expression I couldn't quite read. "He's a good friend," he said simply.

"The best." I set the phone aside. "I should probably head home soon, get changed, figure out what I'm going to tell people about..." I gestured to my neck.

"You don't have to hide them anymore," Ezra said, his voice soft but certain.

The words sent a shiver through me that had nothing to do with being damp from the shower. He was right. I was tired of hiding, tired of pretending I didn't want what was right in front of me.

"We'll see," I said, but we both knew my walls were already coming down.

Chapter Twenty-One

HEART TO HEART

The familiar bell above the diner chimed as Alex, and I slid into our usual booth. The cracked garnet vinyl seats had been patched with duct tape in three different places, and the laminated menu still had "Tomorow's Special" written in faded marker across the top. The place that served coffee in thick white mugs and had been exactly the same for at least twenty years.

"What can I get you today?" Karla asked, appearing at our table with her pen already poised. She was new here, but she'd learned the rhythms of the regular customers quickly.

"Just coffee for me," I said, my stomach too twisted to handle food.

Alex's eyebrows shot up. I always got the clam chowder here—it was my favorite thing on the menu, the whole reason we came to this place. "Clam chowder," he said, still looking at me with concern. "And coffee.

And can we get some of those little oyster crackers on the side?"

"Coming right up."

The fluorescent light above our booth flickered occasionally, casting intermittent shadows across the scratched Formica table. Someone had carved JM + RS 4EVER into the wood near my elbow, and I traced the letters while we waited.

Once Karla had disappeared behind the counter, Alex leaned forward. "Okay, now I know something's really wrong. You never skip the chowder."

I wrapped my hands around the coffee mug when it arrived, grateful for the warmth. The ceramic was chipped at the handle, probably older than I was. "I don't think I could keep anything down right now."

"That bad, huh?" He pushed the bowl of tiny crackers toward me. "Alright, let me have it."

I took a shaky breath, watching steam rise from my coffee. The diner smelled of bacon grease and industrial coffee, comforting in its predictability. "I went to Nereus's club opening last night. Alone. After our dinner date, I went home, but then he called and asked me to come to the grand opening, and I said yes."

Alex paused with his spoon halfway to his mouth. "You didn't text me about that."

"I know. I should have, but..." I shrugged helplessly, still tracing the carved initials. "I didn't want you to worry, or lecture me, or try to talk me out of it."

"Because you knew it was a bad idea?"

"I knew you'd see right through all my justifications for why I was going." The admission tasted bitter, worse than the diner's strong coffee. "I was hurt, Alex. Ezra had been ignoring me, giving me nothing but mixed signals for weeks before that. And here was this guy who wasn't making me guess what he meant every time he looked at me."

Alex nodded slowly, setting down his spoon. The chowder sat untouched while he focused entirely on me. "Okay. So you went to the club. What happened?"

The next part was harder. I pulled one of the tiny crackers apart, scattering crumbs across the table. "Nereus was... very hands-on. We danced, and he was using his siren song on me, and I let him because I was angry and wanted to feel wanted." My face heated with embarrassment. "Ezra was there. With another woman. And when he saw us together, something happened to him. Something was wrong."

"Wrong how?"

"He looked like he was in pain. He left, and I followed him." I stared at the coffee stain on the table, unable to meet Alex's eyes. "I found him in an alley, and he was... different. Changing. He had a fever, and gills, and he could barely stand."

Alex went still, his coffee mug frozen halfway to his lips. "Jesus, Twy. What did you do?"

"I took him home. To his place." The words came faster now, like a dam breaking. "And then... things happened. He said he was in heat—a siren thing triggered by another male showing interest in his...in me. And we..."

"Had sex," Alex finished when I trailed off.

"More than that." I finally looked at him, seeing concern and understanding in his dark eyes. "He changed completely. Became fully siren, and he took me underwater, and we...did the mating act. But in siren terms, there's more to it. The bond isn't complete yet."

Alex was quiet for a long moment, absently stirring his chowder. The spoon clinked against the ceramic bowl in a steady rhythm. "How do you feel about that?"

The question caught me off guard. I'd expected judgment, or at least more questions about the supernatural mechanics of it all. "I don't know. Good? Scared? Overwhelmed?"

"Those all sound like reasonable responses to that." Alex mused. "But that's not really what I'm asking. How do you feel about Ezra? About potentially being bound to him?"

I pulled my knees up under me on the cracked vinyl seat. "I think I love him. But Alex, the things I did with Nereus..." My voice dropped to barely above a whisper. "Before last night. At the club, and after our dinner date. We... I let him touch me. I let him mark me." I gestured to my neck.

"Were you and Ezra together at the time?"

"No, but—"

"Had you two even had a conversation about what you were to each other?"

"No, but I knew I had feelings for him, and—"

"Twyla." Alex's voice was firm but not unkind. The fluorescent light flickered again, casting his face in harsh shadows for a moment. "Look at me."

I turned to face him, seeing nothing but love and understanding in his expression.

"Did he ever tell you he had feelings for you?"

"Not in so many words, but—"

"Not in *any words*," Alex corrected. "You were attracted to each other, sure. You had chemistry. But chemistry isn't a relationship, and attraction isn't commitment. You can't cheat on someone you were never actually with."

The relief that flooded through me was so intense it left me dizzy. I slumped back against the patched vinyl. "But I feel guilty."

"Feeling guilty doesn't mean you did anything wrong." Alex reached across the table and squeezed my hand, careful not to knock over the salt shaker. "You went on dates with someone who was actually interested in pursuing you. That's what single people do."

"Even though I knew I had feelings for Ezra?"

"Especially because you had feelings for Ezra and he wasn't doing anything about it." Alex's voice grew more pointed. "You spent weeks trying to decode that man's signals. You deserve someone who's clear about wanting you."

"But now he is. Clear, I mean. And there's a bond forming, and—"

"What does that feel like?"

I thought about the golden warmth that had spread through me when I'd realized what the bond was. The way it felt like coming home. "Right. It feels right. But also terrifying."

"Why?"

"Because what if he goes back to being distant and mysterious? What if this was just the heat talking and now he regrets it? What if I'm not enough to keep someone like him interested long-term?"

Alex was quiet for a moment, finally taking a spoonful of his chowder. The silence stretched between us, filled only by the clatter of dishes from the kitchen and the inaudible murmur of other conversations.

"Do you want to be with Ezra? Or do you want him to change into someone else?"

The question hit me like a slap. I crushed another cracker between my fingers. "I...what do you mean?"

"I mean, are you in love with who he actually is, or are you in love with the potential of who he could be if he just communicated better and was more emotionally available?" Alex's voice was gentle but relentless. "Because you can't change people. You can only decide if you can accept them as they are."

I stared at the "Tomorow's Special," typo on the menu, watching condensation drip down my water glass. "I think...I think I love who he is. Even the mysterious parts. Even the parts that drive me crazy."

"What about Nereus?"

My stomach twisted. "What about him?"

"You let him mark you. Was that just about hurting Ezra, or was there something there?"

I considered the question honestly, picking at the duct tape on the seat. "He made me feel wanted in a way that was immediate and uncomplicated." I paused. "But looking back, knowing what I know now about his motivations... I think he was using me to get to Ezra."

"How does that make you feel?"

"Used. Stupid. Angry." The emotions bubbled up as I named them. "He made me feel special, but I was just a pawn in some supernatural pissing contest."

"So not someone you'd want to build a relationship with."

"God, no." The thought made me shudder. "But what if I'm just rebounding from one extreme to the other? What if I'm choosing Ezra because he's the opposite of Nereus, not because he's actually right for me?"

Alex set down his spoon and leaned forward. The chipped Formica table creaked under his weight. "I'm going to say something, and I want you to really hear me, okay?"

I nodded.

"You don't have to choose either of them."

The words hit me like a bucket of cold water. "What?"

"You heard me. This isn't a choice between Ezra and Nereus. You could choose neither. You could take time to figure out what you actually want in a relationship before jumping into a supernatural bond with someone."

He smiled slightly. "There are plenty of fish in the sea. Pun intended."

I stared at him, the possibility I hadn't even considered settling into my mind like sediment in still water. "I... but the bond..."

"You said it yourself—it won't fully form unless both parties acknowledge it. And it can fade if you don't. If you decided you weren't ready for this, you could walk away."

"But I don't want to walk away," I said immediately, surprising myself with how quickly the words came. The fluorescent light flickered again, casting strange shadows across the table. "Even thinking about it makes me feel sick."

Alex's smile widened. "Then I think you have your answer."

"Do I?"

"When you imagine your life without Ezra in it, how does that feel?"

The thought made my chest tighten with panic. I pressed my palm against the carved initials in the table. "Awful. Like I'd be losing a piece of myself."

"And when you imagine building a life with him, mysterious artist tendencies and all?"

Warmth spread through me, the same golden feeling I'd experienced when the bond had formed. "Like coming home."

"Sounds like you know what you want." Alex reached across and stole one of my crackers.

I thought about Ezra waiting for me, patient and willing to give me all the time I needed to process. About the way he'd looked at me when the bond had formed, like I was a miracle he'd never expected to receive.

"Yeah," I said, my voice growing stronger. "I think I do."

"Good." Alex flagged down Karla for the check. "For what it's worth, I think you two are good for each other. He needs someone who challenges him, and you need someone who sees you for who you really are."

"What about the supernatural stuff?"

Alex grinned, counting out bills from his wallet. "Twy, you've been dealing with supernatural customers for years. You handle a shop full of magical weirdos every day. I think you can manage one lovesick siren."

I laughed, feeling lighter than I had all day. The coffee was terrible, but it was warm, and Alex was here, and everything suddenly felt manageable again. "When did you get so wise about relationships?"

"When I fell in love with Kronos and had to figure out how to make it work." His expression grew more serious. "Love is love, whether it's human or supernatural. The same rules apply—communication, respect, choosing each other every day."

"And if Ezra goes back to being mysterious and distant?"

"Then you call him on it. You don't let him hide behind his art and his brooding. You make him show up for the relationship." Alex's smile turned wicked. "Besides, something tells me he will not stay away from you now. Mating bonds make Supes a little possessive."

I touched my neck, feeling the tender spots where Ezra had marked over Nereus's claim. "Yeah, I'm getting that impression."

"Come on," Alex said, standing and tossing money on the table. "Let's get you home so you can go have that conversation with your siren."

I slid out of the booth; the vinyl making a sound like a deflating balloon. "Thank you. For helping me figure out what I actually want."

"That's what best friends are for." He pulled me into a hug right there in the middle of the diner, fierce and warm. "I love you, Twy. I want you to be happy."

"I love you too." I squeezed him back, grateful beyond words for his friendship. "And I think...I think I'm going to be."

Chapter Twenty-Two

LIGHT OF MY LIFE

I'd spent the time since my talk with Alex turning everything over in my mind, but I kept coming back to the same conclusion. I knew what I wanted. More importantly, I knew I was brave enough to go after it.

I pulled into Ezra's driveway just as the sun was setting, painting the sky in shades of pink and gold that reflected off his copper roof. The ocean beyond crashed against the rocks below, sending salt spray into the evening air. My hands were steady on the steering wheel, my heart calm despite the flutter of nerves in my stomach. This felt right.

The front door opened before I could even turn off the engine. Ezra appeared, leaning against the doorframe in paint-splattered jeans and a white t-shirt that had definitely seen better days. His hair was mussed like he'd been running his hands through it, and streaks of blue and gold paint decorated his forearms like temporary tattoos.

When he saw me, his face broke into a delighted grin that made my pulse skip.

"Well, look who it is," he said as I approached, his voice carrying that musical quality that always made my skin tingle. "Perfect timing, darling. I was just about to ask you to come over, though I'd planned to clean up first."

The warm evening breeze carried his cologne mixed with turpentine and something purely him. I let my eyes travel over the paint streaks on his tan skin, the way his damp shirt clung to his chest, the satisfied exhaustion of someone who'd been creating for hours.

"I don't know," I said, stopping just close enough to catch the heat radiating from his body. "I kind of like you all dirty and covered in paint."

His smile turned absolutely wicked, pink eyes gleaming in the fading light. "Do you now?"

"Maybe." My heart hammered against my ribs, but flirting felt safer than diving straight into the serious conversation we needed to have. "Are you going to invite me in, or do I have to stand on your doorstep all night?"

"Oh, I'm definitely inviting you in." He stepped back with a theatrical flourish, paint-stained fingers trailing along the doorframe. "I have something to show you."

The house smelled of linseed oil and ocean air, with an underlying hint of whatever expensive candles he preferred. Instead of leading me toward the main living area where we'd been the other night, he guided me down a hallway I hadn't noticed before. His hand found the small of my back, warm and sure, and I could feel that golden thread between us humming with contentment.

"Close your eyes," he murmured, his breath tickling my ear.

"Ezra—"

"Trust me."

I let my eyes flutter shut, hyperaware of his presence beside me, the soft pad of our footsteps on hardwood, and the sound of a door opening. Cool air rushed over my skin, carrying the distinct smell of a gallery space.

"Open them."

I did, and my breath caught in my throat.

We stood at the entrance to a stunning gallery space—high ceilings with perfect track lighting, pristine white walls, and polished concrete floors that reflected the warm glow from above. But it wasn't the architecture that stole my breath. It was the art.

Every single painting was about me.

"Ezra," I whispered, my voice barely audible in the hushed space.

"Welcome to my private collection," he said softly, his hand still resting against my back. "The pieces that matter most to me."

The centerpiece, hung on the far wall where it commanded the entire room, was the seascape I'd helped him finish weeks ago. But it had been transformed completely. The light I'd added wasn't just a splash of gold anymore—it had become the sun breaking through storm clouds, casting divine rays across turbulent waters. The painting practically glowed with life.

My feet carried me toward it without conscious thought, drawn like a moth to flame. Up close, I could see every brushstroke, every careful blend of color. He'd painted over my original addition seamlessly, incorporating my light into something magnificent.

"This was the moment I knew," he said, coming to stand beside me. The gallery lighting caught the gold flecks in his paint-streaked hair.

I turned to look at the next piece and gasped. It was a portrait of me, but not like any I'd ever seen. He'd painted me with an inner glow, as if I was lit from within. My eyes held secrets, my smile promised mysteries. I looked powerful, beautiful, otherworldly—like some kind of modern goddess.

"Is that really how you see me?" I asked, my throat tight with emotion.

"That's exactly how I see you." His voice was low, reverent.

I moved to the next painting, my heels clicking against the polished floor. This one made me laugh with pure delight. It wasn't literal—instead of depicting the vibrant dress I'd worn to the Institute, he'd painted a figure in motion, surrounded by swirls of every vivid hue imaginable. Blues bled into purples, golds melted into reds, all captured in fluid strokes that seemed to dance on the canvas. The movement was so perfectly captured I could almost feel the fabric flowing, could almost hear the music I'd been dancing to that night.

"You remember what I was wearing," I said, amazed by the detail, the way he'd translated fabric and color into pure emotion.

"I remember everything about that night." His fingers found mine, intertwining gently.

There were others—abstract pieces that somehow captured the essence of our encounters better than any photograph could. One was all heat and urgency, pink and gold swirling together in patterns that made my skin tingle with memory. I could feel the moment he was painting, the tension and desire that had crackled between us during those early encounters when we were both fighting the pull.

Another showed two figures—barely suggested, more feeling than form—reaching for each other across space. The longing in it was so palpable it made my chest ache.

And then I saw it. The last piece hung in a place of honor near the entrance, where anyone entering would see it first. Deep blues and silver dominated the canvas, flowing forms that suggested water and movement and something primal and beautiful. Schools of fish swirled in the background like living brushstrokes, and at the center, two forms moved together in perfect harmony. I couldn't make out details, but I could feel when everything had changed between us.

"You painted our mating," I said, heat flooding my face as I stared at the abstract representation of the most intimate moment of my life.

"I painted the most beautiful moment of my existence," he corrected, moving to stand behind me. His reflection joined mine in the glass covering the painting. "The moment I found my match."

I turned in the circle of his arms, overwhelmed by the magnitude of what he'd shown me. The gallery lighting cast dramatic shadows across his face, highlighting the sharp lines of his cheekbones, the soft curve of his mouth. "Ezra, this is...I don't have words."

"I wanted you to see how every moment with you has inspired me." His hands came up to frame my face, thumbs brushing across my cheekbones.

Tears pricked at my eyes, threatening to spill over. No one had ever created something so beautiful for me, had ever shown me so clearly how I appeared in their heart. "Why?"

"I've been a coward." His admission was quiet, honest. "I've been so afraid of scaring you away that I never actually showed you how I felt."

"And now?"

His smile was soft, vulnerable in a way I'd never seen from him. "Now I'm choosing you. Openly, completely, and hoping you'll choose me too."

A sound from deeper in the gallery caught my attention—the soft clink of china, the whisper of movement. I looked past him and noticed warm light spilling from what looked like an adjoining room.

"There's more?" I asked.

"Just a little more." He looked almost shy, which was so endearing on someone usually so confident it made my heart melt. "I thought you might be hungry."

He led me toward the light, his hand warm and sure in mine. The adjoining space had been transformed into an intimate dining room. A table for two sat beneath a chandelier that cast prisms of light across crisp white linens. Real china gleamed in the soft glow, crystal glasses caught the light like captured stars, and white roses—simple, elegant, perfect—filled the air with their subtle fragrance.

"You did all this for me?" I asked, taking in the covered dishes, the perfectly folded napkins, the single candle flickering at the center of it all.

"I wanted tonight to be perfect." He pulled out my chair, ever the gentleman.

I settled into the chair, watching as he moved around the table with fluid grace. Everything about this felt like a dream—the art celebrating our connection, the intimate dinner, the way he looked at me like I was something precious.

"Why now?" I asked as he sat across from me, candlelight dancing across his features.

He was quiet for a moment, pouring wine into my glass with steady hands. The crystal sang softly as he set the bottle down. "Three days ago, you asked me to give you time to think. I realized while you were thinking about us, I should show you what us could look like."

The first course appeared as if by magic—someone must have been waiting in the kitchen. Delicate soup that tasted like the ocean but in the best possible way, like summer and salt air and everything good about the sea.

"This is incredible," I said, savoring the complex flavors. "Where did you find a chef who cooks like this?"

"I have my ways." His eyes sparkled with mischief. "I wanted everything to be perfect for you."

We ate in comfortable quiet for a while; the silence filled with the soft classical music drifting from hidden speakers and the distant sound of waves against the rocks below.

"Can I ask you something?" I said finally, setting down my spoon.

"Anything."

"The bond. If I accept it completely, what does that actually mean? Day to day, I mean."

His expression grew thoughtful. "It means I will always be able to sense you. Your emotions, your well-being, whether you're in danger." He paused, swirling the wine in his glass. "It means no other siren could ever claim you, and I could never be with anyone else."

"Ever?"

"The bond is for life, Twyla." He met my eyes across the candlelit table. "It also means that your natural lifespan would extend to match mine. Not immortal, but...significantly longer than human normal."

That stopped me cold. "I'd live as long as you do?"

"The bond sustains both partners. It's the reason mating isn't taken lightly among my kind." He reached across the table, his fingers finding mine. "There are other changes too. You'd be able to breathe underwater permanently, not just when I kiss you. You'd be able to hear my thoughts if you chose to, and I yours."

The main course arrived—something that looked like art and tasted even better. I barely noticed, too caught up in processing what he'd told me.

"That's a lot," I said finally.

"It is. Too much?"

I thought about it, really thought about it. About living for centuries, about being connected to someone so completely. About never being fully alone again, but also never being fully independent.

"I don't know," I admitted. "It's not something I ever imagined for myself."

"What did you imagine?"

"Normal things. Growing old with someone, maybe. Kids, grandkids. A human life."

Ezra was quiet for a long moment, his thumb tracing circles on the back of my hand. "You could still have children, if that's what you want. The bond doesn't prevent that."

"But they'd be..."

"Half-siren. Powerful, magical, but able to choose their own path." His voice was soft. "Twyla, I don't want you to accept the bond because of what you might gain. I want you to accept it because you want me."

I looked around the gallery, at the evidence of his feelings painted in vivid detail. At the care he'd taken with dinner, with every detail of the evening. At the way he looked at me like I was the answer to every question he'd ever had.

"What do you want?" I asked.

"I want forever with you," he said without hesitation. "I want to wake up every morning knowing you're mine." His voice grew softer.

"And if I'm not ready for forever?"

"Then we take more time." He brought my hand to his lips, pressing a soft kiss to my knuckles. "The bond isn't going anywhere, Twyla. It will wait for you to be ready."

Dessert appeared—something involving chocolate and gold leaf that probably cost more than my monthly rent. But I was too focused on the man across from me to appreciate it.

"I have something to tell you," I said, my heart hammering. "About the other night."

"Hmmm?"

"Alex helped me realize something." I took a deep breath, gathering my courage. "I was feeling guilty about Nereus. About letting him mark me. But Alex made me realize I can't cheat on someone I was never actually with."

Ezra's jaw tightened slightly, but he kept his voice level. "You don't owe me explanations about your past, darling."

"Maybe not, but I want to give them." I met his eyes steadily. "I was hurt. Nereus was direct about wanting me, and I...I enjoyed feeling wanted."

"And now?"

"Now I know what I want." I stood up, moving around the table until I was standing beside his chair. "I want you, Ezra. Just you."

He looked up at me, hope and desire warring in his expression. "Are you sure?"

Instead of answering, I leaned down and kissed him. Soft at first, then deeper when his arms came around me, pulling me closer. He tasted of wine and chocolate.

"Stay with me tonight," he murmured against my lips.

"I guess I could do that." I said playfully, poking him in the side. "Next time you plan a grand romantic gesture, maybe warn a girl. I would have worn something nicer than jeans and a tank top."

His laugh was rich and warm, filling the gallery space. "Darling, you could show up in a garbage bag and still be the most beautiful thing I've ever seen."

"Flatterer."

He stood, gathering me into his arms. As he led me from the gallery toward his bedroom, I felt that golden thread between us singing with contentment. I wasn't ready for the bond yet—that still felt too big. But I was ready for this. For him. For whatever we could build together, one beautiful day at a time.

The paintings watched us go, silent witnesses to a love story told in brushstrokes and color, in light breaking through darkness, in two souls finding their perfect match.

Chapter Twenty-Three

LURE

I slipped out of bed carefully, trying not to wake Ezra. He was sprawled across the sheets, one arm flung over where I'd been lying, his pink hair a mess against the pillow. The moonlight streaming through the floor-to-ceiling windows painted silver streaks across his bare shoulders, and for a moment I just stood there watching him sleep, marveling at how peaceful he looked.

The night had been perfect—dinner, conversation that flowed like wine, and then hours of incredible sex that had nothing to do with supernatural heat and everything to do with two people choosing each other. My body still hummed with satisfaction, but my throat was dry from all the wine and moaning his name.

I padded naked through his house toward the kitchen, my feet silent on the cool hardwood floors. The house felt different at night—larger, more mysterious, with shadows pooling in corners and the distant sound of waves crashing against the rocks below. I found a glass in one of the pristine cabinets and filled it with cold water, the sound seeming unnaturally loud in the quiet space.

That's when my phone buzzed against the marble countertop where I'd left it.

The screen lit up with a text from Nereus.

Nereus: I need to see you. Tonight.

I stared at the message, my good mood evaporating like morning mist. Another text appeared before I could even process the first one.

Nereus: I can't sleep. I keep thinking about you. Please come over so I can apologize.

My stomach twisted. The last place I wanted to be was at his house, especially in the middle of the night.

Twyla: It's 2 AM, Nereus.

Nereus: Please, Twyla. Just for a few minutes. I need to explain.

I glanced back toward the bedroom where Ezra slept peacefully, then down at the phone again. Every rational part of my brain screamed to delete the messages and go back to bed.

Twyla: I'm not coming to your place.

Nereus: Please, Twyla. I swear on my life, I just want to apologize. No games, no tricks. You can leave the second you want to.

I closed my eyes, already knowing I was about to make a mistake. But maybe facing this head-on was better than letting it fester.

Twyla: Twenty minutes, max.

Nereus: I'll leave the front door unlocked. Just come in when you get here.

***

Twenty minutes later, I stood outside Nereus's modernist house, with every instinct screaming at me to turn around and go back to Ezra's warm bed. The building loomed before me, all sharp angles and floor-to-ceiling windows that glowed with soft blue light from within. It looked like something from a magazine—beautiful, expensive, and cold.

I'd left a note for Ezra saying I'd gone for a drive because I couldn't sleep. It wasn't entirely a lie, but it felt like one sitting heavy in my stomach.

The front door was unlocked as promised. I pushed it open, my heart hammering against my ribs.

"Nereus?" I called softly, stepping into the minimalist foyer. The house smelled like expensive cologne and something vaguely oceanic, like high-end air freshener trying to mimic sea breeze.

"In here," his voice drifted from what looked like the living room.

I followed the sound, my footsteps muffled by thick carpeting. The living room was exactly what I'd expected—sleek furniture in shades of blue and silver, abstract art that probably cost more than my car, and windows that offered a stunning view of the harbor even at this ungodly hour.

Nereus sat on a low sofa, elbows braced on his knees, his head in his hands. Gone was the confident, polished siren who'd charmed me at dinner and danced with me at his club. This version looked haggard, his usually perfect hair disheveled, dark circles under his eyes.

"You came," he said, rising to his feet. "I wasn't sure you would."

"I almost didn't." I stayed near the doorway, every muscle in my body coiled to run. "You said you wanted to apologize. So apologize."

He ran a hand through his hair, the gesture so different from his usual smooth confidence that it was almost jarring. "God, where do I even start? I've been such an ass, Twyla. Such a complete and total ass."

"That's a start," I said dryly.

"I used you." The words came out in a rush, like he'd been holding them back for days. "I pursued you specifically because I knew it would get to Ezra. I wanted to prove I could take something he wanted, and I didn't care who got hurt in the process."

"Including me."

"Especially you." His voice cracked slightly. "You were never anything more than a pawn to me, and that 's...that's unforgivable."

I crossed my arms over my chest, partly for warmth and partly as a barrier between us. "Why are you telling me this?"

"I can't live with myself." He started pacing, his movements agitated. "Do you know what it's like to realize you've become everything you hate? I've spent my whole life watching older sirens play power games with innocent people, and I swore I'd never be like that. Then

I saw you with him, saw how he looked at you, and I just...lost my mind."

"So this is all about Ezra?"

"No!" The word exploded out of him, and I took a step back instinctively. He noticed my reaction and immediately gentled his voice. "I mean, it started that way. But somewhere along the line, it became about you too."

"What do you mean?"

He stopped pacing and looked at me directly, his turquoise eyes intense in the soft lighting. "I mean, I fell for you, Twyla. Which made what I was doing even worse."

My stomach churned. "Nereus—"

"I know it doesn't matter now. I know I ruined any chance I might have had. But I needed you to know that my feelings for you became real, even if they started out fake."

"That doesn't make it better," I said quietly. "If anything, it makes it worse."

"I know." He slumped back onto the sofa, looking utterly defeated. "I know it does. But I couldn't let you go on thinking you meant nothing to me. I was jealous and stupid and—"

"And manipulative," I finished. "Don't forget manipulative."

"Yes. That too." He looked up at me with something that might have been hope. "Is there any chance you could forgive me? Not now, but...someday?"

Part of me wanted to forgive him—he seemed genuinely remorseful by what he'd done. But a larger part of me was just tired.

"I don't know," I said honestly. "Maybe someday. But right now, I just want to move on with my life."

"With Ezra."

"With Ezra."

He nodded slowly, like he'd expected that answer. "He's lucky to have you."

"I'm lucky to have him too."

"Is he..." Nereus hesitated, then seemed to force himself to continue. "Is he treating you well? Really well, not just the superficial stuff?"

The question surprised me. "Why do you care?"

"Because despite everything I've done, I care about you. And Ezra has a reputation for being emotionally unavailable."

"He's not like that with me," I said, defensive.

"Good." Nereus smiled, and for the first time tonight it seemed genuine. "I'm glad. You deserve someone who sees how incredible you are."

An uncomfortable silence stretched between us. I glanced at the expensive watch on the wall—I'd been here for almost fifteen minutes already.

"I should go," I said, taking a step toward the door.

"Twyla, wait." Nereus stood up abruptly. "There's something else."

Something in his tone made my skin prickle with unease. "What?"

"Your bond with Ezra," he said, his eyes taking on that predatory ice-blue glow I remembered from the dance floor. "It's not actually complete yet, is it?"

"What are you talking about?" I backed toward the door, alarm bells going off in my head.

"Come on, you bonded during his heat cycle. That's not real consent, Twyla." His voice was taking on a hypnotic quality, but it sounded earnest, like he genuinely believed what he was saying. "You got caught up in some supernatural sex haze. That's not the same as actually choosing."

"That's not true." I fumbled for the door handle behind me. "I chose him."

"Did you though? Or did some ancient siren biology make the choice for you?" He moved closer, but instead of approaching the door, he gently guided me back toward the couch. "Look, the bond isn't locked in yet. You could still choose differently if you wanted to."

I tried to resist, but his song was making my limbs heavy, my thoughts sluggish. "Nereus, stop—"

"Just listen for a second," he said, easing me down onto the couch. "Okay? Just give me five minutes."

Before I could get back up, he was there—hands braced on either side of me against the couch cushions, his knee sliding between my thighs as he leaned over me. Not threatening, but overwhelming, inescapable.

"I get you in ways he never will," he murmured, his face inches from mine. His song wrapped around us, making the air thick and sweet. "We're the same generation. You don't have to translate your whole life for me."

"Nereus—"

"He's been alive for three thousand years, Twyla. You think he really gets what it's like to be twenty-eight in 2025?" His voice was hypnotic but conversational, like we were just having a normal debate. "I do. I know what it's like to grow up with social media and student loans and all the shit that actually matters to you."

His proximity was overwhelming, his natural siren allure making my thoughts fuzzy despite my resistance. "I don't want to choose you."

"You haven't really considered me yet. How could you?" His thumb traced along my jawline, feather-light. "Just think about it. Someone who actually gets your references, who won't look confused when you talk about literally anything from the past decade."

"It doesn't matter," I managed, though his song was making it hard to think clearly. "Let me go."

"It does matters though," he whispered, leaning closer until his breath tickled my ear. "You know how exhausting it is to be with someone from a completely different world? I could be your equal, not some ancient being you have to keep up with."

Chapter Twenty-Four

BREAKING POINT

The blue glow in his eyes intensified, and suddenly his song hit me like a physical force. Without my protection runes, I had no defense against it. The hypnotic melody didn't just wrap around my mind—it invaded it, sliding through my thoughts like oil, making everything slippery and wrong.

My vision blurred at the edges. The room seemed to tilt sideways as his song pressed against my skull like a migraine made of music. I could feel my own thoughts being pushed aside, shoved into dark corners while something else—his will—tried to take their place.

"That's it," he murmured, his voice weaving through the supernatural music like a snake through water. "Just relax and listen to what I'm saying."

I tried to push against his chest to get some distance, but my arms felt like they were moving through cement. Panic clawed at my throat as I realized I was losing control of my body. The bond with Ezra pulsed weakly in the back of my mind—a golden thread being slowly strangled by Nereus's song.

"No," I gasped, the word barely a whisper as his song pressed harder against my thoughts. It felt like drowning in honey—sweet but suffocating.

"You're fighting so hard against something that could be amazing," he said, his thumb brushing across my cheek. The touch sent unwanted shivers through me, my traitorous body responding to his siren allure even as my mind screamed in protest. "We make sense, Twyla can't you see that?"

His song shifted, becoming more insidious. Instead of crushing my thoughts, it whispered to them, planting seeds of doubt in my mind. *He's right,* a voice that sounded like mine but wasn't said. *Ezra is too old, too different. You'll never understand each other.*

"Stop," I choked out, tears streaming down my face as I felt the bond with Ezra flickering like a candle in a hurricane. The golden warmth that had become as natural as breathing was being replaced by something cold and alien.

"I can't stop," Nereus said, leaning closer until his forehead almost touched mine. His proximity made his song more powerful, the vibrations traveling directly from his chest into mine. "I want you to choose me. Let me love you in a way only I can."

The worst part was that his song was making it feel true. My body relaxed against my will, my heart rate slowing to match the rhythm of his music. Part of me—the part he was controlling—wanted to agree with him, to nod and smile and let him erase everything I felt for Ezra.

But buried beneath the artificial calm, I was screaming.

His song intensified, pressing against the weakening bond with Ezra like a crowbar trying to pry it apart. I could feel the connection stretching, fraying, the golden thread that connected us growing thinner with each note. The pain of it was excruciating—like having my soul slowly torn in half.

"Feel that?" Nereus whispered, his breath hot against my ear. "That's you, breaking free from his influence. That's you choosing what you actually want."

No, I thought desperately, clinging to the last threads of my bond with Ezra. *No, this isn't me. This isn't what I want.*

My voice wouldn't work anymore. His song had wrapped around my vocal cords, silencing me as effectively as a hand over my mouth. I could only sit there, trapped in my body, feeling him methodically destroy the most precious thing in my life.

The front door exploded inward.

The sound of splintering wood cut through Nereus's song like a blade through silk, and his concentration shattered completely. I gasped as if I'd been underwater for hours, the crushing weight of his song lifting so suddenly that I nearly collapsed. The bond with Ezra blazed back to life in my mind like the sun coming out from behind storm clouds.

Ezra filled the doorway like an avenging angel.

"Get away from her!" Ezra roared as I scrambled to push Nereus away from me, my limbs finally obeying my commands again.

His eyes blazed with that fierce magenta glow, his hair whipping around his face like he'd flown here on wings of fury. Scales had already begun appearing along his neck and arms, and his fingernails had extended into claws.

"Get. Your. Hands. Off. Her." He snarled, each word dripping with barely controlled violence.

Nereus stepped back from me, his hands raised in mock surrender, but his smile was triumphant. "You're too late. The bond has already begun."

"Like hell it has." Ezra's voice had dropped to something barely human, harmonics weaving through it that made the windows rattle. "I can smell your lies, Nereus."

"Yet," Nereus said with a shrug, his own transformation beginning. Scales erupted across his chest and shoulders, gills opening at his neck. "But the night is young."

Ezra's roar shook the entire house. He launched himself at Nereus with inhuman speed, claws extended, his body already shifting into something more siren than man. They collided in the center of the living room, a tangle of scales and fury and primal violence.

I scrambled for my clothes, my hands shaking as I pulled on my tank top. The two sirens rolled across the floor, their partially transformed bodies crashing into furniture, sending expensive art flying. Nereus's claws raked across Ezra's shoulder, four parallel lines that immediately welled with blood. Ezra responded by slamming Nereus against the wall hard enough to crack the drywall.

"She's mine," Nereus gasped, his song trying to weave between them even as they fought. "I marked her first."

"Temporary marks," Ezra growled, his claws finding Nereus's throat. "I claimed her properly."

They separated and circled each other like predators, both bleeding, both magnificent and terrifying in their partial transformations. The room reeked of blood and saltwater and supernatural power.

"You want to challenge me for her?" Nereus asked, his voice carrying deadly calm. "Fine. Let's make this official."

"Gladly," Ezra replied, and I realized with growing horror that this wasn't just a fight—it was some kind of formal siren combat.

They came together again, faster than my human eyes could follow. Claws and teeth and impossible strength, both of them moving with the grace of apex predators. Blood spattered the white walls, the expensive furniture, the abstract art that probably cost more than my house.

But Ezra was older, more experienced, and he had something Nereus didn't—righteous fury. When Nereus lunged for his throat, Ezra caught his wrist and twisted, the sound of bones breaking audible over their growls. Nereus screamed, a sound that was part human, part something else entirely.

"Yield," Ezra commanded, his claws pressed against Nereus's jugular. "Yield and leave her alone forever."

"Never," Nereus spat, blood running from his mouth.

Ezra's grip tightened, and I saw murder in his eyes. "Then die."

"Stop!" I shouted, finally finding my voice. "Ezra, stop! Don't kill him!"

Ezra's head snapped toward me, his expression wild and barely human. For a moment, I wasn't sure he even recognized me. Then something shifted; the killing rage in his eyes banking slightly.

"He tried to force you," he said, his voice rough with barely controlled violence. "He deserves death for that alone."

"Maybe," I said, pulling on my jeans with shaking hands. "But you don't deserve to become a killer because of me."

Ezra stared at me for a long moment, then looked down at Nereus pinned beneath him. "You have thirty seconds to yield before I change my mind."

"I yield," Nereus gasped, the words clearly costing him everything. "I yield the challenge. She's yours."

Ezra released him with a disgusted sound, stepping back but not relaxing his guard. "Leave. Tonight. Don't come back to this territory ever again."

Nereus struggled to his feet, cradling his broken wrist against his chest. His transformation was already reversing, scales fading back into human skin. "This isn't over, Ezra."

"It is." Ezra's voice carried absolute authority. "You lost the challenge. You have no claim here anymore."

"I mean between us."

"Touch her again and there won't be enough left of you to hold a grudge," Ezra interrupted, his eyes still glowing with lethal promise. "Test me."

Nereus looked at me one last time, something like genuine regret flickering in his expression.

Then he was gone, moving at high speed despite his injuries, leaving only the sound of a door slamming and the overwhelming silence that followed violence.

I stood there in my hastily donned clothes, staring at the surrounding destruction, trying to process what had just happened. Blood stained the white walls, furniture lay overturned, and Ezra stood in the center of it all like some beautiful, terrible god of vengeance.

"Are you hurt?" he asked, his voice gentling as his transformation reversed.

"No," I managed, my voice hoarse.

Relief flooded his features. "Good. That's good."

I looked at the four parallel scratches across his shoulder, still bleeding freely. "You're hurt."

"It's nothing," he said, but I could see the pain in the tight lines around his eyes.

"It's not nothing." I moved toward him, needing to touch him, to reassure myself that he was okay. "God, Ezra, I'm so sorry. I'm so fucking sorry."

"Hey." He caught my hands in his, careful not to let his still-extended claws hurt me. "This isn't your fault."

"I came here. I left you sleeping and came here in the middle of the night because I thought I needed closure." Tears spilled down my cheeks. "I'm an idiot."

"You were trying to do the right thing." He corrected gently.

"The right thing would have been staying in bed with you and blocking his number."

"Maybe, but you're safe now. That's all that matters."

I looked around at the destroyed living room, at the blood on his beautiful face, at the evidence of violence that had erupted because of my stupid decision. "Is it over?"

"He yielded the challenge. In siren law, that means he has no claim to you and can't pursue you again." Ezra's smile was grim but satisfied. "It's over."

"And if he doesn't honor that?"

"Then I'll kill him." He said it so matter-of-factly that I believed him. "But he will. Nereus may be young and stupid, but he's not suicidal."

I nodded, trying to convince myself it was true. "We should get you cleaned up. Those cuts look deep."

"In a minute." He pulled me against his chest, careful of his claws, and I melted into his embrace. "I need to hold you first. When I woke up and you were gone, I felt your fear through our bond..."

"You felt it?"

"I've never been so terrified in my life." His arms tightened around me. "Promise me you'll never do anything that stupid again."

"I promise," I said, holding my fingers up like a scout. "I promise I'll never leave your bed to go meet another man in the middle of the night."

His laugh was shaky but genuine. "Good. I don't think my heart could survive it."

As we stood there in the wreckage of Nereus's house, holding each other, I felt something shift inside me.

I'd almost lost this. I realized that I didn't want to wait anymore. But first, we needed to get out of here and take care of his wounds. The rest could wait until we were safe at home.

Chapter Twenty-Five

CHOOSING FOREVER

"Sit," I ordered, pointing at the edge of Ezra's massive bathtub. My hands were still shaking from the adrenaline, and I clenched them into fists to hide it. "And don't you dare argue with me."

"I'm fine," he protested, but he sat anyway, wincing slightly as the movement pulled at the claw marks on his shoulder. Blood had soaked through his shirt, staining the white fabric crimson in spreading patches that made my stomach lurch.

"You are not fine. You're bleeding all over your expensive bathroom." I turned away from the sight of all that blood and rummaged through his medicine cabinet, my fingers fumbling with bottles and containers. The metallic smell was making me dizzy. "Christ, do you have anything useful in here, or is it all fancy moisturizers and cologne?"

"Bottom shelf," he said, amusement creeping into his voice despite the pain. "Behind the bath salts."

I found a well-stocked first-aid kit and pulled it out triumphantly, relief flooding through me. Thank God he was prepared for this kind of thing. "There we go. Now take off your shirt."

"Bossy," he murmured, but he obeyed, carefully peeling the ruined fabric away from his wounds.

The sight of the four parallel gashes across his shoulder made my stomach clench hard enough that I had to swallow against a wave of nausea. They were deep, still bleeding sluggishly, and they looked like they hurt like hell. My throat went tight. He'd gotten those protecting me.

"This is going to sting," I warned, soaking a cotton pad with antiseptic. My voice came out rougher than I intended.

"I've had worse."

"During which century?" I dabbed at the wounds, trying to be gentle but thorough. The antiseptic foamed pink where it hit the blood, and I had to focus on breathing through my nose to keep from getting sick. He hissed through his teeth but didn't pull away, which somehow made it worse. I hated that I was hurting him, even to help.

"The 1800s were rough," he said, clearly trying to distract himself from the pain. "Lots of territorial disputes."

"Well, next time maybe don't throw yourself into a supernatural knife fight on my behalf." I cleaned each cut carefully, hyperaware of his every wince and sharp intake of breath. Each sound he made felt like a knife twist in my chest.

"There won't be a next time."

"Good. Because watching you bleed is not on my list of favorite activities." I pressed clean gauze against the wounds, applying pressure to stop the bleeding. The white fabric immediately started turning red, and I pressed harder, willing it to stop. "Hold this."

He covered my hands with his, holding the gauze in place. His skin was warm against mine, and I could feel his pulse beating steady and strong under my fingertips. "You're angry with me."

Was I? I took inventory of the churning mess of emotions in my chest. Fear, definitely. Relief that he was alive. Guilt that he'd been hurt because of me. "I'm not angry with you." I pulled tape from the first-aid kit, tearing off strips to secure the bandages, focusing on the mechanical task to keep my hands steady. "I'm angry with myself for being stupid enough to go to his house, and at Nereus for being a manipulative psychopath."

"But not at me?"

I looked up at him, taking in his tousled pink hair, his concerned expression. He was trying so hard to read my mood, like he was afraid I'd bolt. The uncertainty in his face made my chest ache. "How could I be angry at you? You kicked down a door to save me."

"It was a very expensive door," he said with mock seriousness. "Worth every splinter."

I finished taping the bandages and stepped back to admire my handiwork, though my hands were still trembling slightly. "There. You'll live."

"Will I?" His voice had gone soft, uncertain, and something in his tone made my heart skip. "Twyla, what I did tonight...I know it might have scared you."

I stared at him, this beautiful, deadly man who'd just fought another siren with claws and fangs for the right to call me his. The memory of seeing him in full predator mode flashed through my mind—savage and protective and absolutely magnificent. "Scared me?"

"Yes."

"Ezra." I moved to stand between his knees, my hands finding his face. His skin was warm under my palms, real and solid and alive. "Do you want to know what I was thinking when you broke down that door?"

He nodded, his eyes searching mine with an intensity that made my pulse quicken.

"I was thinking, 'Thank God, my siren is here to fuck up the asshole.'"

His eyes widened, pupils dilating. "Your siren?"

"My siren," I confirmed, running my thumbs along his cheekbones. The admission sent a thrill through me, like finally saying something I'd been holding back for too long. "And do you want to know what I was thinking when you had Nereus pinned to the floor with your claws at his throat?"

"What?" His voice had gone rough, and I could feel the tension coiling in his muscles.

"I was thinking how incredibly hot it was that you'd fight for me." I leaned closer, my voice dropping to a whisper. Heat was pooling low in my belly just from the memory. "I was thinking that I'm the luckiest woman alive to have someone who'd go full apex predator to protect me."

"Really?" The hope in his voice made my heart clench.

"Really. And I'm lucky you're all mine."

"What's yours?" he repeated, his voice going low and dangerous in the best possible way.

"I..." I tried to backtrack, but the words stuck in my throat. Because they were true. He was mine, and I was his, and I was tired of pretending otherwise. The realization hit me like a physical blow, stealing my breath.

"Say it again," he murmured, his hands coming up to rest on my hips.

"You're mine," I whispered, the admission sending electricity racing through my veins. "And I'm yours. And I don't want to wait anymore, Ezra. I don't want to be careful or cautious or reasonable."

"What do you want?" His grip on my hips tightened, fingers pressing into my skin.

"I want the bond. All of it. Forever." The words tumbled out of me in a rush, like a dam bursting. "I want to be connected to you for the rest of your ridiculously long life. I want to breathe underwater and hear your thoughts and live for centuries watching you create beautiful things."

His hands tightened on my hips, and I could see something fierce and possessive flare in his eyes. "Are you sure?"

"I've never been more sure of anything in my life." I cupped his face in my hands, looking directly into his eyes, drowning in that blue-green depth. "I choose you, Ezra. I choose us. I choose forever."

The moment the words left my lips, something shifted in the air around us. It felt like the world tilting on its axis, like gravity changing direction. The golden thread I'd felt forming between us suddenly blazed to life, warm and bright and absolutely right. I gasped as the sensation flooded through me—not just my own emotions, but his too. Joy so pure it made me dizzy, relief so profound it brought tears to my eyes, and love so overwhelming I thought my heart might burst from it.

"I can feel you," I whispered in wonder, my voice breaking on the words.

The bond settled into place like the final piece of a puzzle, warm and sure and permanent. I could sense him in the back of my mind, a comforting presence that felt like coming home after a lifetime of wandering.

"So that's it?" I asked, slightly breathless from the intensity of it all. "We're mated now?"

"We're mated now," he confirmed, pulling me down for a kiss that tasted like forever and promises and everything I'd ever wanted. "No take-backs."

"Good," I said against his lips, my heart racing with joy and terror and absolute certainty. "Because I'm planning to be very high-maintenance for the next few centuries."

"I wouldn't have it any other way."

I settled onto his lap carefully, mindful of his bandaged shoulder, and let myself really absorb what had just happened. The magnitude of it was staggering. I was bonded to a three-thousand-year-old siren. I was going to live for centuries. Everything I'd thought I knew about my life had just changed completely.

"This is insane," I said, but I was smiling so hard my cheeks hurt.

"The best things usually are." He tucked a strand of hair behind my ear, the gesture so tender it made my chest ache. "Any regrets?"

I thought about it seriously, taking inventory of everything I was leaving behind. About the life I was giving up, the normal human existence I'd never have. About growing old and dying like everyone else I knew. About never seeing my friends age past me, never having the simple mortal life I'd always assumed was my destiny.

"Only one," I said finally.

His face fell, and I could feel his anxiety spike through the bond. "What?"

"I regret not having done this sooner." I grinned at his expression, loving how the relief washed over his features. "Did you really think I was going to say I regretted choosing you?"

"For a terrifying moment, yes."

"Never." I kissed him again, sweet and full of promise, tasting the smile on his lips. "Though I do have some conditions about this whole eternal bond thing."

"Name them."

"First, I get to redecorate parts of this house. It's gorgeous, but it needs some personality."

"Done."

"Second, you're teaching me to paint. I want to create beautiful things with you."

"I'd love nothing more."

"Third, we're getting a dog. A big, slobbery, completely unrefined dog that will shed all over your fancy furniture."

He laughed, the sound echoing in the bathroom's acoustics and vibrating through the bond in a way that made my toes curl. "A dog?"

"A dog. I've always wanted one, and now I have time to spoil it." I traced patterns on his chest, careful to avoid his injuries, marveling at the solid warmth of him. "What do you think? Can the sophisticated siren handle a pet?"

"For you? I can handle anything."

"Good answer." I stood up, offering him my hand, steadying myself as the bond hummed contentedly between us like a purring cat. "Come on, let's get you some painkillers and then I want to test out this whole telepathic communication thing."

"What do you want to say?"

I helped him to his feet, steadying him when he swayed slightly. "All the filthy things I'm going to do to you once your shoulder heals."

"You can't say things like that when I'm injured." He groaned, his eyes already darkening with interest, and I could feel his arousal spike through the bond.

I grinned wickedly, delighting in this new ability to affect him so completely. "Better get used to it, darling."

As we made our way to his bedroom, the bond humming contentedly between us, I felt a profound sense of rightness settle in my bones. This was it. This was my life now—beautiful and strange and magical and absolutely perfect. Everything I'd never known I wanted, all wrapped up in one impossible, wonderful package.

I was Twyla Knight, bonded mate to a siren, future immortal, and the happiest woman in any century.

And I wouldn't change a single thing.

Well, except maybe I'd invest in a better first aid kit. Something told me life with Ezra was going to be anything but boring.

Epilogue

Six Months Later

"I still can't believe you got a Great Dane," Alex said, watching as our new puppy—who was already the size of a small horse—bounded through the waves at our feet. "When you said big dog, I was thinking maybe a golden retriever."

"Go big or go home," I replied, laughing as Neptune—yes, I'd named him Neptune, much to Ezra's amused resignation—shook seawater all over Kronos's perfectly pressed pants.

"He's going to be enormous," Kronos said, but he was smiling as he scratched behind the puppy's ears. "Though I suppose that's fitting for this household."

"Ezra needs someone to keep him humble." I glanced back toward the house where said siren was undoubtedly in his studio, working on his latest masterpiece. Ever since we'd bonded, his art had taken on a new quality—warmer, more alive, filled with hope instead of beautiful melancholy. The gallery showings had been incredible, with collectors from around the world clamoring for pieces from his "Light Series"—what the art world was calling his recent work, though they had no idea the light came from me.

"And how is married life treating you?" Alex asked, settling onto the driftwood log beside me.

"We're not married," I corrected. "We're bonded. It's different."

"How different?"

I considered the question, absently reaching out through the bond to check on Ezra. He was paint-splattered and content, completely absorbed in his work. The warmth of his presence in my mind was as natural as breathing now.

"Marriage is a promise," I said finally. "This is a fact. Like gravity or the tide. It just is."

"Sounds terrifying."

"It should be," I admitted. "But it's not. It's like...finding out you have a superpower you didn't know you needed."

Neptune came bounding back, shaking sand and water everywhere, and I laughed as Alex yelped and tried to protect his coffee from the spray.

"Speaking of superpowers," Alex said, eyeing me curiously, "how's the whole enhanced human thing working out? Any cool new abilities I should know about?"

I grinned, holding up my hand. My nails, now permanently etched with protection runes that glowed faintly in certain light, caught the sun. "Well, I can breathe underwater indefinitely now, which makes beach days interesting. And apparently I have supernatural strength when I'm really pissed off—found that out when some tourist tried to shoplift from the store last week."

"You didn't hurt him, did you?"

"Just scared him. A lot. Turns out when you're bonded to a siren, you develop some of their... intensity." I flexed my fingers, watching the runes shimmer. "Plus, I can sense other supernatural beings now. It's like having a built-in creep detector."

"Nice," Kronos observed, still wrestling with Neptune over a large stick. "Has anyone else given you trouble since Nereus?"

The name still made me tense slightly, though the bond with Ezra immediately flooded me with reassurance. "No. Word got around pretty fast about what happened. Apparently, challenging an ancient siren to formal combat and losing hurts your reputation."

"Good," Alex said fiercely. "That bastard had it coming."

I was quiet for a moment, watching Neptune chase seagulls along the waterline. "I mean, what he did was unforgivable," I said carefully. "But I think...I think he was just lonely. That doesn't excuse the manipulation or the attempted coercion, but I can understand how someone might get desperate enough to make terrible choices."

Alex gave me a look. "You're too kind, Twy. He tried to force a bond on you."

"I know. And I'll never forgive him for that." I shrugged. "But understanding someone's pain doesn't mean excusing their actions. Two things can be true at once."

Kronos nodded thoughtfully. "Loneliness can make people do terrible things. It doesn't justify them, but it explains them."

"Exactly." I stood up, brushing sand off my jeans. "Anyway, enough about ancient history. I should go check on my sea creature. He gets cranky when he's hungry, and I promised to make dinner tonight."

"You? Cook?" Alex looked genuinely shocked. "The woman who once tried to make toast and somehow set off the smoke alarm?"

"I'm learning. Turns out I have centuries to perfect my culinary skills." I grinned. "Plus, Ezra's very patient when properly motivated."

"Actually," Alex said, standing and dusting off his own jeans, "I should come help. I promised Ezra I'd show him how to make that pasta dish Kronos likes. Apparently he wants to surprise you with it next week."

"Aw, that's sweet." I looked at Kronos. "You don't mind if we steal your boyfriend for kitchen duty?"

"Not at all," Kronos said, but there was something in his expression—a nervous energy that hadn't been there before. "Actually, I was hoping to have a word with Twyla. If you don't mind."

Alex glanced between us, clearly picking up on the sudden tension. "Everything okay?"

"Fine," Kronos assured him, leaning over to press a soft kiss to Alex's lips. "Just some boring logistics about the gallery. Go teach Ezra how to properly cook for his mate."

After Alex headed toward the house with Neptune bounding after him, I turned to Kronos with raised eyebrows. "Okay, what's really going on? You look like you're about to throw up."

Kronos ran a hand through his hair—a nervous gesture I'd rarely seen from him. "I need your opinion on something."

"Shoot."

Instead of answering, he reached into his jacket pocket and pulled out a small velvet box. My heart immediately started racing.

"Oh my god," I breathed. "Kronos, is that—?"

He opened the box, revealing the most beautiful ring I'd ever seen. It wasn't flashy or ostentatious—instead, it was elegant and understated, with a simple platinum band and a perfectly cut diamond that caught the late afternoon light like captured starfire.

"Oh my god," I repeated, louder this time. "You're going to propose?!"

"Shh!" Kronos glanced toward the house nervously. "Not yet. But...soon. I hope."

I grabbed his arm, excitement bubbling up inside me. "Kronos, this is amazing! When? How? Do you have a plan?"

"I'm still working on the details," he admitted, closing the box and tucking it safely back into his pocket. "I want it to be perfect. Alex deserves perfect."

"He deserves you," I corrected. "And you deserve him. This is so exciting! How long have you been planning this?"

"Months," Kronos confessed. "I had the ring custom made. The diamond is from a mine my family owns, and I had it cut specifically for him."

"He's going to *die*. In the best possible way." I bounced slightly on my toes, unable to contain my enthusiasm. "Can I help? Do you need ideas? I know all his favorite places, his favorite foods—"

"Actually," Kronos said, his nervousness giving way to a small smile, "I was hoping you might help me figure out the timing. You know him better than anyone."

"What are you thinking?"

"I want it to be meaningful. Somewhere that matters to both of us." He looked out at the ocean, his expression thoughtful. "Maybe here? This place has become important to all of us."

"That could be perfect," I agreed. "What about during one of our beach dinners? You could coordinate with Ezra to make it extra special."

"You think he'll say yes?" The vulnerability in Kronos's voice made my chest tight.

"Are you kidding me? That man is so gone for you it's not even funny. He's going to say yes before you finish asking the question."

Kronos's smile was brilliant. "I hope so. I can't imagine my life without him."

"You won't have to," I assured him.

He glanced toward the house, where we could hear Alex's laughter drifting through the open windows. "Should we head in? I don't want him getting suspicious."

"In a minute." I grinned at him. "I'm still processing the fact that my best friend is about to get engaged. This is huge, Kronos."

"I know. I just hope—"

"Twyla! Kronos!" Alex's voice carried across the beach as he appeared on the deck, waving a pair of oversized grilling tongs in the air. "Get your asses up here! Ezra's about to burn the fish, and I need backup!"

We could hear Ezra's indignant response from inside the house, though the words were muffled.

"Duty calls," I said, still grinning. "But seriously, I'm so happy for you guys."

Kronos pocketed the ring box and smiled. "Just remember—not a word to Alex until after."

"My lips are sealed," I promised, miming zipping my mouth shut.

As we trudged up the sandy path toward the house, Neptune bounding ahead of us, I couldn't help but feel like everything was falling perfectly into place. Alex was about to get the proposal of his dreams, Ezra and I were building something beautiful together, and apparently my siren could almost cook fish without setting the kitchen on fire.

I found Ezra in the kitchen, looking slightly frazzled as he tried to manage what appeared to be three different dishes at once. His pink hair was tied back in a messy bun, and he had flour somehow streaked across one cheek despite the fact that we weren't making anything that required flour.

"How exactly did you get flour everywhere?" I asked, wrapping my arms around his waist from behind.

"I have no idea," he admitted, leaning back against me. "Alex attempted to teach me to make breadcrumbs from scratch. It...escalated."

"I can see that." I reached up to brush the flour from his cheek, then pressed a kiss to the spot. "Need help?"

"Always," he murmured, turning in my arms to capture my lips in a proper kiss. "Though I think we have everything under control now."

"Famous last words," Alex called from where he was expertly managing the grill outside, Kronos and Neptune both hovering nearby like eager assistants.

Through the bond, I felt Ezra's contentment, his quiet joy at having our little family gathered together. It was a feeling I'd grown addicted to—this sense of belonging, of being exactly where I was meant to be.

The shop was thriving under the joint management of Alex and myself, though I'd had to hire additional staff now that I split my time between Cypress City and traveling with Ezra to various gallery showings around the world. Mira had become our unofficial supernatural consultant, helping customers who needed more specialized magical items.

"What are you thinking about?" Ezra asked, his fingers finding the protection runes on my nails and tracing them gently.

"Just...all of this," I said, gesturing around the kitchen where evidence of our domestic chaos was scattered everywhere. "Six months ago, I never could have imagined this life."

"Regrets?" he asked, though I could feel through the bond that he already knew the answer.

"Only that it took us so long to figure it out," I replied, stealing another kiss.

"Dinner's ready!" Alex called, and soon we were all gathered around the large outdoor table on the deck, Neptune sprawled beneath it hoping for dropped food, the sunset painting everything in shades of gold and pink.

As Kronos and Alex bickered good-naturedly about the proper way to grill fish, and Ezra described his latest painting idea with the passionate enthusiasm that always made my heart flutter, I couldn't help but think about how perfectly imperfect this all was.

This life was nothing like what I'd planned, nothing like what I'd expected.

It was so much better.

Life was funny that way.

But as Ezra's hand found mine under the table, his thumb tracing over my hand, I couldn't imagine wanting it any other way.

After all, normal was overrated.

And forever was just getting started.

www.ingramcontent.com/pod-product-compliance
Lightning Source LLC
Chambersburg PA
CBHW032353310726
48973CB00007B/1984